THE PIRATES
IN THE DEEP
GREEN SEA

BLOOMSBURY READER

Discover books by Eric Linklater published by
Bloomsbury Reader at
www.bloomsbury.com/EricLinklater

THE PIRATES IN THE DEEP GREEN SEA

ERIC LINKLATER

BLOOMSBURY READER

LONDON · NEW DELHI · NEW YORK · SYDNEY

This edition published in 2013 by Bloomsbury Reader

Bloomsbury Reader is a division of Bloomsbury Publishing Plc,

50 Bedford Square, London WC1B 3DP

ISBN: 978 1 4482 0582 0
eISBN: 978 1 4482 0551 6

For
Magnus and Andro

Contents

Chapter One

For three days there had been a gale from the west, but now it was nearly calm again and the sea was blue. The Atlantic swell still broke on the cliffs, thudding and slapping and splashing great fountains high in the air, but in the bay there was smooth water. The tide was out, and Timothy and Hew and Sam Sturgeon were looking for treasure. The bottom of the sea was a strange and secret land that no one had ever explored, but sometimes the sea itself disclosed some of the curious things that lay hidden in its caves, or in forests of ribbon-weed, or among the green timbers of long-lost ships. Sometimes a gale brought ashore old bones, gold coins, and cannon-balls. In North Bay, it was said, lay the wreck of a pirate ship, and part of the skeleton of a great whale had once been thrown up by a winter storm on the beach of Inner Bay.

Far above the water's edge there was a little wall of seaweed, running all round the bay, that had been broken from its roots and carried inland by the storm. Timothy and Hew and Sam Sturgeon, with bare feet and a very serious expression on their faces, were trampling the seaweed, and pulling it apart and feeling it with their toes. It was dry, crackly, and dusted with sand on top, but underneath it was cold and slippery. They had been treasure-seeking for an hour, and found nothing, when suddenly Timothy gave a yelp of pain like a frightened dog, and danced on his right foot, and cuddled the other in both hands. He had found a cannon-ball, and his big toe was very sore in consequence.

He was a neat and nimble boy, not very big for his age, which was eleven, but he was quick on his feet and his mind was quick too. His brother Hew was two years younger and three inches taller, and when they fought together Hew was usually the winner. But they seldom quarrelled—not more than once a month or so—because Timothy was good-tempered and Hew respected him. Sometimes, however, Hew would wake in the morning and think how tall and strong he was, and out of pure happiness and the desire to show off his strength, he would throw a pillow at Timothy and shout, 'Let's have a fight!'

Then five minutes later, sitting on Timothy's chest, he would probably say, 'I'm very, very sorry, but I'm afraid you're going to have another black eye. I really didn't mean to hit so hard. Honestly I didn't.'

And Timothy would answer, puffing and panting, 'You're a stupid, clumsy, hulking brute. You ought to have been a cart-horse, and then you might be some use in the world. But as it is, you're just a nuisance. And now get off my chest, because your nose is bleeding and it's dripping on me.'

Later in the morning they would tell Sam Sturgeon about the fight, and Timothy would say, 'We fought for about half an hour at the very least, I think.'

'It must have been longer than that,' Hew would protest. 'It couldn't have been less than three-quarters of an hour, and perhaps it was more.'

'And I wish I'd been there to see you at it,' Sam would answer. 'You've got a nose like an old tomato that someone's trod on, and it must have been a nice straight punch that did that to you. And you caught Timothy a proper good 'un, didn't you? His right eye looks like a nice spoonful of blackberry pudding, if you ask me. Oh, it's a shame I wasn't there to see you at it!'

Sam Sturgeon was a tall man with long arms who looked rather like a hare. He had a small head, great pointed ears, and a receding chin; and his big round eyes were dark and melancholy. He was forty-five years old, and for more than half his life he had been in the Royal Marines. He knew a great deal of geography, and could draw useful maps of the West Indies, the coast of Africa from Cape Town to Zanzibar, the Mediterranean, the China Sea, and the Yangtse-kiang. He was also well acquainted with Captain Horatio Spens, late of the Royal Navy, whose servant he had been for many years; and that was even more useful than his knowledge of geography, because Captain Spens was a very difficult man. Timothy and Hew were not afraid of him—they were indeed quite fond of him—but sometimes they watched him as carefully as if he were a kicking horse. He was their father, and he, more than any of them, would be excited by the cannon-ball that Timothy had found.

Having rubbed the pain out of his toe, Timothy picked up the round iron ball, and Hew and Sam Sturgeon came hurrying to look at it.

'That makes seven altogether,' said Hew, 'and it's the same as the others.'

'Father's right,' said Timothy. 'There must be a ship in North Bay.'

Sam Sturgeon whistled a little tune and said, 'The Old Man won't half be pleased when he sees that. There'll be half a crown apiece for you, when you get home, and a nice glass of rum for me.'

Very solemnly they all stared at the cannon-ball. It was about four inches in diameter, a rusty-red and cracked with rust, and it closely resembled six others that had been found on the beach in the last ten years. There was a very old story in the island that a pirate ship, coming home from a seven years' voyage, had been wrecked on the west coast; and though most of the crew had come safely ashore, it was said, they had all been captured by sailors of the Royal Navy, and taken to Execution Dock, where they were hanged. Captain Spens believed the story, because, he said, the master of the ship, who had been drowned, was his ancestor; and he had spent a lot of time and trouble and money in looking for the wreck. Ten years before, soon after the first cannon-ball had been found on the beach, he had picked up a human skull with a little slit in the top of it, like the opening of a money-box, and seventeen gold coins inside. The skull stood on the Captain's writing-table, on a pedestal that Sam Sturgeon had carved from a piece of old oak, but the seventeen gold coins had been spent long ago. For the Captain was by no means rich, and certainly not rich enough to save any money.

Hew and Timothy—Timothy with the cannon-ball in his hands—all stood silent, and thought about the Captain. He was a very good man, but he had a very bad temper. He had fought in two wars, and in one he had lost his left eye and his left hand, and in the other his left leg had been shot off just below the knee. To a stranger who saw him for only a little while, Captain Spens still seemed to be quite an ordinary sort of man, for he wore a handsome glass eye in place of that which he had lost; he had an imitation hand that was always covered with a brown leather glove; and his artificial leg was so good that he could walk five

4

miles. But the people who had to live with him—who were Timothy and Hew and Sam Sturgeon and Mrs. Matches the housekeeper—knew that when he lost his limbs he had lost his temper too.

'It just ran out of him through all the wounds he got,' Mrs. Matches used to say.

'He's a very nice gentleman in reality,' Sam would explain, 'but when he starts shouting, well, you take my advice, and clear out!'

So now all three of them—Timothy with the cannon-ball in his hands—stood in the seaweed and seriously considered what they should do next. Presently Timothy said, 'It must be about eleven o'clock. He'll be reading history-books or studying his charts. I don't think we ought to interrupt him just now. Let's go for a swim first, and show him the cannon-ball at lunch-time.'

'That's sensible,' said Sam Sturgeon, and immediately took off his coat and shirt and trousers. Underneath he wore red woollen bathing-drawers and some very handsome pictures that had been tattooed on his back and chest and arms. On his chest there was a full-rigged ship sailing on a calm sea with two mermaids watching her. Sea-serpents, twining and twisting, decorated his arms, and on his back a white man and a negro were boxing in a very fierce but scientific style. Hew and Timothy wore only jerseys and short trousers, and nothing at all when they ran down the beach and into the sea.

They were all good swimmers, and without any trouble or stopping for a rest they swam to the outermost limit of calm water, and farther than that Sam Sturgeon would not let them go; for beyond the bay the sea was dancing again, and the tide, which had turned and begun to flow, was setting strongly to the north. So in the smooth green water they floated, or dived like ducks and came up again, and talked about the treasure that might be lying beneath them. Then Hew, bobbing out of the water, cried, 'Oh, look! Look there! Who's that?'

One after another they bobbed as high as they could, and each in turn saw a remarkable and unexpected sight. In the rougher water beyond the shelter of the bay, among bright waves that rose and fell with ragged silver tips, there floated at ease a man with a bald head, a red nose, red patches of hair above his ears, and red side-whiskers, and in his mouth a short clay pipe from which came little puffs of smoke as if he were a steamer.

"Well, bless my immortal soul,' said Sam Sturgeon, 'if it isn't Gunner Boles!'

'I thought it was,' said Hew, spluttering because he had swallowed a mouthful of water.

'You don't remember him,' cried Timothy, bobbing again. 'You were too young.'

'No, I wasn't!' answered Hew indignantly. 'I remember him as well as you do.'

'You can't. You were only five.'

'Well, you were only seven!'

'Pipe down!' said Sam Sturgeon. 'There's no one wants to hear you talking. Not when there's Gunner Boles out there, as large as life and pining for intelligent conversation. Pipe down, I say!' And treading water he waved his long right arm like a semaphore, and shouted as loudly as he could, 'Ahoy there! Ahoy there, Gunner Boles! Good morning to you, Gunner Boles, and what are you doing up here in these high latitudes?'

Chapter Two

A long, long time ago, more than four years ago, Timothy
and Hew and Sam Sturgeon had been afloat on a raft in the
South Atlantic. It was a very small raft, and as it tilted this way
and that in the lift and the fall of the sea, the grey salt water came
spilling over its floor. Timothy and Hew were tied to the planks—
not tightly, but not very comfortably either—and Sam Sturgeon,
balancing like a proper sailor, stood and searched the horizon
for any sign of help.

Captain Spens had been stationed in Ceylon, and for some
time they had all been living there in great comfort. But then the
Captain had gone back to sea, and their mother had decided to
come home, though everybody knew how dangerous that was in
time of war. But Mrs. Spens liked to have her own way, whether
there was a war or not, so presently they embarked in a large
ship called the *Blue Moon*, and Sam Sturgeon came with them,
because Captain Spens had left him behind to look after them.
And that was very lucky for Timothy and Hew.

After she had been at sea for about two weeks, the *Blue Moon*
was torpedoed one evening by a German submarine, and before
she could sink everybody took to the boats. Mrs. Spens, who was

playing bridge in the saloon, was carried on deck by a tall man with a black moustache who put her into one of the largest of the boats, though all the time she was struggling in his arms and protesting that she must go and look for her two sons. But the man with the black moustache paid no attention, and the large boat pushed off, and Mrs. Spens sat in the bottom of it and cried most bitterly. She would have wasted her time, however, and perhaps even lost her life, if she had stayed aboard the *Blue Moon*. She would never have found Timothy and Hew, who were both in the engine-room with Sam Sturgeon.

Mrs. Spens had forbidden them to go there, because she thought it was dangerous. But Sam Sturgeon saw how disappointed they were, and made arrangements with an engineer with whom he was friendly, and one night after Mrs. Spens had put the boys to bed, he came and helped them to get dressed again, and took them down to the depths of the ship. And that was the night when the *Blue Moon* was torpedoed by a German submarine.

The engineers and the stokers were very kind to Timothy and Hew, and helped them up the long steel ladders that led to the deck, but it took them several minutes to get there, and by that time all the life-boats had gone. There were plenty of rafts, however, and Sam Sturgeon, having chosen a good one, had time to go down to a steward's pantry and bring up a large tray of sandwiches and six bottles of lemonade. Then, as the *Blue Moon* was sinking fast and the deck was slanting down to the water's edge, they launched the raft, and got aboard, and pushed off.

The weather was warm, and though the sea was rather rough and they all got soaking wet, they did not suffer much during the night; and they enjoyed having lemonade and sandwiches for breakfast. But they were rather worried when they looked this way and that, and nowhere could they see any of the life-boats, and nowhere another raft. The sun came up and the sky was clear, and on all sides the sea was bright blue with white lines of foam upon it; but it was quite empty. During the night the life-boats and the other rafts had been blown far away, and they were all alone. They had some more sandwiches and another bottle of lemonade for lunch, and they could see that Sam Sturgeon was getting worried. He said nothing that would make them feel worried, and they, of course, were careful to avoid worrying him by showing him that they knew he was worried. But when they saw the stern expression on his face, they began to count the remaining sandwiches and wonder how long they would last. Timothy found a piece of string in his trouser-pocket and a pin in the collar of his coat, and made a fishing-line that he baited with a crust of bread; but he did not catch anything.

The sea was growing smoother, and by tea-time it was almost flat. The sun went down in the west, and when it touched the rim of the sea they were dazzled by the great light that seemed to flow from it like a golden road. Timothy blinked, and looked the other way—and to his immense surprise, about two hundred yards from the raft, he saw floating at ease a man with a bald head, a red nose, red patches of hair above his ears, and red side-whiskers, and in his mouth there was a short clay pipe from which came little puffs of smoke as if he were a steamer.

'Look!' he exclaimed. 'Oh, look, Sam! Who's that?'

Sam looked in the direction to which he pointed, and stared very earnestly at the red-haired man.

'Well, scratch my back with a garden rake,' he said, 'but that's very odd, now isn't it? Here we are, eight hundred miles from the nearest land, and there's an old fellow with a bald head out

9

bathing! Now what do you make of that?'

'Have you always got to use a garden rake when you want to scratch your back?' asked Hew.

'Don't you ask troublesome questions, or I'll give you a clip over the ear,' said Sam; and putting two fingers in his mouth, whistled shrilly. 'Ahoy there!' he shouted. 'You with the crimson whiskers! Come alongside, will you, and give us your news?'

The man with the bald head turned towards them, and in the glow of the setting sun they could see upon his face a look of gaping astonishment and great alarm. His eyebrows rose on his wrinkled forehead, his mouth opened, and his pipe fell into the sea. He looked wildly to the north and the south, as though fearing he had been surrounded by rafts, and then dived like a duck to retrieve his pipe. He came up again within twenty yards of them, and now his expression was mild and curious.

'You gave me a regular surprise, you did,' he said in a deep rolling voice. 'I might have lost my pipe, all on account of you. Now what are you doing out here, alone on the South Atlantic sea?'

'That's what we might be asking you,' said Sam.

'Ah!' said the bald-headed man. 'But this is where I belong. You're only visitors, I suppose, and from the look of you you're survivors of some great ship that's been sunk in the depths of the ocean!'

'That's so,' said Sam. 'The *Blue Moon* it was. Sunk by a German submarine.'

'And these little boys,' said the bald-headed man, 'what were they doing out on the broad sea in time of war, when they ought to be in their warm beds or getting up and doing their lessons, like little boys must, the poor unhappy things they are?'

'They were going home,' said Sam. 'Their father's a naval

officer, Captain Spens, R.N., a fine man with a bad temper who lost his left hand and the sight of his left eye in the last war——'

'Like Lord Nelson,' said the bald-headed man.

'Just so,' said Sam.

'And you yourself,' said the bald-headed man. 'What were you in civil life?'

'I never was in civil life!' said Sam indignantly. 'I'm a Royal Marine, and have been for twenty-six years, and that's all the life I know!'

'So you're in the Service,' said the bald-headed man, 'and these little boys are the chicks of an old cock who's in the Service too. Well, that makes a difference, so it does.' And climbing on to the raft he sat on one corner of it, with his legs in the water, and looked sadly at his pipe. 'You've spoiled the good smoke I was having with the fright you gave me,' he said.

'Try a fill of this,' said Sam Sturgeon, and offered his own tobacco-pouch.

Now Timothy was only seven at this time, Hew only five, and neither could properly remember the conversation that followed, because both fell asleep before it came to an end. The sun went down, and though their clothes were wet the air was warm, and they were very tired. The raft lay quietly on a calm sea, and they fell fast asleep. But Timothy remembered—quite definitely remembered—the bald-headed man lighting his pipe, and sucking hard at the stem, and saying to Sam Sturgeon, 'Boles is the name. Gunner Boles. And if you've ever learnt anything about history, you won't have forgotten the battle of Trafalgar?'

It was after that that Timothy's memory became vague and uncertain, and whether it was a dream he remembered or the real truth he could never quite decide. But if he were not dreaming, then Gunner Boles actually said that he had taken part in the battle of Trafalgar, in Admiral Collingwood's ship, the *Royal Sovereign*, and had been hit on the breast-bone by a musket-ball from the Spanish ship *Santa Ana*.—And if that were so, thought Timothy, he should have been killed; and even if he had survived so desperate a wound, he must have been, when they saw him swimming calmly in the South Atlantic Ocean, about a hundred and seventy years old; which was most unnatural. So Timothy, when he thought about the matter, had gradually come to the conclusion that he had indeed been dreaming, and Gunner Boles—well, there was another difficulty, for no one could say that Gunner Boles was quite an ordinary person, because of Cully.

Cully was an octopus, who had made his appearance on the following morning.

Timothy remembered the events of the morning very clearly. He had wakened up feeling hungry, and seen that there were still five sandwiches on the tray. He had said to Sam: 'Sam! Oh, Sam! Can I have a sandwich for my breakfast, please?' And Sam had answered: 'Yes, and only one. And you can take two sucks of lemonade out of the last bottle there, and only two.'

Sam Sturgeon and Gunner Boles were standing amidships on the raft, and looking straight ahead. The morning was fine, the sea was calm, and the raft was moving quickly through the water. Sam unfastened the line by which he had tied Timothy to the planks—to prevent him from falling overboard—and Timothy also stood up to look at the view. There was nothing to be seen except blue water all round, and ahead of them a rope tied to some strange creature that was towing them. The creature could not properly be seen, because it was entirely under water except for its head.

Hew woke up, and was given a sandwich for his breakfast. Then the creature that had been towing the raft stopped swimming, and came alongside, and exclaimed, 'Oh dear, I'm so tired! I'm terribly, terribly tired!'

He had large pale eyes and a great orange beak like the beak of a giant parrot. His body and his limbs lay in the water like a silver shadow that was always changing its shape. Sometimes his body seemed no larger than a tea-tray, and then quite suddenly it became as big as a flower-bed. And at one moment his legs and arms were long and slender, and a moment later they seemed short and stumpy. He opened his beak, and closed his eyes, and in a soft warbling voice, rather like a flute, said again, 'Oh, how tired I am! And I'm very hungry too!'

'Give him a sandwich,' said Timothy.

'What a charming little boy!' said the creature. 'What a thoughtful, kind, and considerate little boy! Won't you introduce us, Gunner Boles?'

'Well,' said Gunner Boles, 'this is an old friend of mine, a well-known octopus in the South Atlantic, who goes by the name of Cully——'

'No, no, *no*!' screamed the octopus, and covering his head with his legs and his arms, sank quickly out of sight. But Gunner Boles hauled strongly on the rope to which the octopus was tied, and by and by he reappeared. As soon as his beak was above water he exclaimed in a bubbling voice, because there was some water in his throat, 'That was very rude of you! Most unmannerly, and quite discourteous! I won't be referred to in that familiar way! You know my name perfectly well——'

'No, I don't,' said Gunner Boles in his deep voice. 'It's far too long a name for a simple sailorman like me to remember. Cully is what I call you, and what's good enough for me ought to be good enough for you.'

'But it isn't!' cried the octopus. 'I've got a very beautiful name, a very distinguished and honourable name, an historic name——'

'All right, all right,' said Gunner Boles. 'You tell them!'

'I shall!' cried the octopus, and rising a little way out of the sea he said to the boys, 'I am delighted indeed to make your acquaintance, and I trust we shall become very good friends. My name, I must tell you, is Culliferdontofoscofolios Polydesteropouf.'

'Or Cully for short,' said Gunner Boles.

Sam Sturgeon bent and whispered to them, 'Now nod your heads and say *How do you do* like gentlemen.'

'How do you do,' said Timothy and Hew together, and Hew added, 'Won't you have a sandwich?'

'Oh, how kind, how very kind!' exclaimed Cully, and lifting three of his arms out of the sea, removed very neatly from the tray the three sandwiches that remained.

He gulped them down, and a moment later said, 'Now I feel much stronger. Oh, much, much stronger! Now I shall take you wherever you want to go. Where shall I go, Gunner Boles?'

'Nor'-nor'-east,' said Gunner Boles.

So Cully began to swim quickly in that direction, the raft moved swiftly through the water, and Gunner Boles explained to the boys: 'We've been friendly for a long time, him and me. He was only a little fellow when I first came across him. No bigger than a soup-plate he wasn't, and in a rare pickle, too. He'd been practising tying knots, you see, using his limbs or feelers to practise with, and the result was that he'd done himself up in four different kinds of knots, all very well tied, and couldn't undo them again no matter how he twisted and turned. So I came to his rescue and set him free, and ever since then he's followed me

14

about and done what I told him. He's grown a lot, in the course of years, and now he's the biggest and best-educated octopus in the South Atlantic; but he's become a little bit conceited in some ways, as you've seen for yourselves.'

Timothy and Hew were very much impressed by his story, and for some time they watched Cully swimming powerfully through the water, and towing the raft behind him, with the liveliest interest. It was very grand, they thought, to be towed by the best-educated octopus in the South Atlantic, and they made up their minds to stay awake all night in case there should be any chance of further conversation with him.

But as it grew dark they became sleepy, and Sam Sturgeon and Gunner Boles were sitting side by side, talking in a low tone of voice, and the sound of their voices was sleepy, like the sound of the sea rushing softly under the raft, and somehow or other, in spite of their resolution, the very next thing of which Timothy and Hew became aware was the rising sun, a calm sea, and a dazzling golden path to the east.

The raft lay motionless. Cully was floating on his back, splashing the water with his eight arms, and singing a little song in a rather screechy, high-pitched voice:

'There was a little dog-fish, oh dear me!
The naughtiest dog-fish in the sea.
He bit his little brothers and his pretty cousin Kate,
He wouldn't get up early, and he stayed up late.

'"Freddy," said his father—that was his name—
"You're a naughty little fish, and your mother is to blame!"
"Freddy," said his mother, "it makes me very sad,
If your father was a better fish, *you* mightn't be so bad!"

'Freddy ate his breakfast, and wouldn't hurry up—
"Freddy," said his teacher, "you're an idle little pup, And if
you're late for school again, I'll beat you without fail!"
But that made Freddy angry, so he bit his teacher's tail.

' "Freddy," said his father, "biting teachers is a sin,"
So Freddy bit his father behind the dorsal fin.
"Oh, Freddy," said his mother, "your conduct makes
    me ill!"
But Freddy said he didn't care, and bit her on the gill.

'Freddy went off swimming, and stopped to have a look
At a worm in the water—and bit a fish-hook!
The fisherman was angry, for fishermen all wish
To catch a forty-pounder, and despise a little fish.

' "Oh, try again," said Freddy, "and bait your hook anew,
My mother's twice as long as me, and you can catch her
    too;
And father likes a limpet best, so bait your hook with that,
You'll be very pleased with father, who is fine and big and
    fat!" '

When Cully saw that Timothy and Hew were awake, and
listening to his song, his expression changed and he tried to look
very serious and respectable. He came nearer to the raft, and
addressed them in a most dignified voice: 'Good morning, dear
boys! I do so trust you have slept well and had a good night's
rest?—You have? Oh, how glad I am! That's splendid! Splendid,
splendid! And I hope, dear boys, that you didn't hear the absurd
little song I was singing?'

16

'We heard it all,' said Timothy. 'It was very interesting.'

'But what happened?' asked Hew. 'Did the fisherman catch Freddy's father and mother?'

'Oh, no!' cried Cully in great distress. 'No, no, no, no! It isn't a true song, it's just nonsense really, because no one could possibly be as wicked as that, could they? I learnt it from a friend of mine, another octopus, a very clever creature, but not quite respectable, I'm afraid, and I sometimes sing it because it has a pleasant tune. I often sing the silliest songs if they have good tunes, because I'm very musical. But you mustn't think for a moment that I *believe* what I sing! Oh, dear me, no! No, no, no, no! I'm a good octopus, I really am, and if I sing horrid songs, it's just because they happen to have nice tunes. That's all.'

His big grey eyes were full of tears, and some were rolling down his orange-coloured beak. He was wiping them away, with his second arm on the right-hand side, when Gunner Boles shouted to him: 'Ahoy there, Cully! Show a leg, my boy! Slip your cable, Cully, it's time to go!'

'Oh dear!' said Cully. 'He's always in such a hurry. I like to take my time about things, but Gunner Boles is most impatient. A busy man, with such a sense of duty.—Well, I must leave you now, dear boys, and I do hope you'll remember that in spite of my silly songs I really am a good octopus, and you must be good too, because to be good is the most important thing in the world. Be clever if you can, be very clever if it's possible, but above all be good.—And now I must bid you adieu, but some day, I trust, we shall meet again in happier circumstances.'

'That's what all grown-up people tell us,' said Hew glumly as Cully swam round to the other side of the raft. 'Be good, they say.'

'It will be very tiresome,' said Timothy, 'if being grown-up simply means being good.'

17

'Perhaps it doesn't,' said Hew. 'Perhaps it only means that you want other people to be good.'

'Well, that's all right,' said Timothy. 'I shouldn't mind that.'

Gunner Boles was already in the water, holding on to the edge of the raft and exchanging a last word with Sam Sturgeon. Now he climbed on to Cully's back, and having shaken hands with Sam, said to the boys, 'Good-bye, my dears, good-bye to you both, and I hope you have a good voyage. You'll be all right now, have no fear of that. But let me give you a piece of advice before I go: say nothing about me and Cully when you get home again! Not a word. Nobody would believe you, even if you did!'

'Isn't it sad,' exclaimed Cully, 'to think that people wouldn't believe in *me*!'

'You're talking too much,' said Gunner Boles, and pushed Cully's head under the water. 'So long,' he said to Sam.

Then Cully, indignant at being treated so rudely, dived deeply down into the blue-black depths of the sea, taking the Gunner with him, and they both disappeared from view in a swirl of water.

'But why have they gone?' asked Timothy.

'Look down there to the south'ard,' said Sam Sturgeon; and there they saw, rising above the edge of the sea, some eighteen or twenty little plumes of smoke, as though in the distance the fires had been lighted in the fire-places of eighteen or twenty houses in some small town. 'Don't you see,' said Sam, 'there's another convoy coming up?'

So an hour or two later they were all rescued from the raft, and after a comfortable voyage in a large ship where they were well treated, they landed in Liverpool. There they were met by their grandfather, their mother's father, who took them to his house in Hampshire. But their mother, who had been saved by an outward-bound ship going to Cape Town, stayed in South Africa. She always liked to have her own way, and she had decided to remain there till the war was over.

The war came to an end, and still she did not return. Captain Spens, having been wounded again, retired from the Navy and lived in his own home on the island of Popinsay, off the north coast of Scotland; and Timothy and Hew lived with him. Mrs. Spens wrote a letter every week to say they should all come out to South Africa; and every week Captain Spens replied that nothing would ever make him leave Popinsay again—for he liked to have his own way just as much as she did. So that was how matters stood, and Timothy and Hew were quite content to be looked after by Sam Sturgeon and Mrs. Matches the housekeeper.

They went to the village school, and they learnt much that was useful from Sam: such as swimming and the names of the stars, and how to tie knots and sail a boat and snare a rabbit, and when it would be high tide next Wednesday—and matters of that sort. Sam had also told them, very seriously, what Gunner Boles himself had said: that never must they speak of their strange experience in the South Atlantic Ocean. Nor had they, except to each other, and as time went on they thought of it more and more as a dream, or a story they had heard, rather than as something which had really happened to them.

But now, when again they saw Gunner Boles's bald head and red whiskers bobbing up and down in the bright sea, they remembered their days on the raft quite clearly; and Timothy and Hew both wondered if Cully had also come to their island.

Chapter Three

'Ahoy there!' shouted Sam, and Gunner Boles turned an astonished face towards them—they could see his bushy red eyebrows rising high on his forehead, and his mouth open, and his pipe fall out—and suddenly he disappeared.

'He'll be up again in a minute,' said Sam, still treading water, and eagerly they waited, and waited a little longer, but still there was no sign of him.

'Perhaps you frightened him,' said Timothy.

'Gunner Boles isn't the man to get frightened,' said Sam, and at that moment Hew, pointing farther out to sea, shouted, 'There he is!'

In a big wave rising and curving and curling over like a green hood, he had seen him come up and poke out his head from the crest of it—and then the wave had fallen in a crash of white water.

'Oh, he'll be hurt!' exclaimed Timothy.

But Sam Sturgeon said in a comfortable voice, 'Gunner Boles can look after himself'; and a moment or two later he reappeared no more than ten yards away, took another look, and dived again. Then his bald head came up in the midst of them, and shaking the water from his whiskers he shook hands first with Sam, and then with Timothy and Hew.

'You might have scared me out of my wits, with that shout of yours,' he said. 'I thought you were strangers, and it gave me such a turn I nearly lost my pipe.—And how are you keeping, Mr. Sturgeon? And the two little boys? But bless my soul, they've growed enormously! They're big lads now!'

'Hew's bigger than me,' said Timothy, 'though he's a lot younger.'

'But Timothy's cleverer,' said Hew modestly.

'A nice nature counts for a lot too,' said Gunner Boles, 'and who lays claim to that?'

'They've both got nice natures,' said Sam Sturgeon, 'or otherwise they'd get a clip over the ear from me.'

Gunner Boles nodded approvingly: 'That's the way I was brought up too.'

'But he never gives us a clip over the ear,' began Timothy indignantly.

'Now, now!' interrupted Sam. 'Not so much chatter from you when your elders and betters have got something to talk about. Won't you come ashore, Mr. Boles, and sit down comfortably, and let's hear your news?'

'It's against orders, in the usual way,' said Gunner Boles, 'but as I'm on special duty at present, well, I dare say I might stretch a point and see what it feels like to sit on dry land again. There's a pretty piece of shore over there.'

'That's the Hen of Popinsay,' said Timothy. 'Nobody lives there except a lot of rabbits.'

'Then it will suit me very well indeed,' said Gunner Boles, and they all swam towards the beach of the little island that was called the Hen. As they were going ashore, Hew asked where

Cully was, and Gunner Boles looked extremely grave and said that Cully hadn't been behaving very well, and was doing extra duty by way of punishment.

'I wish we could see him again,' said Hew. 'He's the only octopus I've ever spoken to.'

'Well,' said Gunner Boles, 'it all depends on Cully himself. If he's good and nothing unforeseen occurs, I dare say I could give him shore-leave in a few days' time—he's not very far away, I'll tell you that much—but duty comes first, of course, and everything finally depends on what we call the exigencies of the service. But I'll tell him you were asking for him, and that will please him, it will indeed; for he's often spoken of you both.'

'And now,' said Sam Sturgeon, 'you take a run round the island and warm yourselves up a bit. You're looking white and cold, and what you need is exercise; and while you're taking a run, Mr. Boles and I'll have a chance to talk.'

Timothy and Hew were most unwilling to go, and miss an interesting conversation, but Sam refused to let them stay; so they ran along the beach to a ruined sheep-fold at the edge of the turf, where they stopped and looked back, and saw Gunner Boles drawing what appeared to be a picture on the level sand— or it might be a map or a plan—which Sam Sturgeon, stooping with his hands on his knees, examined with close attention. Then they talked together, very seriously, and every now and then Gunner Boles pointed to some particular part of the plan, or bent down to draw some new detail with a little stick he had found.

'What do you think they're talking about?' asked Timothy.

'I don't know,' said Hew, 'but it may be the pirate ship. Perhaps Gunner Boles knows how to find it.'

'He said he had come here on special service, and that Cully was doing extra duty for punishment. I wish I knew what their duty was.'

'And where does he live?' asked Hew. 'He can't spend all his time in the sea, can he?'

'He was hundreds of miles from land the first time we met him.'

'Was he dressed in the same way?'

'I can't remember,' said Timothy.

They had both admired the bathing-suit which Gunner Boles was wearing. It consisted of a white vest with two pockets, buttoned with brass buttons, and dark-blue trunks made of a thin rough material like shark-skin, on which the water-drops glistened when he sat in the sun; and on his vest was printed, in neat blue letters, 'H.M.S. Royal Sovereign.' He wore a broad red belt, with a small satchel on one side and a sheath for a long knife on the other; and on his feet were curious large slippers that made his feet look like the feet of an enormous frog.

'It's all very mysterious,' said Timothy, 'but perhaps Sam will explain if we ask him very confidentially.'

'He won't,' said Hew. 'He would never let us talk about Gunner Boles, or Cully either.'

Timothy shivered and said, 'I'm feeling cold. Let's run round the Hen.'

They set off up-hill, over the springy turf that covered the little island with a green carpet, tufted here and there with cushions of pink thrift, and holed with sandy burrows where rabbits lived; but near the cliffs to the west and the north some of the burrows had been deserted by the rabbits, and puffins nested in them. They ran at a steady pace till they came to the eastward side of the island, that looked across Inner Bay to the beach

23

where they had been seeking for treasure; and there they heard someone shouting.

'It's Father,' said Timothy.

'He's found the cannon-ball,' said Hew, as their father shouted again.

Captain Spens had a very loud voice, and the noise of it boomed across the bay, but they could not quite distinguish his words.

'I suppose he wants us to come ashore,' said Timothy.

'We'll have to go and tell Sam and Gunner Boles,' said Hew. 'They can't see him from where they're sitting.'

'And we'd better hurry, or he'll be angry,' said Timothy.

They waved, to let their father know they had heard him, and ran back to the bay where Sam Sturgeon and Gunner Boles were still talking together about something that was, to judge from their appearance, very important indeed. But as soon as Sam heard that Captain Spens was waiting for them—and shouting—he said, 'Well, we'll have to go now,' and Gunner Boles bent down and wiped out the plan he had drawn.

'I'll be seeing you again, Mr. Boles?' asked Sam.

'I'll keep a look-out for you,' said Gunner Boles, 'and if I need help I shan't be slow in coming to ask for it.'

'Good luck to you,' said Sam.

'Thank 'ee,' said Gunner Boles, 'and so-long to you, boys. I'll remember you to Cully, shall I?'

'Yes, please,' they replied.

They shook hands and ran down to the sea, leaving the Gunner sitting all by himself on the sand. When they were half-way across the bay Hew asked, 'What sort of duty is it that Mr. Boles has to do, and what were you talking about, Sam?'

'You mind your own business,' said Sam in his gruffest voice, 'and let other people mind theirs. And remember this, both of you: you mustn't say anything about Gunner Boles to the Old Man. You understand that?'

'Of course,' said Timothy. 'We never have spoken about him.'

'And we never will,' said Hew indignantly.

'I was just reminding you,' said Sam in a milder tone.

Captain Spens was waiting for them at the very edge of the sea, with the cannon-ball in his hands. He was very excited, and his glass eye looked as though it might fall out at any moment.

'Where did you find it?' he demanded. 'Why didn't you come and tell me at once? Don't you realise how important it is? That gale last week, all that hard weather, Sam, may have exposed the wreck. It may be breaking up!'

'Yes, sir,' said Sam, 'it was a proper gale, there's no doubt about that. I wouldn't be surprised if it had moved things about on the bottom of the sea almost as much as it did on top.'

'Have you searched the whole beach?'

'We went along that bank of seaweed pretty carefully. I don't think there's anything else come ashore, sir, except that cannon-ball.'

'But that's evidence, isn't it?' exclaimed the Captain, and gave the evidence to Timothy to carry. 'You don't find cannon-balls coming out of nothing, do you? Cannon-balls come out of ships, and cannon-balls like that come out of old ships. I wish I had some of those long-winded, self-important, addle-pated so-called experts here, who won't admit that my great-great-great-great-great-great-great-great grandfather ever wrecked his ship on Popinsay; or if he did, they say, he wasn't Aaron Spens the pirate, and so there was nothing of any value in it.—Experts, my wooden foot! A lot of scoundrels and nincompoops, that's what they are.'

For a long time the Captain had corresponded with

historians and learned people of that sort, telling them that he was a descendant of Aaron Spens, a famous pirate whose crew had been hanged at Execution Dock in 1712; and trying to convince them that Aaron Spens had wrecked his ship, and gone down with it, under the cliffs of Popinsay. All the historians, without exception, refused to believe his story, and the more firmly they denied it, the more strongly the Captain declared it to be true. Whoever opposed him—in this or any other matter—was in his opinion a scoundrel or a nincompoop. When he was in a bad mood, indeed, he appeared to think that nearly everybody in the world, except his own particular friends, was either one or the other; and sometimes, after he had been reading the newspapers and come to the conclusion that everything was being horribly mismanaged, and getting worse and worse, Timothy and Hew would hear him striding to and fro in his study, and exclaiming, 'Scoundrels and nincompoops, that's what they are! A set of scoundrels and a pack of nincompoops!'

His voice would grow louder and louder until it thundered through the house like someone beating a big drum. He was not a big man—he was, indeed, quite small and thin, with a fierce red face and bright blue eyes—but when he was angry his voice was like that of a giant, and the walls of the house would shake and tremble as he bellowed, 'SCOUNDRELS AND NINCOMPOOPS!'

Now, however, though he shouted from time to time, he was in a very good humour as they walked up from the beach. Timothy and Hew had quickly dressed themselves, and calling them into his study he gave each of them half a crown for finding the cannon-ball. Then he unlocked a big black cupboard, and taking out a bottle of rum poured a large drink for Sam; who took it and said, 'My best respects to you, sir, and very happy to be still under your command.'

Timothy and Hew were allowed to stay and listen while the Captain and Sam discussed diving operations. The Captain owned a fishing-boat called *Endeavour*. It was about thirty-five feet long, broadly built and deep in the keel, and very seaworthy. Before the war he had often used it for diving, and Sam in a diver's suit had gone down into the deep green sea to look for the pirate ship, while one of the crew pumped air to him, and another stood ready to haul him up again when he gave the signal that he was ready. But Sam's old diving-suit had worn out, and the Captain had found it difficult to get an up-to-date new one of the sort he wanted.—His difficulty, he said, was due to the fact that everybody in charge of anything was either a scoundrel or a nincompoop.—At last, however, the new suit had arrived, and the *Endeavour*, which had gone south to have its engine over-hauled, was due back in Popinsay within a few days. And then, said the Captain, they would waste no more time but quickly put Sam overboard, and wait above him until he had found pirate gold! He had discovered, he thought, the exact place where the wreck must be lying.

He unstrapped a large portfolio and spread a chart on the floor. Stiffly, because of his artificial leg, he knelt down, and Sam, breathing heavily, knelt beside him. The two boys leaned over their shoulders.

'There!' said the Captain. 'That's where she lies, I'll bet a fortune on it!'

He pointed to a spot in North Bay, under the west cliffs of Popinsay and about two cables north of the Hen. He began to explain why that must be the exact place where the wreck lay, and Timothy and Hew listened eagerly, though they could not understand all he said.

In an attic of the house, in a sea-chest full of old papers, he had lately discovered a tattered manuscript in which there was a story about Aaron Spens the pirate; and on another page of the manuscript, more than half of which had been torn away, there was a rough drawing of what, he felt sure, was North Bay and the Hen. He spoke also about the set of the tide, which he had studied very carefully, and said that the cannon-balls and the skull with the gold coins in it, which had been washed ashore in Inner Bay, could only have come from that part of the coast which he now marked, on the chart, with a pencilled cross.

It was this part of the argument that Timothy and Hew could not follow, and they grew rather tired of listening; but Sam understood everything the Captain said, and seemed much impressed by it.

They were twice interrupted by Mrs. Matches the housekeeper, who came in to say that lunch was ready. 'Go away!' said the Captain. 'Go away, Mrs. Matches, we're busy.'

When she came in for the third time she merely beckoned to the boys with a long skinny forefinger, and they, because by now they were very hungry, got up quickly, and tiptoed out, and had lunch with her in the kitchen.

Mrs. Matches was six feet tall and very thin; and she was the only woman on the island who could put up with the Captain's bad temper. Fourteen other women had tried to be his housekeeper, but all had left him because they could not bear to be shouted at. No one, they said, could bear being shouted at in such a terrible way. So Mrs. Matches became the Captain's housekeeper just to prove they were wrong and show that she could bear it. 'Faith!' she said, 'there's not a man alive that can daunt me with his shouting!' And for ten years she had put up with the Captain, and quite often shouted back at him. The Captain still treated her badly, and never came to a meal in time if he was busy with anything else; but he always expected his meals to be hot when he did come. He often said, however, that Mrs. Matches was a fine woman; and so she was.

She was not a very good cook, but she always cooked twice as much as anyone could eat, and whenever the boys had lunch with her in the kitchen they ate too much. So now, after lunch, they felt rather tired, and went outside to sleep in the sun under a dyke.

But before they went to sleep Timothy said to Hew, 'I understood nearly everything that Father said about the ship, and it was very interesting, and if we discover a cargo of gold—well, that will be most exciting. But what I can't understand is what Gunner Boles has got to do with it. Why has he come here, just at this very moment?'

'And Cully too,' said Hew. 'I wonder what Cully's doing, and why he had to be punished?'

Timothy tried to think of an answer, but yawned instead; and Hew followed suit. So they lay down in the warm grass and went to sleep.

Chapter Four

The island of Popinsay was twelve miles long and nearly eight miles broad at its broadest part. Its population numbered about three hundred and fifty people, and nearly all the men were either fishermen or farmers or shopkeepers in the little village of Fishing Hope at the south end. Captain Spens owned the northern half of Popinsay, and the small islands that were called the Calf and the Hen; but all the best land was in the south. There were several farms on the Captain's property, but none of them was worth very much, and that was why he was so anxious to find the pirate's treasure; because his barns and byres and stables were in danger of falling down, and he could not afford to repair them.

Popinsay House, where he lived, was the largest house on the island. A little wood grew behind it, and from a distance it looked very handsome. But the roof leaked, the chimneys smoked, the bedroom floors had holes in them, and bees nested in the roof and could not be driven out. If he found a treasure-chest full of gold, he could make it a very fine house indeed; but otherwise it would become more and more uncomfortable to live in, and already it was quite uncomfortable enough, especially in winter-time. That was why Mrs. Spens preferred to live in South Africa.

The Captain and Sam Sturgeon and the boys all waited with growing impatience for the return of the fishing-boat *Endeavour*, and every afternoon Timothy and Hew walked round Inner Bay, and swam over to the Hen—or walked across, if the tide was out—and searched the cliffs there, hoping to find some new treasure or to meet Cully. But they found nothing, and met no one except people whom they knew very well, until the third afternoon. Then, when they were walking up from the beach of the Hen to the cliffs on the north side, they heard a strange, thin, reedy voice singing a little song. They stopped in surprise, and listened for a few seconds. Then they got down on their hands and knees, and cautiously, but as quickly as they could, crawled towards the cliffs.

Not far away there was a narrow cleft in the rock, as though the cliff had been split in two. From either side the turf sloped down to it, and then there were ledges of bare rock, like great stone steps. In some places the cleft was no more than a yard across, but, thirty or forty feet below the ledges, the green sea rose and fell, and grumbled in little caves.

Crawling down the nearer slope, Timothy and Hew looked into the cleft and saw a curious sight. Cully—they recognised him at once—was hanging over the sea as if he lay in a hammock, and swinging to and fro. With four of his long thin arms he held on to a ledge on the near side of the cleft, and with the other four to a ledge on the far side. He looked very comfortable, and as he swung out and in, he began to sing again:

> 'The Captain of the *Saucy Kate*
> Gave these instructions to the Mate:

31

"We're sailing through the Downs to Deal,
So have a good man at the wheel;
And to avoid a total wreck,
Please keep the Starboard Watch on deck;
Let a sailor go to the masthead,
And let another heave the lead;
And do remember, Mr. White,
To see your lamps are burning bright!"

'But Mr. White, he shook his head,
"Dear Captain, I am tired," he said,
"We've worked your ship from Port o' Spain,
And I'm never going to work again!"

'Lazy, lazy! Let's have a holiday!
It's quite crazy to work all your strength away!
You'll lose your breath if you hurry,
There's nothing to win from worry,
But take your ease, and do as you please—
I want to go out and play!'

'I've heard that tune before,' said Hew.

'It's not all the same,' said Timothy, 'but part of it is just like *A Bicycle Built for Two.*—Listen! He's going to sing some more.'

Cully cleared his throat, and sang some more verses:

'The Captain of the *Saucy Kate*
To the Bo'sun did ejaculate:
"We do not want to have a wreck,
So keep the Starboard Watch on deck;

Let a sailor go to the masthead,
And let another heave the lead;
And do remember, Bo'sun Kite,
To see your lamps are burning bright!"

'But Bo'sun Kite, he shook his head,
"Dear Captain, I am tired," he said,
We've worked your ship from Elsinore,
And I'm never going to work no more!"

'The Captain of the *Saucy Kate*
With a Seaman then had some debate:
"Let a sailor go to the masthead,
And let another heave the lead;
And do remember, Seaman Twite,
To see your lamps are burning bright!"

'But Seaman Twite, he shook his head,
"Dear Captain, I am tired," he said,
 "We've worked your ship from Portland, Maine,
And I'm never going to work again!"

'The Captain of the *Saucy Kate*
To the Cabin Boy his case did state:
"Now do remember, Boy McKnight,
To see your lamps are burning bright!"

'But Boy McKnight, he shook his head,
"Dear Captain, I am tired," he said,
"We've worked your ship from Singapore,
And I'm never going to work no more!"

'The *Saucy Kate*, she ran aground,
And all the sailormen were drowned;
And the Captain and the Bo'sun too,
And Mr. White, and all the crew,
No longer work, no longer care—
And here's a song with a pleasant air …'

Then, swinging to and fro like a swing-boat at a fair, he repeated the chorus:

'Lazy, lazy! Let's have a holiday!
It's quite crazy to work all your strength away!
You'll lose your breath if you hurry,
There's nothing to win from worry,
But take your ease, and do as you please—
I want to go out and play!'

Timothy and Hew crawled a little nearer, till they were looking straight down at him. Then they spoke together. 'Good morning, Cully,' they said politely.

Cully gave a little scream and disappeared.

'He's gone!' said Hew.

'Yes,' said Timothy, 'but he's still holding on.'

They leaned over the cliff, and saw that Cully had dropped down to the level of the sea, but his long arms—four on each side—still clasped the ledges of rock from which he had been swinging. His arms had stretched like elastic, and the weight of his body had pulled them out till they were nearly as thin as elastic bands.

'Cully!' they shouted. 'Come up again and talk to us!'

Cully's voice sounded very small and far away. 'No, I won't,' he cried. 'I won't come near you till I know who you are. I'm not

34

in the habit of talking to strangers!'

'But we're not strangers,' shouted Timothy, 'we're Timothy——'

'And Hew!' shouted Hew. 'Oh, do come up again, Cully!'

Slowly the elastic bands grew thicker, and shorter, as Cully hauled himself to the top of the cliff, and at last his big orange beak appeared above the edge, and his large pale eyes, that were as big as saucers, looked coldly at Timothy and then at Hew. They were quite taken aback to see that his expression was far from friendly. They had naturally expected that he would be as glad to see them as they were to see him; but when he spoke his voice was as cold and disagreeable as his eyes.

'My friend Gunner Boles told me you were here,' he said, 'and I was looking forward to meeting you again. But I did expect—and I had the right to expect!—that you would remember my name, and address me with proper courtesy, instead of shouting down the cliff, without caring who heard you, "Cully, Cully, Cully!" as if I were a common sea-urchin or something like that.'

'But Cully *is* your name,' said Timothy.

'It is not! My name is Culliferdontofoscofolio Polydesteropouf. And please remember that in future.'

It's a very long name to have to remember,' said Hew.

'Long!' exclaimed Cully. 'It's one of the shortest names I know. Among the octopuses, that is. Why, there's a friend of mine—and a charming young lady she is—called Dildery Doldero Casadiplasadimolodyshenkendorf Rustiverolico Silverysplash. That's a lot longer than my name, and she would be most offended if you forgot a single syllable of it. And another of my friends, who's a great sportsman, is called Donicocharlidipendomoranty Suspenderabatsicorolagornover

35

Abrolicocasm. And I had an uncle, but he's dead now, whose name was Gerrumfogeraster Gerrubbulagillimore Gasteroplasterostikonnatoffico Sukkumansee. Both of those names are much more difficult than mine, and in any case it's very, very rude to criticise a person's name, no matter what it is.'

Timothy and Hew apologised for their lack of courtesy, and promised they would do their best to remember Cully's full name in future; but Cully interrupted them and said, 'Oh, well, you can call me Cully if you want to. Nearly everyone does,' he added with a sigh, 'though I really don't like it. I don't like it a bit.'

Hoping to please him, and make him more cheerful, Hew said they had heard the song he had been singing, and liked it very much. 'I wish you would sing it again,' he said.

'What song?' asked Cully in a trembling voice; and Timothy and Hew both whistled the tune.

A look of dreadful dismay appeared on Cully's face. 'Oh, not that song!' he exclaimed. 'Surely you didn't hear me singing that? Oh dear, oh dear! It's a most improper song, and you mustn't think for a moment that I approve of it. I'm a great believer in work. Work is a noble occupation, and I wouldn't say a word against it—not a word!—but the song has a pretty tune in spite of the horrid sentiment it expresses, and that is why I was singing it; thinking, of course, that I was all alone. I wouldn't dream of singing it in company! But we octopuses are such musical creatures.—*Octopodes*, I should say. That is the proper form of the plural, isn't it? I always say *octopodes* unless I forget.— Yes, we are both musical and artistic, and hard workers too, of course. Very hard workers.'

'What sort of work do you do?' asked Timothy.

Loosening his hold on the far side of the cleft in the rock,

36

Cully hauled himself on to the cliff beside the boys, and settled down to talk in comfort. He arranged his eight arms round about him, and sat in the middle of them as though he were in a sort of nest. He looked very much at his ease, and at the same time extremely important.

'My work,' he said slowly, 'is absolutely indispensable. You know what that means, I hope? It means that you can't get on without me. Do you realise that there are occasions when the safety of the whole world depends on me? On me alone! I don't boast about it—in fact I never speak of it—but that is the simple truth. Yes, my dear boys, there have been times when I have held the safety of the world in my eight arms!'

'But how?' asked Hew.

'What do you do?' said Timothy.

'That is a secret,' said Cully. 'I couldn't tell that to anyone. No, not even to you. All I can say is that I am always on duty, and when things are dangerous, I have *to hold on!*'

'What do you hold on to?' asked Timothy.

'That is the secret,' said Cully.

'Are you on duty now?' asked Hew.

'Now, and always,' said Cully in his most dignified voice. 'From time to time, of course, I take a little rest, or recreation, but that doesn't interfere with my duty. Oh, no, no, no! No, no, no, no, no! Not at all.—But we mustn't speak only about my affairs, we must talk about yours too. Tell me, what have you been doing since last we met in the middle of the South Atlantic Ocean?'

Timothy and Hew were very pleased to talk about themselves for a change, and tell Cully about Popinsay and their Father and Sam Sturgeon and Mrs. Matches; and they talked for a long time.

Cully listened quietly to all they had to say, and never interrupted except to ask Hew for the loan of his handkerchief. This he spread over his eyes to keep the sun out of them, he explained. The boys thought he was deeply interested in what they had to say, and went on talking until a little breeze blew the handkerchief away. Then they saw that Cully had fallen asleep.

They were disappointed, of course, but Timothy said that Cully had probably been working so hard that he was tired out.

'If he's always on duty, he must be very tired,' said Hew.

They could not decide whether to wake him, or to go quietly away and leave him; and while they were wondering which would be the kinder thing to do, they heard a great voice shouting from somewhere out at sea.

'Cully, you rogue! Cully, you idle vagabond!' roared the voice. 'Where are you skulking, you lazy, good-for-nothing, insubordinate, skrimshanking lump of sinful sloth? Cully, I say! CULLY!'

'That's Gunner Boles,' said Timothy, and stood up to look for him.

'There he is,' said Hew, pointing to the northwest; and there, a hundred yards or so from the shore, they saw the Gunner bobbing up and down in the sea, his bald head shining in the sun.

Cully too had heard him. Cully was now wide awake and looking rather frightened.

'Don't tell him I'm here!' he cried. 'Don't let him know that you've seen me, will you? He's a good man, but very unreasonable. Very, very unreasonable. With a dreadful temper and a sense of duty—what a pity they so often go together! So keep it dark, dear boys. Keep our little party a secret between ourselves, will you?'

Hurrying in an oozy way to the edge of the cliff, Cully let

himself down like a ball at the end of four pieces of elastic, and just before he disappeared he looked up and said, 'Good-bye, dear boys, for the present—and remember to keep it dark, won't you?'

Then he let go, and they heard a soft splash as he dropped into the sea. From the north-west Gunner Boles shouted to them: 'Ahoy, my lads! Is that worthless octopus there? He's absent from duty again, and I'd wring his dirty neck, if he had one!'

'No,' shouted Timothy, 'he isn't here.'—'But it's a good thing he didn't ask if he *was* here,' he said to Hew.

'A very good thing,' said Hew.

'Well, if you happen to see him,' roared the Gunner, 'tell him I'm going to court-martial him, keel-haul him, cut his claws, and clap him in quod—and that's only a beginning of what I'm going to do.'

'Poor Cully,' said Hew. 'He doesn't seem to be such a hard worker as he pretends.'

'If Gunner Boles is right, he certainly isn't on duty all the time.'

'But I like him just the same,' said Hew.

'So do I,' said Timothy. 'It's something to be friendly with an octopus, even if he isn't a very good one.'

They watched the Gunner swimming to and fro in the bright sea, and then they saw something like a little whirlpool in the water, quite near to him. The Gunner shook his fist, and was evidently very angry; the whirlpool began to splash.

'That's Cully now,' said Hew.

'They're having an argument,' said Timothy.

The argument lasted for about half a minute, and then, quite suddenly, the Gunner disappeared as though someone had seized him by the ankles and dragged him under.

'Cully's won,' said Hew.

'I'm not so sure about that,' said Timothy. 'If Gunner Boles is his superior officer, then Cully's only making things worse by giving him a ducking. Try to imagine what would happen to anyone who gave Father a ducking.'

'Poor Cully!' said Hew again. 'It was a very nice song that he sang.'

'Yes, I liked it too,' said Timothy, 'though, as Cully himself said, you couldn't possibly approve of it, could you?'

'I'm sure Father wouldn't,' said Hew, 'but then Father isn't likely to hear it.'

Presently they went home, and from Sam Sturgeon learnt the important news that the *Endeavour* was due to arrive in two days' time. They said nothing to Sam about their meeting with Cully.

Chapter Five

In the morning everyone got up early, and soon after breakfast the diving-apparatus was loaded into one of the farm-carts and taken down to the pier at Inner Bay; and two young men from the home-farm went with them to man the pump and the ropes. Sam Sturgeon was going to test his new diving-suit and make sure that everything was in good working order.

They helped him to get into his heavy trousers, and put on his lead-soled boots. He put on the upper part of the suit, and forced his hands through tight rubber cuffs. A pad was placed on his shoulders to take the weight of the great copper helmet, his corselet was screwed on, and the helmet was screwed to the corselet. Lead weights were fastened to his shoulders, and last of all the face-glass in the helmet was closed. Then Captain Spens tapped the top of the helmet, and Sam raised his hand as a sign that everything was in order.

Slowly he descended the iron ladder at the end of the pier. 'Heave round the pump!' said the Captain, and for the third time that morning made sure that the young men from the farm understood the signals that Sam might make.

If he pulled once on the air-line, it meant they were pumping too hard and giving him too much air; if he pulled twice, it meant that he wanted more air. A single pull on the breast-rope, which was made fast in a bowline under his arms, meant 'Stop,' or 'Hold on.' Two pulls meant 'Haul up,' and three 'Veer away'—or pay out more rope.

Captain Spens and Timothy and Hew sat at the end of the pier and dangled their legs, and a pair of screaming terns followed the line of bubbles that showed where Sam was walking, as if they expected a fish to appear.

'How far can he see under water?' asked Timothy.

'Visibility's good on a dull day like this,' said the Captain. 'At fifteen fathoms—and he's no deeper than three or four now—he could see fairly well for about thirty feet.'

'And what would happen to him,' asked Hew, 'if the air-line was cut?'

'He would get a very bad fright,' said the Captain, 'but if he closed his air-valves he could last for twenty minutes, I dare say.'

After a quarter of an hour Sam could be seen again, like a stumpy broad-shouldered monster moving in the clear green water at the end of the pier, and when he had climbed the ladder, and they had unscrewed his helmet, he said that everything had worked very well indeed, and he was quite satisfied with his new suit. So they decided to go home again.

Captain Spens was in excellent humour as they walked back to lunch, and Timothy and Hew both wondered why they had ever thought he was a bad-tempered man. For when he was cheerful he would make as many jokes as he could think of, and even if they were not very good jokes they showed that he wanted everyone else to feel as happy as he did. He would also listen quite patiently to other people when they made jokes, and he would try to laugh at the proper time. Sometimes he was in a good mood for three or four days on end, and Timothy and Hew would feel tired with having to laugh so much; while their mother, if she were at home, would say she had a headache and go to bed. But on this occasion Captain Spens's good humour lasted only until the postman came.

Timothy and Hew were upstairs, washing their hands, when they heard the crash of something falling, and knew that their father had pushed his writing-table over. He often did that when he lost his temper, because in such a state he could not sit still but had to get up and walk about the room. The boys hurried to the landing at the top of the stairs, and leaning over the banisters listened with great interest. They heard their father exclaim, loudly and bitterly, 'Oh, the nincompoops! What nincompoops they are!' Then he opened the door of his study, and shouted for Sam.

Sam came quickly and said, 'Yes, sir. What's gone wrong now?—Why, your writing-table's fallen over.'

'Pick it up, Sam. Pick it up,' said the Captain, and Timothy and Hew looked at each other in astonishment. For now, when they could hear it clearly, they realised that their father's voice was more sad than angry, and that was a note they had never heard in it before. But they could only guess, or try to guess, what had made him sad, for he shut the door of his study—more quietly than usual—and talked to Sam without shouting at all.

'It must have been something in a letter that upset him,' whispered Timothy.

'Did you see the letters before he took them in?' asked Hew.

'No.'

'There may have been one from South Africa.'

'That's what I was thinking,' said Timothy.

They sat side by side on the top stair, silent and rather

43

frightened, for both were wondering if their mother had written to say she was ill, or had been knocked down by a motor-car, or something like that. Or perhaps someone else had written. Perhaps she was seriously ill. They felt very unhappy.

After about ten minutes the study door opened, and Sam Sturgeon came out with a serious expression on his face. He went half-way down the passage that led to the kitchen and shouted: 'Mrs. Matches! Captain's orders. You're wanted on the quarter-deck.'

Then he came upstairs and saw the boys. 'You too,' he said. 'The Captain wants to speak to you.'

They found their father sitting at his writing-table, looking stern and very solemn. He was reading a letter, perhaps for the fourth or fifth time, that was, they could see, in their mother's handwriting. Mrs. Matches, whose sleeves were rolled up and whose hair was coming down behind, said she had dished the potatoes and they would be getting cold; but the Captain paid no attention to her.

'They're mashed,' she said. 'Just wait a minute and I'll run out and put them in the oven——'

'Stay where you are,' said the Captain. 'I have important and unhappy news for you. But tell me first if you could look after these boys, for two or three weeks perhaps, if I were to go to South Africa?'

'A fine question!' exclaimed Mrs. Matches in a scornful voice. 'If I can look after you and the boys as well, how should I not be able to look after them, if they were left to themselves, and we hadn't you about the house to hinder us all?'

'I want no impertinence!' shouted the Captain.

'It's not impertinence I'm giving you, it's the simple truth. But if I don't get leave to go to the kitchen it's cold potatoes you'll be getting, and you won't like that.'

'Confound your potatoes!' roared the Captain.

'And that won't improve them either,' said Mrs. Matches.

Captain Spens made a great effort to control himself, and in a quieter voice—though it was still angry—demanded: 'Will you listen to me, woman? I tell you that I've important news for you. News of my wife. Terrible and horrible news! She says that she's made up her mind to live in South Africa. She isn't coming back to Popinsay, she says. She's going to settle down in Cape Town. In Cape Town!'

'And never come home again?' cried Hew.

'Is she ill?' asked Timothy.

'If you want my honest opinion,' said the Captain, 'she's mad.'

'Oh, no, sir, I wouldn't say that,' Sam Sturgeon interrupted. 'That's going a bit far, sir. Headstrong—that's what she is. She always was a lady that liked to have her own way.'

The Captain turned in his chair and looked fiercely at Sam. 'Do you remember,' he asked, 'the sort of hat she was wearing when you first saw her?'

'I shan't ever be able to forget it,' said Sam.

'What was it like?'

'It filled me with admiration, sir.'

'What!' cried the Captain.

'With admiration for you, sir,' Sam explained. 'It took a brave man to go out walking beside a hat like that. Its colour would have made a delicate person sea-sick, and in shape it was like a Chinese gong with a hole through the middle and bits of mosquito-netting hanging down from the brim. To this day, sir, I can't think of that hat without a shudder.'

'She made it herself,' said the Captain moodily, 'and now she wants to start a shop in Cape Town. A hat-shop. A shop to sell the hats that she's going to make! Hats like the one that you remember, Sam, and worse, if possible. She's going into partnership with a woman called Blinkingroof, or some such name, and Mrs. Blinkingroof's husband, who must be a nincompoop if ever there was one; and his name's Blinkingroof too, I suppose.—But I shan't allow it, Sam! It wouldn't be fair to South Africa! South Africa's a fine country, a loyal country, and the South Africans are splendid people. To let my wife make their hats, and fill them with confusion and despair, would be a crime, Mrs. Matches! A crime, I say!'

'Then make her come home,' said Mrs. Matches. 'Go out, and bring her back with you.'

'That is exactly what I propose to do,' declared the Captain, 'though Heaven knows I can't afford to. I must borrow money, I'll have to mortgage my pension—but to save South Africa I'm prepared to go to any expense! I mean to leave at once. I shall fly out, meet my wife, talk things over and try to make her see reason—and if she won't see reason I'll stuff her in a sack and bring her home as cargo!'

'She wouldn't be very comfortable in a sack,' said Timothy.

'Though I suppose you could put a bottle of lemonade and some sandwiches in with her,' said Hew.

'Listen to me!' exclaimed the Captain. 'You want your mother to come home, don't you?'

'Yes, of course we do!' they answered, both together.

'Then home she shall come! I'll rescue her from the scoundrels and nincompoops into whose hands she has fallen—I'll save South Africa from the anarchy and misery your mother would create if she started selling hats there—and she'll come back to Popinsay either sitting decently beside me in the aeroplane, or in a sack among the luggage!—That's settled, that's all arranged. I've made up my mind, and there's nothing more to say. Is there, Sam?'

'No, sir.'

'Then we can have our lunch.—Come along, Mrs. Matches, don't you see what time it is? How much longer are you going to keep us waiting?'

Mrs. Matches, who was an active woman, had grown more and more impatient while the Captain was talking. She had passed the time by rolling down her sleeves, by tidying her back hair, by taking off her apron and tying it more neatly round her waist, and by pulling up her stockings, which were inclined to fall in wrinkles about her ankles; but she had never stopped worrying about the potatoes, which were getting cold, and a rhubarb pudding which had been too long in the pot. So now, when she heard herself accused of idling, she started as if she had been stung by a wasp.

'*Me* keep you waiting!' she exclaimed. 'Me that's been itching to get away and see to the potatoes that'll be as cold as a stone, and the pudding that'll be as soft as a wet sponge, while you sat there blethering as though time would stand still to let you finish! *Me* keep you waiting! May the Lord forgive you, man, but if the pudding's spoilt, I never will!'

Her thin face was red with anger, and as she flung open the study door, and marched indignantly away, her back hair fell down again and fluttered like a pennant in a breeze.

Sam followed her, and the Captain, frowning a little, said, 'There goes a most unfortunate woman. A woman who can't control her temper! It's a bad fault, my boys, and I hope you'll avoid it. Try to keep your temper in all circumstances.'

Then he walked briskly into the dining-room, followed by Timothy and Hew, and began to carve what was left of a cold leg of mutton. He carved slowly, because his artificial hand was not much use to him, and he had cut only two slices when Mrs. Matches appeared again, carrying a large china dish on which lay a rhubarb pudding, steaming hotly, that looked as if it had fallen out of an upper window. And Mrs. Matches was very angry indeed.

'There!' she said, holding the dish under the Captain's nose. 'That's what you've done with your talking and chattering! That was as fine a pudding as ever went into the pot, and look at it now. Ruined, just ruined! And it was you that did it!'

Her voice was so angry, her expression so fierce, and she thrust the pudding so close to the Captain's nose that he grew somewhat alarmed. He thought she was going to throw it at him. So he retreated a step or two, and picked up the leg of mutton. He held it as if it were a club, and shook it in Mrs. Matches' face.

'Stand back,' he exclaimed. 'Stand back, Mrs. Matches!'

And now it was Mrs. Matches' turn to be alarmed, for the Captain was waving the leg of mutton in a very threatening manner.

'And you call yourself a gentleman!' she cried. 'But what sort of a gentleman would hit his housekeeper with a leg of mutton, I'd like to know?'

'And you call yourself a housekeeper,' shouted the Captain. 'But what sort of a housekeeper would throw a rhubarb pudding at her employer?—Get back to your kitchen, Mrs. Matches. Back to your kitchen, and learn to keep your temper!'

Mrs. Matches' spirit failed her. The Captain's voice was used to command a thousand men, and Mrs. Matches was overawed. Step by step she retreated before him, and was driven from the dining-room. The Captain, breathing deeply but otherwise calm, replaced the leg of mutton on the sideboard, and having

48

wiped his hands on a napkin, again set to work on it.

He said to the boys: 'You have just seen a good example of the power of the human eye. A man who is sure of himself can dominate a wild animal merely by looking at it in a resolute and determined fashion. That is how I looked at Mrs. Matches when she threatened to become violent and throw a rhubarb pudding at me. I fixed her with my eye, and dominated her completely.'

'It didn't look like that,' said Hew.

'It looked as though you fixed her with a leg of mutton,' said Timothy.

The Captain was about to explain that the leg of mutton was of no consequence at all, when Sam Sturgeon brought in a dish of cold potatoes; so instead of arguing, the boys and their father sat down to lunch.

Chapter Six

In the afternoon it began to rain, and a gale sprang up. The wind rattled the windows, and the rain came through the leaky parts of the roof, and Mrs. Matches brought all her buckets and basins up to the drawing-room and the bedrooms, and set them down where they would catch the drops. Then she had to go and iron some shirts for the Captain, who was busy packing, and kept everyone else busy too.

Sam Sturgeon had carried eighteen or twenty suitcases, valises, gladstone bags, hold-alls, and portmanteaus down from the attics before the Captain could find exactly what he wanted, and every now and then Mrs. Matches had to come and look for socks or handkerchiefs or collars or pyjamas. Captain Spens did not want to stay more than a few days in South Africa, because the longer he stayed the more money he would have to spend, and the trip was going to cost him far more than he could afford in any case. So to begin with he decided to carry very little luggage. Enough, perhaps, for three days in Cape Town. But then he thought it might take longer than that to make his wife see reason, so he packed a larger suitcase with enough clothes to last him a week. And a little while later he grew more doubtful still, and made Mrs. Matches look for more socks and more collars, and told Sam to fetch the gladstone bag that, an hour before, he had thought he would not need. 'For if she's in a difficult mood,' he said, 'I may have to stay as long as a fortnight.'

Timothy, who was helping his father, looked very thoughtful and said, 'Why can't you fix her with your eye, and make her come at once?'

'Well,' said the Captain, 'that might be a little difficult.—Go and get my white buckskin shoes, Sam. I'll probably need them too.'

He waited until Sam had gone, and then admitted, 'The fact is that your mother's got an eye of her own, and once or twice in her life she has fixed me!'

'You'd better take a sack with you,' said Hew. 'You may need it.'

'That's very sound advice,' said the Captain, and when Sam brought in his white shoes, he told him to go and look for the biggest sack he could find.

At night the wind blew harder, and howled in the chimneys, and thundered on the window-panes. Doors rattled, floors creaked, and in all the upper rooms the rain fell *drip-drop, plish-plash*, into the buckets and basins that stood under the leaky parts of the roof.

Timothy and Hew lay in bed, unable to sleep because they were excited by the thought of their father flying to South Africa to bring their mother home.

'But she won't enjoy living here in weather like this,' said Timothy.

'Not unless the roof's mended,' said Hew.

'And there's something wrong with the windows too.'

'And with the doors.'

'It would cost hundreds of pounds to repair everything that needs to be repaired.'

'But if we can find the wreck,' said Hew.

'And if there's treasure in it——'

'Then we can afford it, and mother won't have anything to complain about.'

Presently they fell asleep, and in the morning rose early to go with their father to Fishing Hope, where he went aboard the little steamer that crossed every day to the mainland.

'Be good boys,' he said, 'and take care of yourselves.—And don't do anything rash while I'm away, Sam. If you like to use *Endeavour* to go out and do some general exploration, well and good. But keep an eye on the weather and take no risks.'

'Oh, no, sir,' said Sam. 'Of course not.'

'And when I come back,' said the Captain, looking very grim indeed, 'I'll have Mrs. Spens with me—and the Government of South Africa ought to pay me handsomely for bringing her home!'

The gangway was pulled aboard, the little steamer backed out into the harbour, and turned and headed to the south. The boys stood on the pier and waved till their father was out of sight.

The wind was still blowing hard, though the weather was improving and Sam said it would be a fine evening. But it was cold on the pier, and before the steamer had reached the harbour-mouth they hurried back to the old shooting-brake in which they had driven down from Popinsay House.

Then, just as they were about to start, Timothy cried, 'Stop! Stop, Sam; don't you see who's coming in?'

He pointed to the mouth of the harbour, and there, with the broken waves dancing like fountains before her, was the fishing-boat *Endeavour.* Her skipper, Old Mattoo Marwick—his Christian name was Matthew, but everyone called him Old Mattoo—had not waited for the gale to go down, but had brought his boat across from the mainland in spite of rough weather, and as soon as they saw her plunging in the tide-rip at the harbour-mouth, Sam Sturgeon and Timothy and Hew jumped out of the shooting-brake and ran back to the head of the pier to wait her arrival.

She came quickly in through the sheltered water of the harbour, and as she approached the pier the sun broke the clouds and cast a vivid light on her; and Timothy and Hew and Sam Sturgeon all agreed that nowhere could they have seen a prettier picture. For not only had the *Endeavour's* engine been overhauled, but she had been newly painted from masthead to keel, and her topsides were a pale bright green like new leaves, with a golden bead running from stem to stern; and below the water-line she was a dark red that gleamed through the green sea; and her little deck-house was primrose yellow with a brown roof; and the small sail she carried was the colour of autumn leaves. So they waited in great excitement till she came alongside and tied up to the pier, and then hurried aboard to shake hands with Old Mattoo, and James William Cordiall who was the mate and the engineer as well.

Sam Sturgeon had a long discussion with Old Mattoo and James William Cordiall about the state of the engine, while Timothy and Hew admired the new paint, and finally it was decided that *Endeavour* should lie that night in Fishing Hope and sail round to Inner Bay on the following morning. And after that had been settled, Sam Sturgeon drove the boys home, and for the rest of the day they did nothing in particular. But late at night they were wakened by a curious noise.

Timothy was the first to get up. He slipped out of bed and shook Hew's arm. Hew whispered, 'I heard it too. What do you think it is?'

'It sounds like people laughing,' said Timothy.

A dead calm had followed the gale, and the night was utterly silent except for the sound, like very distant thunder, of the sea breaking on the western cliffs. But then, while they listened, the silence was broken by a great din as if someone in the house were playing a trombone. Or was it a bass drum? Or could it be somebody—somebody with lungs of leather and a throat of brass—leaning back in his chair and roaring with laughter?

'Oh, what can it be?' asked Hew,

'Let's go and see,' said Timothy.

Very quietly they opened the bedroom door and stepped out into the corridor. There was a lighted lamp, turned very low, on the landing at the top of the stairs, and under the door of their father's room there showed a narrow glow of light, and from behind the door came the sound of deep voices, talking.

'Burglars?' whispered Hew.

'Let's go and see,' said Timothy again.

He opened the door. They went in together, and to their great surprise saw Gunner Boles, magnificently dressed in red silk pyjamas, in their father's big mahogany bed; and Sam Sturgeon, in his ordinary clothes, in an arm-chair facing him. On a small table, convenient for both, were two tall tumblers half-full of a splendid-looking drink, with slices of lemon afloat on top, and beside them a china bowl from which rose a little steam and a strong sweet scent.

'Well, now,' exclaimed Gunner Boles in a hearty voice—and the boys stood, astonished, at the foot of the bed—'Well, now, we're going to have a party, I do declare! Here come the old gamecock's young chickens, and a welcome sight they are, to be sure. Come in, my sweet boys. Come in and have a sip of this fine drink that Sam Sturgeon has made for me. There's nothing in it but rum and hot water and honey and lemon-juice, and it won't do you any harm, my dears. Say what you think of it, Timothy. Take a taste of it, Hew. Take a taste of it from an old sailor's glass.'

'Now, now, Gunner Boles,' said Sam, 'get back under the clothes and behave yourself.'—For Gunner Boles had come down to the foot of the bed and was holding out his tumbler of rum punch to Timothy and Hew, who weren't quite sure whether they should take it or not.—'The boys are in my charge,' said Sam, 'and they're not old enough to be drinking rum, not for ten years yet. Milk or lemonade's what they like, and milk or lemonade is all they're going to get while I'm responsible.'

'I thought we were going to have a party,' said Gunner Boles in a disappointed voice. 'It's my birthday, boys, and no one's remembered to give me a present but my dear friend Sam Sturgeon.'

'If we'd only known,' said Timothy——

'I'm a hundred and seventy-two to-day,' said the Gunner proudly.

'Then you're old enough to know better,' said Sam, 'and if you don't get back into bed you won't have no more rum punch.'

'Whatever you say, Sam, just whatever you say,' answered the Gunner, and settling himself comfortably against the pillows again, pulled up the blankets. Then he lighted his pipe and puffed away as vigorously as an old steamer.

'Now I dare say,' said Sam, 'that you boys are wondering what right we've got to be drinking rum punch in your father's room when he's far away.'

'Not to speak of taking our pleasure in his red silk pyjamas,' added the Gunner.

'We thought you were burglars,' said Hew.

'Well, it isn't as bad as that,' said Sam, but he looked rather uncomfortable and a little guilty.

Timothy said nothing. He was thinking how angry his father would be to find an unknown sailor in his bed, and how he would roar till the windows rattled to see the sailor wearing his good silk pyjamas. Captain Spens's bedroom was a dignified and rather solemn apartment, with long curtains and heavy mahogany furniture, and a photograph of King George V in a silver frame on the chest of drawers, and a coloured engraving of the battle of the Nile over the mantelpiece. Gunner Boles, smoking a pipe and drinking rum in bed, looked out of place in it.—But Timothy didn't want to offend the Gunner, or to say anything that would upset Sam Sturgeon, so he kept his thoughts to himself and remained silent.

Sam got up and softly shut the door. 'We don't want Mrs. Matches coming in to interrupt us, do we?' he said. 'And now, to resume the conversation, what we were talking about was Gunner Boles's birthday——'

'A hundred and seventy-two,' said the Gunner complacently, 'and I started life as a little squalling baby, just like you did.'

'Just so,' said Sam. 'And when Mr. Boles told me that he hadn't slept in a proper bed since the year before the battle of Trafalgar——'

'In 1805,' said Timothy.

'It seemed to me,' said Sam, 'that he deserved a birthday treat. And the nicest treat I could think of was a good lie-down in a Captain's bed, with a glass of rum in his hand and a hot-water bottle at his feet, which is what he's got.'

56

'And very nice it is, Sam,' said the Gunner contentedly.

'Moreover,' said Sam, 'Mr. Boles has brought important news that required something in the nature of a celebration. He has discovered, or so he has reason to believe'—Sam was talking in a very solemn and impressive manner—'the whereabouts of something that we've been hoping to find for a long time past.'

'The pirate ship!' said Timothy.

'Where did he find her?' demanded Hew.

'In North Bay,' said Sam, 'not far from where your father calculated she'd be found.'

'Is there any treasure aboard?' asked Timothy.

'That's what we're going to find out,' said Sam.

'Now you be careful, Sam,' said Gunner Boles, 'and remember what I told you. On the main deck, under the break of the poop, there's no weed at all. On all other parts of her, wherever she's showing above the sand, there's great long tangles of weed, and her timbers are green as grass. But under the break of the poop she's clean, and it looks to me as though she'd been swept clean. It looks suspicious to me.'

'It was the storm that did it,' said Sam. 'It was the storm that swept her clean.'

'That may be, and it may be otherwise,' said Gunner Boles.

Timothy and Hew had a dozen questions to ask, and a dozen plans for exploring the wreck without delay. They paid no attention to Gunner Boles's warning of danger, and they had quite forgotten their surprise at finding him in their father's bed. It now seemed quite natural that he should be drinking rum in red silk pyjamas, with Sam Sturgeon in an arm-chair beside him. There was nothing in the situation that was now astonishing, except that Sam and Gunner Boles were in no hurry—or so it appeared—to begin treasure-hunting.

57

'But when are we going to start?' cried Hew.

'When are we going to look for it?' asked Timothy. 'The treasure, I mean?'

'We needn't wait till Father comes back, need we?'

'We can begin to-morrow morning, can't we?'

'It's quite light at four o'clock.'

'Or even earlier ...'

Sam listened patiently to all they had to say, and promised to do his best to satisfy them, and waste no time. Then Gunner Boles interrupted them, and spoke rather sharply.

'Sam,' he said, 'it looks to me as if my glass was empty. It looks to me, Sam, as if you were forgetting what day it is to-day.'

'I'm not forgetting anything,' said Sam, and filled the Gunner's glass again from the china bowl on the table. 'It's your birthday, Mr. Boles, and I'm sure we all wish you many happy returns!'

Gunner Boles smacked his lips, and smiled happily, and said, 'A hundred and seventy-two to-day, and my heart's as young as ever it was!'

'A long time ago,' said Timothy, 'when we first met you on a raft in the South Atlantic, you told Sam—at least I think you did, but I may have been dreaming—that you were in a ship called the *Royal Sovereign* at the battle of Trafalgar, and got hit on the breast-bone by a French musket-ball.'

'And very painful it was, too,' said Gunner Boles.

'Then why weren't you killed?' asked Hew.

'In any case,' said Timothy, 'it's very unusual to live till you're a hundred and seventy-two, even if you don't get hit by a musket-ball.'

'Ah!' said Gunner Boles. 'It wants a lot of explanation, doesn't it?'

'You boys are asking too many questions,' said Sam. 'It's time you were going back to your beds.'

'But I want to know,' said Timothy.

'And so do I,' said Hew.

'Well,' said Gunner Boles, 'you've heard about cats, haven't you? Everybody knows about cats, and a cat's got nine lives, hasn't it?'

'That's what people say,' said Timothy.

'And in the old days,' said Gunner Boles, 'our sailors went on long voyages in little ships that tossed and tumbled on the great waves of the wild green sea, and when the storm-winds blew, the sailormen had to go aloft in the darkness of the night and wrestle with the sails, that were hard as a board, and conjure with ropes, that were swift as serpents. They had to live on biscuits that were full of weevils, and salt-horse that tasted only of the brine, and ale that was sour as vinegar. They had to fight with Frenchmen and Spaniards, with Dutchmen and Moors, with buccaneers and privateers. They said good-bye to their mothers when they were young boys only, and they didn't come home again till there were great beards on their chins. They sailed into the northern seas where every rope was cased in ice till it looked as thick as the fore-topsail yard, and they lay becalmed in the southern ocean where the sea-worms ate the timbers beneath them, so when they came home through the chops of the Channel they were leaking like an old woman's basket. They sailed all over the world, and where-ever they went they had hardship and danger for their messmates, and found bitter enemies lying in wait for them. Sometimes, when their seafaring was over and done with, they retired with a pocket full of gold, and sometimes with a wooden leg. Sometimes the people came down to the quay and cheered 'em, and told 'em they were heroes; but often they got no reward at all. And such being their life, old sailormen weren't like ordinary mortal folk. Their skin grew tough as sailcloth and their cheeks were as hard as the main-course. Their bones were like oak-trees, and their veins were full of Jamaica rum. They had hearts of pure valour, and fingers like meat-hooks. They had bright blue eyes that could see a mile on the darkest night, and they weren't afraid of nothing. And like cats—which both of you know about—they had nine lives apiece, and needed them. Nine lives at least.'

'So even though you were killed at Trafalgar,' said Timothy, 'it didn't mean that you were—well, that you were *quite* killed?'

'You're asking too many questions,' said Sam again, 'and you're losing your sleep. Now off you go, and no more argument. Off to your beds, or I won't take you to sea to-morrow.'

They protested still, and pleaded for permission to stay and talk to Gunner Boles a little longer. But Sam would not listen, and made them say good-night and return to their room. But it was some time before they went to sleep, because their minds were filled with thoughts of the pirate ship that lay under the sea, and of Gunner Boles's hard life in olden times. And when at last they were too sleepy to think even of treasure and battles long ago, they were kept awake—but not for long—by strong hoarse voices raised in song. Gunner Boles and Sam Sturgeon were singing now.

'I hope Mrs. Matches won't hear them,' said Hew.

'Even if their skin's as tough as sailcloth,' answered Timothy sleepily, 'and their bones are like oak-trees, and their veins are full of Jamaica rum, Mrs. Matches wouldn't care. Mrs. Matches would be very, very angry with them.'

Chapter Seven

S am had been right when he said that the wind would soon go down, for the following morning was calm and grey; but Sam himself was by no means so calm as the sea, though he looked almost as grey in consequence of sitting up too late with Gunner Boles. He was in a difficult mood, and would not tell the boys what he meant to do. The *Endeavour* came in to Inner Bay during the morning, and Sam had a long conversation with Old Mattoo and James William Cordiall, but the boys were not allowed to listen. There was nothing they could do but wait until Sam should tell them his plans, and to wait and wait throughout a long morning, and do nothing, was very tiresome when they thought of the pirate ship that lay within a couple of miles of them, under the smooth water of North Bay. So tiresome and so trying, indeed, was their idle morning that presently they fell into a bad temper too, and going down to the beach they had a short fight in which neither was much hurt, and neither could say that he had won. After that they felt a little better.

In the early afternoon Sam said to them, 'You'd better hurry if you want to come with us. We're starting right away, and we've got no time to wait for those that aren't ready.'

'We've been ready since breakfast-time,' said Timothy indignantly.

'You're too fond of talking,' said Sam, and set off for the pier without waiting for a reply. The boys followed him, and no one said another word until they were at sea. Sam's diving-suit and his big copper helmet lay on the forward deck of the *Endeavour*, with coils of rope and the little ladder that would be slung over the side for his descent. Everything was ready for him to go down and explore the wreck, and Sam became much more cheerful as soon as they put to sea. Inner Bay lay smooth and calm, but off the western cliffs of the Calf the *Endeavour* rolled in the long Atlantic swell, and danced a little where the tide ran strongly. When they turned into North Bay they were again in calm water, and they headed inland until they were not far from the tall cliffs of Popinsay. Then they turned south at slow speed while Sam and Old Mattoo pored over a chart in the little deckhouse.

'It's here, or hereabout,' said Sam at last, and Old Mattoo stopped the engine, and James William Cordiall let go the anchor.

'Well, this is where I get dressed for the party,' said Sam, 'and I hope I shan't be late.'

'What do you mean?' asked Hew.

'I hope no one's been there before me and gone off with the cake—that's what I mean.'

'But nobody knows about the wreck except us.'

'Let's hope not,' said Sam.

'And we haven't exactly been invited to the party, have we?' asked Timothy.

'So you needn't expect to find anyone at home,' said Hew.

'Except the cake,' said Sam, and began to put on his heavy diving-suit.

They helped him into it, and Old Mattoo set the copper

helmet in position and screwed it down. Then the little ladder was thrown over the side, the boys manned the pump, and when Sam was ready he climbed slowly down and gradually disappeared under the water while James William Cordiall paid out the rope that would guide him under the sea and help him aboard again. The water was dark and the sky was cloudy. They lost sight of his copper helmet when he was only a fathom down and then for a long time they waited, and still James William Cordiall paid out more rope.

No one spoke very much, and there was nothing they could do to pass the time, but keep on pumping. They could only wait and wonder how Sam was getting on, and try to picture him moving to and fro on the bottom of the sea, or among the green timbers of the wreck. The minutes passed very slowly, and they all thought that Sam was staying under far too long when James William Cordiall felt two pulls on the breast-rope and exclaimed, 'That's him now! Lend a hand and haul away.'

He and Old Mattoo hauled together, and presently James William muttered, 'He's terrible heavy!'

'He's heavier than he used to be,' Old Mattoo agreed.

'Perhaps he has found something, and is bringing it up with him,' said Timothy.

'The treasure-chest,' said Hew. 'The cake!'

'Maybe, maybe,' said Old Mattoo, and hauled away at the breast-rope. Timothy and Hew leant over the side to watch for the first appearance of Sam's copper helmet, and presently through the dark water they saw a little gleam of light, and below it a pale moving body.

'There he is,' cried Hew.

'He's got something with him,' cried Timothy. 'He's got— he's got—Oh, Mattoo, come here! He's got another man!'

Sam's head appeared above the water, and in his arms they could plainly see the half-naked form of a stranger. Old Mattoo and James William Cordiall were so startled that they let go the breast-rope, and Sam Sturgeon and his mysterious burden— whatever it might be—disappeared again in the darkness of the sea.

'You are a stupid old man,' exclaimed James William Cordiall indignantly. 'Why did you let go the rope?'

'And you are a very feeble, useless kind of man,' retorted Old Mattoo. 'For it was you who let go first, and a man who cannot hold on to a rope should never come to sea at all. He should stay at home among the women and the little children.'

'Oh, never mind whose fault it was,' cried Timothy. 'Haul him up again as quickly as you can. Quickly! Quickly!'

'The boy has more sense in him than you have,' said James William Cordiall.

'It was his fault in the beginning,' grumbled Old Mattoo. 'It was he that gave me a fright in the beginning, by shouting and saying that Sam had found another man in the sea.'

Again they hauled, and again the boys, looking over the side, could see the gleam of a copper helmet and the pale shape of a strange body moving beneath it.

'He's still there,' whispered Timothy. 'Sam's got him still.'

As Sam's helmet broke the surface, Hew quickly made the rope fast with a couple of turns round a big cleat on the deck, and it was a good thing that he did so, because Old Mattoo and James William Cordiall were so frightened by the sight of Sam's burden that they would certainly have let the rope run out again if it had not been secured. But Sam's feet were now safely on the ladder, and with one hand he was holding the side of the boat while in his other arm he supported one of the strangest and ugliest men that any of them had ever seen.

Both Old Mattoo and James William Cordiall were very unwilling to touch the stranger, but through the glass front of Sam's helmet they could see him grimacing fiercely, and it was clear that he wanted them to relieve him of his curious burden. Timothy and Hew were as reluctant as the others to lay hands on the stranger, and at last it was Old Mattoo who leaned over and took him below the shoulders, and hauled him in.

'Man and boy,' said Old Mattoo, 'have I been taking fish from the sea, and many strange ones have I seen. I have seen the Great Sea Serpent itself, though no one ever believed me when I said so. But never have I seen the like of this before, and I hope I will never see it again!'

The stranger lay on the deck. He appeared to be unconscious, and he was dressed in much the same manner as Gunner Boles, though his vest was red and his trunks—that seemed to be made of shark-skin—were purple with ragged edges. He wore the same sort of curious slippers that Gunner Boles had worn, and from the belt round his waist hung a little satchel at one side and a sheath-knife at the other. His shoulders were broad, his arms muscular, and his face looked as if it had been badly carved out of some rough grey stone.

Sam climbed in over the side, and Old Mattoo and James William Cordiall, still keeping an eye on the stranger, unscrewed his helmet. Then they all began asking him questions at once, but the first thing that Sam said was, 'You'd better get a rope's end and tie him up. I hit him on the head and knocked him out, but when he comes to again he may be dangerous.'

Old Mattoo tied the stranger's wrists behind his back, and James William Cordiall lashed his ankles together, while the boys helped Sam out of his diving-suit. Then the questions began again, and everyone wanted to know who the stranger was, and what he was.

'Who he is,' said Sam, 'I don't know, but I'll tell you what happened. I didn't have much trouble finding the wreck. She's lying between us and the shore, not more than fifty yards away in a patch of sand under a long shelf of rock. There's part of her deck that's pretty clean, though the rest of her looks like a jungle, there's so much weed growing on her. I looked about me, and under the break of the poop, where the deck seemed to have been swept——'

'That's where Gunner Boles said it had been swept,' interrupted Hew.

'You keep your mouth shut,' said Sam angrily, and Hew remembered that no one knew of Gunner Boles's existence but Timothy and himself and Sam Sturgeon. Old Mattoo and James William Cordiall had never heard of him, and it would be as difficult to explain to them who he was as to account for the stranger on the deck. So Hew said no more, and felt ashamed of himself for having said so much.

'Well, as I was telling you,' Sam went on, 'the deck looked as if it had been swept, and there was a little door leading off it into the after quarters. I tried to open it, but it seemed to be made fast on the inner side. So I took a turn forward, to see if I could find some sort of hatch or opening under the weed, and then I happened to look back. And there was the door, that I thought was shut from the inside, beginning to open! Well, that gave me a bit of a surprise, as you can well imagine. But moving as quickly as I could, I got back to the break of the poop and stood there, waiting quietly, on the blind side of the door. If there was anyone behind the door, he was moving slowly, and very cautiously. But by and by I saw a head coming out, as though it might be the head of a turtle coming out of its shell, and a very nice chance he gave me to tap him on the napper with the back of the axe I was carrying. Which I did, and down he fell. Then I took a quick look through the door, and found an alley-way that led to a sort of saloon and a fair-sized after-cabin. There was no one else there—at least, as far as I could see—but both those rooms looked as though they had been cleaned up and made tidy. There was weed growing from the deck above, but there wasn't any weed on the floor, and a big table in the saloon was so clean you could have eaten your dinner off it; except, of course, that it was under water. Well, I didn't want to stay too long, because I thought it best to get rid of this chap here. So I came out again and picked him up, and gave you the signal to haul away. And except for the nasty drop you gave me when I was half out of the water, that's all that happened.'

Old Mattoo and James William Cordiall looked very much ashamed of themselves, and Old Mattoo began to explain that they had naturally been a little surprised when Sam returned from the depths of the sea with a stranger in his arms. But his apology was interrupted by Timothy, who suddenly pointed to the man who lay on the deck. They looked and saw that his eyes were open, and he was watching them with a cold and horrid glance. He did not seem to be upset by the plight he was in, or in any way afraid. Sam pulled him up into a sitting position, and set him fairly comfortably with his back against the foreward hatch.

'And now,' he said, 'perhaps you'll be so good as to tell us who you are, and what your business is in these parts?'

The stranger made no reply. He looked at them coldly, and his lips moved a little as if he were muttering to himself. But he said nothing that they could hear.

'Perhaps he can't speak,' said Hew.

'He could speak if he wanted to,' said Sam, and stared thoughtfully at his prisoner.

Timothy came close to Sam and whispered in his left ear, 'He's wearing the same sort of shoes that Gunner Boles wears.'

'Keep quiet,' murmured Sam. 'We don't want to say anything about him. Not yet, at any rate, though we may have to some day.'

Old Mattoo and James William Cordiall had by no means recovered from the fright which the stranger's first appearance had given them. Their sunburnt faces were a little pale, and they stood side by side looking down at Sam's prisoner as if they could not quite believe what they saw. James William Cordiall, indeed, was rubbing his eyes and groaning as if he had had a nightmare, and was trying to wake up and forget it.

'I saw the Great Sea Serpent once,' said Old Mattoo again, 'but nobody believed me when I told them. And nobody will believe me when I tell them about this man here.'

'You don't want to tell anyone about him,' said Sam sharply. 'There's something going on that we don't know about, and maybe we couldn't understand it if we did. But you won't do any good by talking about it, and frightening other people. So keep your mouth shut when you go ashore, and don't say nothing. Not a word, do you understand that?'

'We should only be called liars if we did talk,' said Old Mattoo with a sigh, 'so maybe it is best to say nothing, and save our breath.'

'Take him below,' said Sam, 'and put him in the fish-hold.'

Old Mattoo and James William Cordiall picked up the stranger—they handled him as though he might bite, or as if his flesh was poisonous, but he made no attempt to resist them—and carried him below. Sam began to put on his diving-suit again.

'What are you going to do?' asked Timothy.

'I'm going down to have another look at the wreck,' said Sam.

Both Timothy and Hew thought that was a very dangerous thing to do, and looked rather worried. Old Mattoo and James William Cordiall, when they came on deck again and saw what Sam's intention was, were much more upset; and Old Mattoo told him he was mad to think of such a thing. They begged him to be reasonable, they pleaded with him to come back to harbour. But Sam had made up his mind. Sam was not easily frightened, and having found the wreck he wanted to see what was in it. So in spite of all they could say he put on his diving-suit again, and presently climbed over the side and disappeared into the sea.

When he had gone down for the first time the others had waited for his reappearance with some anxiety, but now they were twenty times as worried, and every minute seemed longer and longer. James William Cordiall kept looking at his watch and saying, 'He's been down for eight minutes now.—For nine minutes.—For ten minutes. But my watch must have stopped! It is longer than that, far longer than that! What does your watch say, Mattoo?'

'Just the same as yours,' Old Mattoo answered. 'But maybe there is something the matter with it too.'

'Twelve minutes,' said James William Cordiall. 'Thirteen—fourteen.'

He was following the second-hand with his big thick forefinger when Hew cried shrilly, 'The rope! The rope's broken!'

Sam's breast-rope hung loosely down the side of the boat, and when Old Mattoo began to pull it, it came in easily. The air-line came in too, without resistance.

'They're broken,' said Hew again.

'Or someone has cut them,' said Timothy.

Now they stared at each other in utter dismay, and Timothy's face and Hew's were as white as a sheet, and even the weather-burnt cheeks of James William Cordiall and Old Mattoo looked as grey as old canvas. For two or three minutes nobody spoke, because nobody was willing to say what he thought. But every-one of them had the same idea, and that was that Sam had been trapped in the wreck, and there was nothing they could do to help him.

From this state of sheer despair they were roused by a curious and quite unexpected sound. Someone or something, a short distance to seaward of them, was singing a little song in a little, thin, sharp, reedy voice. Timothy and Hew recognised it at once, and hurrying to the side of the boat cried, 'Cully, Cully! Come quickly, Cully! Come and help us!'

But James William Cordiall and Old Mattoo, when they saw what sort of a creature it was that Hew and Timothy were talking to, fell into a greater fright than ever. Old Mattoo's whiskers were waving on his cheeks as if a gale were blowing, and James William Cordiall felt such a weakness in his legs that he could not stand and had to get down on his hands and knees. He crawled to the side of the boat and again looked at Cully, who was no more than twenty feet away. And when he saw that there was no doubt about it, but there in the sea was a singing octopus, he had to rest his chin on the rail to keep his teeth from chattering.

Timothy and Hew were shouting as hard as they could, but Cully paid no attention. Quietly and happily he was singing a song that went like this:

70

'I've the tenderest heart in the whole of the sea,
  From the Strait of Belle Isle to New Britain;
I've a gift of affection like honey for tea,
  And I'd love to be stroked like a kitten;
But nobody ever can sit on my knee,
  For I haven't a knee she could sit on!

'I've been well educated, I've courteous ways,
  I don't often talk indiscreetly;
I've eight sensitive arms, and I've learnt how to play
  Upon four grand pianos quite neatly—
And yet ladies avoid my embrace, for they say
  They don't like to be *hemmed-in* completely.

'I've an up-to-date mind, I appreciate art,
  I'd make an extremely good parent;
But a very grave handicap keeps me apart
  From all social pleasures—I daren't
Appear in a place where one has to look smart,
  For my stomach, you see, is transparent!'

Then Hew lost his patience, and taking an apple from his pocket threw it at Cully, and hit him squarely on his orange beak. Cully stopped singing, leapt half-way out of the water, and looked north and west and south before he turned and saw the *Endeavour* and the boys leaning over her side. Then he raised one of his feelers, and shook it at them in a disapproving manner.

'Naughty, naughty!' he exclaimed. 'Has no one ever told you to show consideration for others? Don't you know that good little boys respect the repose of their elders? Don't you realise that we who work ceaselessly, tirelessly, and indefatigably need some rest and relaxation? Can't you understand that to rob us of the sleep we require is a rough, rude, brutal, unforgivable thing to do? There was I, after spending a long and weary night on duty, taking an hour or two of rest, enjoying a little nap, a little sleep on the surface of the sea——'

'You can't have been asleep,' interrupted Hew, 'you were singing.'

'And what of that?' asked Cully. 'There are people who snore in their sleep, aren't there? Some of them make horrible grunting noises, others make the most alarming whistling noises, and some wheeze and snuffle in a quite revolting manner. If I choose to sing in my sleep, that's an improvement on the usual custom which every sensible person ought to welcome, and copy if they can.'

'Cully,' said Timothy, 'you talk very nicely, but please stop talking now, and come and help us. We're in dreadful trouble.'

'Oh dear,' said Cully, 'what a world it is, to be sure! Trouble here, trouble there, trouble on all sides. Even I, a respectable hard-workings octopus, can't escape it, and as for you poor human beings—well, well, well! But tell me all about it.'

He swam quickly to the boat, and raising two of his feelers, hooked them over her low side, and pulled himself partly out of the water. Then he rested his beak on the rail, and looked at them with an attentive and friendly stare.

James William Cordiall gave a shrill cry of fear, like a dog that had been kicked, and tumbled into the fish-hold as fast as he could; and Old Mattoo, trembling all over, followed and fell on top of him. But neither Cully nor Timothy nor Hew paid any attention to them, for Timothy was telling Cully as quickly as he could what had happened to Sam Sturgeon. Cully listened attentively and behaved very sensibly. He asked only a few questions, and then in a reassuring voice said, 'Leave it to me, dear boys. I will go down and get him up again in two shakes of an eel's tail.'

Swiftly he disappeared under the surface of the sea, and both Timothy and Hew were much comforted by what he had said.

'But how are we going to explain about Cully to Old Mattoo and James William Cordiall?' asked Timothy.

'We were told to say nothing about him,' said Hew. 'Nothing about him and nothing about Gunner Boles. They're part of something that we had to keep an absolute secret.'

'Well, Cully isn't a secret any longer,' said Timothy, 'and I don't think Gunner Boles is either, because the man that Sam brought up is wearing the same sort of clothes and the same sort of shoes, so he must be part of the secret too. I think we should tell them how we first met Cully.'

In one corner of the fish-hold the man whom Sam had found in the wreck was leaning against the bulkhead and staring at Old Mattoo and James William Cordiall with a cruel sneer on his face. They, huddled together in the opposite corner, as far from him as they could be, were holding each other's hands and still trembling.

'You'd better come up on deck,' said Timothy. 'We've something rather important to tell you.'

'Is that beast with the orange beak and eyes like a saucer still there?' asked James William Cordiall in a quavering voice.

'No, he's gone down to rescue Sam.'

'It was a terrible sight to see him staring over the rail,' said Old Mattoo.

'Not at all,' said Hew. 'He's a very friendly octopus when you get to know him.'

Old Mattoo stood up and began to climb the ladder out of the hold, and when he had looked carefully round and made sure

73

that Cully was no longer on board, he came out on deck, and James William Cordiall followed him.

'We've got something to tell you,' said Timothy, 'but it's rather difficult to explain because I don't suppose you'll believe it.'

'There's nothing I would not believe after what I have seen to-day,' said James William Cordiall.

'No, nothing,' said Old Mattoo. 'The Great Sea Serpent itself, that I once saw when I was a young man, was a simple homely creature compared with him down there in the fish-hold and that beast with the eyes like a pair of saucers.'

Timothy repeated what he had already told them—that Cully was a friend of theirs, and had gone down to look for Sam and rescue him—and then he described their voyage from South Africa, when they were wrecked and made their first acquaintance with Cully as they lay drifting on the raft. Old Mattoo and James William Cordiall listened without saying a word until the story was finished. Then Old Mattoo shook his head sadly and said: 'There's not a man, woman, or child in Popinsay that would believe a word of it.'

'But you've seen Cully, and heard him speak, so you know it's true,' said Hew indignantly.

'That's the worst of it,' said Old Mattoo with a sigh. 'That's by far the worst of it.'

'You may think so,' said Timothy, 'but Hew and I are very pleased to have an octopus for a friend, and it's a good thing for Sam, too, for none of us could have helped him.'

'We don't know yet,' said James William Cordiall, 'whether the beast is going to help him.'

'Don't call Cully a beast,' said Timothy.

'And don't look so glum and gloomy,' cried Hew, 'for there they are!'

74

A few yards from the boat there was a great swirling in the water, and Cully rose to the surface with Sam in his diver's suit held firmly in two of his right-hand tentacles, and on the other side, in two of his left-hand tentacles—

'Save us, save us!' cried James William Cordiall. 'He's found another of them!'

Struggling in Cully's grasp there was indeed another man in a red shark-skin vest and ragged purple trunks, as ugly as the one whom Sam had brought up, and Old Mattoo's whiskers were waving on his cheeks again like an old grey shirt hung on the line to dry, and James William Cordiall's teeth were chattering loudly. Timothy and Hew wished that Sam were aboard to tell them what to do, but Sam in his diving-suit could not help them, and it was Cully who took charge of the situation.

'Now, now,' he cried, 'look alive there, and try to be helpful! Don't stand gaping, but do something! I've had a very difficult time, a very trying experience indeed, and I'm nearly exhausted. Mr. Sturgeon weighs a great deal in his diving-suit, poor man, and this horrible, brutal creature in my other hands is doing his best to get away—but take Mr. Sturgeon first, please, and get his helmet off as quickly as you can.'

In spite of what he said, Cully did not seem to be in the least exhausted, for without any difficulty he lifted Sam as high as the rail, and Old Mattoo and James William Cordiall were able to pull him aboard. Timothy and Hew quickly helped him to get out of his diving-suit. Sam was very tired and could hardly speak. His first words were, 'Take care of that, for there may be something in it'—and he gave Timothy an object that looked like a piece of coral all overgrown with seaweed. Then he sat down on the deck and for some time said nothing more, but Cully made up for his silence.

Cully was master of the situation, and knew it; and he was thoroughly enjoying himself. No one else had a chance of saying anything, for he talked without a moment's pause and seemed likely to go on talking for ever. He pulled himself halfway up the side of the boat, as he had done before, and lifting the second stranger from the sea, set him down rather roughly on the deck. But he still kept a firm hold on him, and whenever the man struggled too violently, squeezed him a little tighter.

'Just look at him!' cried Cully in his shrill voice. 'Have you ever seen such a villainous, ugly, uncivilised, and brutal person in all your lives? He gave me a terrible fright when I first saw him. I very nearly screamed, I wanted to swim away as fast as I could! But then I remembered that poor Mr. Sturgeon was somewhere in the wreck, so I plucked up all my courage, and made a dash at that dreadful creature, and by sheer good luck I was able to get hold of him before he hit me. I don't know what I would have done if he had hit me, because I can't bear getting hurt! And I don't think he likes getting hurt either, because after I had squeezed him a little he told me just where to go and look for Mr. Sturgeon. Poor Mr. Sturgeon had gone into a cabin, or some such place, and this fearful ruffian had cut his life-line, and closed the door on him and jammed it with a sort of wedge. But I managed to open the door, and let poor Mr. Sturgeon out. He wasn't feeling at all well, because I think he had had a fight with this great hulking scoundrel before he got shut in the cabin. So I had to swim all the way back here carrying both of them in my poor delicate little arms, an invalid on the one side, and a prisoner on the other. You can guess how tired I am! Terribly, terribly tired! So please hurry up, and find a piece of rope, and tie this creature's wrists and ankles as tightly as possible, and then I can let him go and have a little rest.'

76

The second prisoner was tied up, and when he was satisfied that the ropes were tight enough and all the knots properly made, Cully loosened his hold. Old Mattoo and James William Cordiall carried the man down, and laid him beside his companion in the fish-hold. Then they came on deck again, and Cully smiled at them in what was intended to be a very friendly and agreeable manner. But Old Mattoo and James William Cordiall, who by this time had got over their first fright, found his new expression extremely alarming, and Old Mattoo whispered to Timothy, 'Tell him to stop *oggling* at us like that. I'm an old man, and my nerves can't stand it when he oggles.'

'You mean ogles, don't you?' asked Timothy.

'Whatever I mean, tell him to stop it!' said Old Mattoo.

But before Timothy could make any such suggestion, Cully was talking again and inviting himself to tea.

'I don't want to make a nuisance of myself,' he exclaimed, 'but it just happens that I'm very, very hungry, and I'm almost sure it must be tea-time. I had a very small lunch, and if it wouldn't be too much bother for you—well, I should love to stay! There's nothing I enjoy more than a party, especially a really good party where there's lots and lots to eat.'

'I don't think there's very much food on board,' said Timothy, 'but I daresay there's some bread and jam.'

'Bread and jam!' exclaimed Cully. 'Did you say *jam*? Oh, but I adore jam—and cake—birthday cake, especially—and choco-late biscuits, and hot crumpets, and mince-pies—but please don't apologise if you haven't everything that I like on board, because I shall be perfectly satisfied with bread and jam, especially if there's plenty of jam.'

James William Cordiall brought up a loaf of bread, a dish of butter, and a pot of raspberry jam. Cully took slice after slice, as fast as he could cut and spread them, and presently he was holding four slices—two in his left-hand tentacles, two in the right—from which he took bites in turn. He lay half in and half out of the water, resting very comfortably on the rail, and ate all the bread and jam that Old Mattoo and James William Cordiall offered him. They were very pleased to see what a good appetite he had, and James William asked him if he would like a boiled egg. Cully said he would, and they felt still more friendly towards him. An octopus who ate bread and jam could not, they thought, be very dangerous, but must be a good simple creature with homely tastes like their own. So James William boiled an egg, and then he and Old Mattoo sat down beside Cully, with another loaf of bread and a new pot of jam between them, and they all became the best of friends.

Sam Sturgeon, in the meantime, had slowly been recovering his strength. Timothy and Hew had been watching him rather anxiously, but now he seemed quite well again, and in good spirits. For he winked at them and said, 'Well, that was a close call, so it was! If it hadn't been for Cully, I'd be down there still.'

'Did Cully save your life?' asked Hew.

'There's no denying that,' said Sam. 'I was at my last gasp when he found me, and he ought to have a medal by rights.—But what are we going to do now? That's the question, and I wish your Father was here to answer it. I'd be glad to have his advice, though I don't suppose he's ever had much experience with fellows like those two down in the hold, and he might be just as much puzzled and bewildered as we are.'

'Do you think there are any more of them in the wreck?' asked Timothy.

'There weren't so far as I could see,' said Sam.

'But you aren't sure?'

78

'I wouldn't take my oath on it,' said Sam, 'but we'll soon find out.—Cully,' he called, 'would you take another trip down below, and see if there's any more of those fellows in the wreck?'

'Oh, how tiresome!' cried Cully. 'Surely I can stay and finish my tea first?'

'You can finish it when you come up again,' said Sam.

'Well, it rather spoils the party,' said Cully reproachfully, 'but if you insist, I suppose I must. It's a hard life we lead, a hard, hard life! Nobody knows what it is to be an octopus with a sense of duty!'

He put another slice of bread and jam in his mouth, all at once, and sliding off the boat, disappeared below the water.

'Where's that skull I brought up with me?' asked Sam.

'A skull?' asked Timothy.

'It was all overgrown with weed,' said Sam.

'Is this it? I thought it was a lump of coral.'

'Just wait a minute and you'll see what it is,' said Sam, and borrowing a knife from Old Mattoo began to scrape off the weed. In a few minutes he had cleaned it thoroughly. The bone was stained and green, and two front teeth were missing from the top row. Timothy took it and looked at it closely.

'There's writing on the forehead,' he said, 'and there's something inside it.' He shook it, and it rattled like a money-box with a few pennies in it.

'That's what it is!' he cried. 'It's a money-box, and it says so.'

He pointed to the words which had been carved on the forehead, and slowly read: '*Jon Flet hys monie box.*'

Sam took it and said, 'It's another of the same sort that your father found on the beach a long time ago—and here's where you put the money in,' he exclaimed.

On the top of the skull a little strip of bone had been cut out, and so carefully fitted in again that it could scarcely be seen; but when Sam pressed hard on one end of the strip with the blade of a knife, it opened. He held the skull upside down, and shook it, and one by one eight gold coins fell out.

'That isn't much of a treasure,' said Hew.

'But there may be a lot more money-boxes in the wreck,' said Timothy. 'I wonder who Jon Flet was?'

'He may have been the captain's steward,' said Sam. 'I found that skull behind a panel in the saloon when I got shut up there. I was feeling round to see if I could get out again, and one of the panels in the wall was rotten. I put my hand through it, into a sort of cupboard, and that's what I found. It wouldn't be one of the crew that kept his money there, but the captain's steward might have thought it was a good hiding place.'

Old Mattoo and James William Cordiall were shaking their heads over the greenish skull, and Hew was counting the money again, when Cully reappeared in the sea beside them. He pulled himself up the side of the boat and exclaimed, 'You'll never believe it, but I feel almost as hungry as I did to begin with! That little swim has given me such an appetite again! Don't tell me that the jam's all finished? Don't tell me that, I couldn't bear it!'

'I'll soon get some more,' said James William Cordiall, and hurried below.

'And what did you find?' asked Sam.

'Nothing,' said Cully, 'nothing at all. It was merely a waste of time going all that way and back again. There's nothing in the wreck except some crabs and eels and creatures like that, and I'm quite sure that no one else would ever want to go there. It's one of the gloomiest wrecks I've ever seen.'

'I hope you like black-currant,' said James William Cordiall, coming up with a new pot in his hand.

'Black-currant!' screamed Cully. 'It's absolutely and faraway and completely my favourite! Oh, what a good party this is!'

But Sam interrupted him and asked, 'When do you go on duty again?'

'Not till eight o'clock this evening,' said Cully. 'I've got plenty of time for my tea, and there's no need to hurry at all.'

'I wasn't thinking about your tea,' said Sam. 'I was thinking about Gunner Boles. I want you to give him a message. I want you to tell him that I'm very anxious to see him as soon as possible on a matter of great importance. I don't know when he'll be able to come ashore, but tell him I'll be waiting for him, on the little beach on the Hen, from ten o'clock onwards. Can you remember that, do you think?'

'I can remember everything,' said Cully with his mouth full. 'We octopuses—or *octopodes*, I should say. Everybody who's had a really good education calls us octopodes, and I do think it sounds better, don't you?—Well, we octopodes have all got excellent memories, and we never forget anything at all.'

'I don't want to hurry you,' said Sam, 'but I'll be much obliged if you'll give Gunner Boles my compliments, and tell him what I've just been saying to you, as soon as ever you can; so that he can make his arrangements. And then we'll up anchor and get home again.'

'And what are you going to do with those two fearful creatures in the hold?' asked Old Mattoo.

'They'll need to stay there,' said Sam. 'You and James William Cordiall will be sleeping on board, so you can look after them.'

'Not me!' exclaimed Old Mattoo. 'I wouldn't be left alone with those two, no, not for all the gold in the ocean!'

'Nor me,' said James William Cordiall. 'I'd never get a wink of sleep if I thought those two ugly, desperate fellows were lying only a yard or two away.'

Sam argued with them for a quarter of an hour, but nothing he could say would make them change their minds; so at last it was decided that the two strangers should stay in the hold till evening, when Sam would take them up to Popinsay House in a farm-cart—hidden under a tarpaulin—and smuggle them into the house, and lock them in a cellar. By that time Cully had finished his tea, and there was nothing left to eat on board. So Cully said 'Thank you,' in his politest manner and Sam thanked him for saving his life. Timothy and Hew said good-bye, and Old Mattoo and James William Cordiall said they hoped they would see him again some day when they were out fishing. Then Cully slid down into the sea, the anchor was hauled up, the engine started, and the *Endeavour* headed for home.

Chapter Eight

Late at night Sam came into the boys' room, and woke them, and told them to keep quiet.

'Gunner Boles is downstairs in your father's study,' he said, 'and he's got something very important that he wants to tell you. So put on your dressing-gowns and come down, but don't make any noise. We don't want Mrs. Matches interrupting us.'

Gunner Boles was standing in a corner of the study where a big globe of the world stood on a table. But he turned when the boys came in, and shook each of them by the hand in a very polite and formal manner. He looked extremely serious. Sam closed the door behind them, and they sat down. All the curtains were closely drawn, so that no light could be seen from outside.

'Now, first of all,' said Gunner Boles, 'I've got to explain about a lot of things that you don't understand as yet. And then when I've finished explaining, I'm going to ask you a difficult question. I'm going to ask you to do something that's very important, and there's no one here can do it but you. But it's dangerous, I'm bound to admit, and if you don't feel inclined to take it on, then nobody's going to make you, or try to persuade you.'

'What sort of a thing is it?' asked Timothy.

'You'd better listen to the explanation first,' said Sam.

'That's good advice,' said Gunner Boles, 'and to begin with I'll have to give you a lesson in geography. But it isn't the kind of geography you learn in school. It's real geography, if you see the difference.'

He got up and took the globe of the world from its table, and set it down on the floor in front of the boys.

'Now,' he said, 'you see all those lines that go round the world, don't you? There's some that go down from the North Pole to the South Pole, and some that go round the middle. But has anyone ever told you what they're called?'

'The parallels of latitude,' said Timothy.

'And the parallels of longitude,' said Hew.

'That's right,' said Gunner Boles. 'And now can you tell me what those parallels do? What are they for, and what good are they?'

'Well,' said Hew, a little doubtfully, 'they help you to know where you are.'

'They're used in navigation,' said Timothy.

'So far, so true,' said Gunner Boles, 'and that's what you were told in school, I suppose. But they never tell you enough in school. They never tell you the really interesting things. Now just you look at this globe again, and tell me what you see.'

'I could see New Zealand if you hadn't got your thumb on it,' said Timothy.

'And what's New Zealand?' asked Gunner Boles.

'It's two islands.'

'Right,' said Gunner Boles. 'And if you look at it properly, you'll see that all the world is just a lot of islands. Some of them, like Australia, are big islands; and some of them, like Popinsay, are little islands; and some of them, like Asia and America, are usually called continents. But there's water all round them, and so, strictly speaking, they're islands too. Now what is it, do you think, that keeps them all in place and holds them together?'

'I suppose they've got good foundations,' said Timothy.

'Well, of course they have,' said Gunner Boles. 'They've got very good foundations, and what's more than that, they've got the parallels of latitude and longitude. Those lines that you see on the globe—and this is what you were never told in school— represent great big strong cables lying at the bottom of the sea, made fast at either end to some island or continent. And what they do is to hold the world together and keep everything in place.'

'And who looks after them?' asked Timothy.

'Ah, ha!' said Gunner Boles. 'Now there's a bright boy if ever I saw one! He's gone right to the very point of it, hasn't he, Sam? He's put his finger on what truly matters. That's what we are all concerned about, Timothy, my boy. Who looks after them?'

Timothy felt rather embarrassed, because Sam and Gunner Boles were looking at him in a very admiring way, as though he had said something particularly clever; and Hew was trying to look extremely wise, as though he too understood what it was all about.

'Who looks after them?' said Gunner Boles again. 'That's what we're all worried about, and more especially about who's to look after the knots.'

'What knots?' asked Hew.

'The knots where the parallels of latitude cross the parallels of longitude, of course. Wherever you see them crossing on the globe, there's a big strong knot at the bottom of the sea, and everyone of those knots has to be watched and guarded night and day.'

85

'Is that what you do?' asked Timothy.

'That's my job,' said Gunner Boles, 'and has been these many years.'

'Is there a knot near Popinsay?' asked Hew.

'If you look at the map,' said Sam, 'you can answer that for yourselves. Don't you see where the 59th parallel of north latitude crosses the 4th parallel of west longitude, and isn't that just a mile or two north-west of the Calf?'

'And who's looking after it now?' asked Timothy. 'You said that all the knots had to be guarded night and day.'

'Why, Cully's on duty now,' said Gunner Boles. 'That's how he's useful to me. He's been with me ever since he was a little octopus, and I've taught him all sorts of things in the last thirty or forty years. He can do the job well enough so long as he doesn't fall asleep, as he's inclined to, or go off and take a holiday, which is what he likes to do.'

'But why have the knots got to be guarded?' asked Hew.

'Now there's another bright boy!' said Gunner Boles. 'They're two fine lads, these are, Sam. They both see deep into the nature of things, and ask sensible questions.—Now, I'll tell you, Hew, and that in one word, what we've got to guard the knots against at this present moment; and that's pirates!'

'Those two men you found in the wreck,' said Timothy, 'are they pirates?'

'They're two of Dan Scumbril's lot,' said Gunner Boles.

'You're going too fast,' said Sam. 'You haven't told them how the trouble started yet.'

'Give me time, and don't hurry me,' said Gunner Boles. 'I was just coming to that.—Now, the fact is, you see, that there's quite a lot of us old sailors living down on the bottom of the sea, and some of us are honest, and some aren't. Some of us do our job in the proper way, and others try to interfere. Some of us attend to our duty like a sailor should, and others are just a set of black-hearted pirates. There's often been a little trouble down there, the same as there often is up here. And then a few months ago the trouble got more serious. There were some who thought they weren't getting as much attention as they deserved. They weren't satisfied with doing an ordinary job, but wanted to get control of things and manage affairs at the bottom of the sea in their own way. So they began to say that the knots which we'd always used for tying together the parallels of latitude and the parallels of longitude weren't the proper sort of knots; and ought to be changed for a newer sort which they'd invented. So there's been a bit of argument lately, and a bit of fighting too; and it seems as though there's going to be more.'

'Do you want us to fight?' asked Timothy.

'Not if you can help it,' said Gunner Boles, and Hew looked disappointed.

'Gunner Boles,' said Sam, 'came up into these northern latitudes just three weeks ago, when it was reported that there wasn't anyone watching that knot off the north-west of the Calf. The man who had been there had disappeared. So Gunner Boles came along, and took his place. And the next thing that happened was that I found those two fellows down in the wreck——'

'Two of Dan Scumbril's lot,' said Gunner Boles.

'They're in the cellar now,' said Sam. 'We brought them up one at a time, and the first one wouldn't speak, but the second couldn't hold his tongue. His mates, he said, would be up here in next to no time, and Gunner Boles would go the same way as the last man who'd been looking after Knot 59 N., 4 W.—That's the one out there.—Within a month, he told us, Dan Scumbril's lot and Inky Poops's lot would be in control of all the parallels of latitude from Popinsay to Greenland, and all the parallels of longitude from Norway to North America. And they'd start to change all the knots, he said, and put in the new sort they fancy, and which aren't any good.'

'Inky Poops,' explained Gunner Boles, 'is another of those pirates. He and Dan Scumbril are the worst of them. They're the leaders.'

'Scumbril and Inky Poops,' said Timothy. 'That sounds funny, doesn't it?'

'It reminds me of Father when he's in a bad temper,' said Hew.

'Scoundrels and nincompoops!' shouted Timothy, imitating his father's voice.

'They're the people that Father used to complain about,' explained Hew.

'And a very good description of those that we complain about,' said Gunner Boles. 'But complaining isn't enough, d'you see. We've got to stop them, and we've got to do it quick.'

'But how?' asked Timothy.

'Well, that's where you come in,' said Gunner Boles. 'We've got to get reinforcements, d'you see. We've got to send news of the plot we have discovered, and we've got to get help from the Loyalists. But I can't go, and Cully can't go, because we've got to watch the knot. And Sam can't go, because I want him to stay here on Popinsay in case things get awkward in the next few days. We've been wondering, Sam and I, whether we could trust the message to a couple of Powder Monkeys——'

'Who are they?' asked Hew.

'You'll find out soon enough,' said Sam. 'At least, I expect you will.'

'They're the little boys that used to carry powder to the guns in the great sea-battles of Lord Nelson's time,' said Gunner Boles. 'There's a good many of them living along with us at the bottom of the sea, and there's Cabin Boys too; but they're on the other side. Well, we thought about the Powder Monkeys, as I've just told you, but they're wild youngsters, and I wouldn't care to trust them with what's so very, very important.'

'So you want us to take the message,' said Timothy.

'I'm not going to persuade you to take it,' said Gunner Boles, 'and there's no one here that can order you to go. But I shan't deny that Sam and I are looking for volunteers.'

'But where should we have to go?' asked Hew.

'To Davy Jones's Locker,' said Gunner Boles.

'And where's that?'

But before the Gunner could answer they were startled by the sound of someone screaming at the top of her voice. It was a fierce and angry voice, but frightened too. They they heard—*thud, thud*—the sound of heavy blows, and something falling, and another scream, and then something else that fell.

'That was Mrs. Matches,' said Timothy, but already Sam had opened the door and was hurrying out, followed by Gunner Boles. They ran down the passage to the kitchen, and there on the kitchen floor lay the two pirates who had been captured in the wreck, unconscious, with Mrs. Matches, also unconscious, lying across the legs of the taller one. Firmly grasped in her right hand was the kitchen poker.

Chapter Nine

It was lucky for Mrs. Matches that quite early in life she had formed the habit of taking the kitchen poker to bed with her. This was not because she was frightened, but because she was prudent.

'I've never seen a burglar,' she used to say, 'and I hope I never will. But if I do, I want to have something to hit him with.'

Once upon a time, in the early days of her married life, she made a slight mistake when her husband came home late one night; and after he had spent three months in hospital he went to Australia, and she never saw him again. But that did not break her of the habit.

While Sam and Gunner Boles and the boys were discussing geography in the study, Mrs. Matches had been wakened by a noise in the kitchen, which lay immediately below her bedroom. It sounded as if someone had knocked a saucepan off the stove, and then Mrs. Matches thought she heard voices. She got up at once and put on her dressing-gown, and firmly grasped the poker which lay ready on the chair beside her bed. She opened her door, and tiptoed carefully down the back stair.

In the kitchen the two pirates, who were members of Dan

Scumbril's party, if Gunner Boles was right, were eating cold mutton and a gooseberry-pie. The long lean pirate had teeth like a shark's. They were very sharp, and triangular in shape, and that was how they had got out of the cellar in which Sam Sturgeon had imprisoned them. The long lean pirate had bitten through the rope which bound his companion's wrists, and when they had untied each other, they discovered that the door of the cellar—which was fastened on the one side with a heavy lock—could be lifted quite easily off its hinges. So they had escaped without much difficulty, and being hungry they sat down in the kitchen to have some breakfast before going back to sea.

When Mrs. Matches opened the door—very cautiously, inch by inch—and peeped round, and saw the two of them sitting at her table, she would have been very frightened indeed if she had not had a poker in her hand. But being well-armed, she flung open the door, and screaming wildly, attacked the two pirates before they could do anything to defend themselves. With three or four well-aimed blows she struck both of them senseless to the floor, and then with a final scream she fainted, and fell across the legs of the long lean one.

A moment later Gunner Boles and Sam Sturgeon and the boys came in, and the two pirates were quickly bound hand and foot again, and taken back to the cellar. And now Gunner Boles put a gag between the tall pirate's teeth, to prevent him biting through the new ropes with which they were tied, and Sam Sturgeon fastened the cellar door with a screw-driver and two large screws.

Mrs. Matches recovered quickly from her fainting-fit, and Timothy and Hew tried to explain to her who the pirates were. They had by no means satisfied her when Sam Sturgeon and Gunner Boles came up from the cellar, and then they had to explain to her who Gunner Boles was. This was no easier than explaining the pirates, but Gunner Boles himself was extremely helpful. He sat down beside Mrs. Matches, and took her hand, and said to her very earnestly, 'You're a fine, brave woman, ma'am. You're as good a hand with a poker as any I've ever heard of, and I've had a lot of experience in my time. You're the sort of woman that Lord Nelson himself would admire, if he was with us to-day, and I can't give you higher praise than that. We're deeply indebted to you for what you did, Mrs. Matches, and I do assure you that we're all your very devoted and obedient servants, ma'am.'

Mrs. Matches was greatly impressed by this polite and handsome speech. She realised at once that Gunner Boles was not only a good man but a true sailor, and after that she did not really mind where he came from or how he had arrived at Popinsay House. So she cleared away the remains of the pirates' meal, spread a clean cloth on the table, and began to fry bacon and eggs and make a pot of tea.

'For if you've been at sea for all those years, as the boys were telling me, Mr. Boles, you must feel very hungry now that you've come ashore,' she said.

Now Sam was in a difficulty. He did not want to go on with their conversation about the trouble at the bottom of the sea in front of Mrs. Matches, because she would certainly declare that the boys must not be mixed up in it. But he could not tell Mrs. Matches that they had been discussing something very important, and would she excuse them if they went back to the study—because that would offend her. So after thinking the problem over, he said, 'Well, you go on with your breakfast, Mr. Boles, and I'll put these boys to bed again. It's no time for the like of them to be up, as you'll agree—and so will you, Mrs. Matches.'

But as he spoke he winked at the boys, to let them know that he was on their side, and they went up to bed—or so Mrs. Matches thought—without grumbling at all, or arguing even for a minute. Sam went with them, and when they were in their own room he sat down on Timothy's bed and asked them, 'Well, now, have you made up your minds yet?'

'About going for help, you mean?' asked Timothy.

'That's right,' said Sam.

'To Davy Jones's Locker?' asked Hew.

'You've got the address right,' said Sam.

'But where is it?' asked Timothy.

'At this time of year,' said Sam, 'Davy Jones brings his Court up to a place about three hundred miles off Mizen Head, which is down at the bottom left-hand corner of Ireland. In the winter he lives well below the Equator, but when the weather gets better, in May or thereabout, he comes up to his summer place off the south-west coast of Ireland.'

'But how can we get there?' asked Timothy. 'And how could we live under the sea?'

'We've been making some arrangements,' said Sam, 'just in case you'd agree. No one's compelling you to go—remember that—and I'm not even trying to persuade you. But if you like to volunteer—well, you'll get Mr. Boles and me out of a great difficulty, and perhaps you'll be able to save the situation down below. Which, it seems to me, is pretty serious.'

'I think we ought to volunteer,' said Timothy gravely.

'Of course we're going to volunteer,' said Hew. 'I made up my mind long ago.'

'But what are the arrangements you've made?' asked Timothy.

'You'll have to wait for Gunner Boles to tell you about them,' said Sam, 'and the first thing you'll have to do is to take an oath.'

'An oath of loyalty?' asked Timothy.

'Not exactly,' said Sam. 'You'll have to swear that you'll never tell what it is that gives Mr. Boles—and you yourselves, of course—the power of living down there in the depths of the green sea, and feeling as comfortable on the bottom of the ocean as ordinary human beings up here on dry land. That's the secret you must promise to keep, because if it came to be widely known there'd be such a crowd of visitors and holiday-makers going down to have a look for themselves, that the old sailors wouldn't hardly have room to turn. And they like their privacy; they like to have the sea to themselves, those old sailormen.'

'You mean it's quite easy to live under water?' asked Timothy.

'It's not so difficult as you might think,' said Sam.

'Then when do we start?' asked Hew.

'Take your breakfast to-morrow in the ordinary way,' said Sam, 'and then come out to the little beach on the Hen. I'll be there waiting for you, and maybe Gunner Boles will be with me, or Cully. I'll have to go now, and tell him the good news. It's time he was getting back to duty, and he'll go with a good heart when he hears that you've decided to help us. So tuck yourselves up and get some sleep if you can, because you're going to have a busy day to-morrow.'

Then Sam turned out the light, and closed the door behind him.

Chapter Ten

etween the Calf of Popinsay and the Hen there was a deep
channel through which the tide ran strongly. The rocks
under the low cliffs of the Hen were worn into strange shapes,
and here and there, when the tide was out, deep pools remained
in the rose-pink stone as round and smooth as pudding basins,
but as big as a double bed. Floating in one of these pools, in the
morning sunlight under a cloudless blue sky, Cully lay as comfortably as if he were indeed in bed, and sang a little song while three
oyster-catchers, two arctic terns, and four ringed-plover stood
round the pool and listened to him.

'The Seal is sitting on the rock,
    So cool and calm;
The seaweed, growing on the rock,
    Waves like a palm.

'The Seal looks at his watch, and sees
    It's half-past three;
The Codling, swimming past him, sees
    It's time for tea!

'Oh dear, oh dear!—Some think their life
    Is just a treat—
They do not know a Codling's life
    Is just as sweet!

'They never feel, poor little Cod,
    Doubt or remorse,
Nor indigestion after cod
    And parsley sauce.'

When he had finished the birds all nodded their heads and congratulated him on his fine voice. He was about to sing again when a young herring-gull, walking up to see what was going on, hopped on to a little brass pot which stood on the rock a yard or two from Cully's pool. The pot fell over, and Cully suddenly became extremely angry. He hauled himself out of the pool and screamed at the frightened gull, 'Go away, go away, I tell you! Don't touch that pot! How dare you come and listen to me without asking my permission!'

He was very angry indeed, and waved his eight arms in all directions. The birds flew away, and Cully put the brass pot in a safer place in a crevice in the rocks. It had a lid which screwed on, and when he lifted it, it made a gurgling noise like a bottle half-full of water when it is shaken.

It was only seven o'clock, and as yet there was hardly anyone to be seen in the fields or on the roads of Popinsay. For the people of Popinsay did not believe in getting up too early. In some of the houses, however, the fire had been lighted and smoke was rising from their chimneys. Cattle on the pastures were hard at work eating the summer grass, and young horses were chasing each other round the fields as if they were in a circus. A cock crew, a dog barked, and Sam Sturgeon was walking across the sand from Inner Bay to the Hen. The tide was out and the cream-coloured sand lay firm and dry. He walked across the Hen to the low cliffs on its western side, and presently discovered Cully; who lay in his pool again, and had been enjoying a little nap in the morning sun. The oyster-catchers, the terns, and the ringed-plover had come back and were standing round the pool, hoping that Cully would entertain them with another song. The oyster-catchers gave a warning cry when they saw Sam approaching, and Cully woke in time to greet him.

'Good morning, Mr. Sturgeon,' he exclaimed, 'and what a lovely morning it is, to be sure! What a glorious world we live in! It makes you feel all the better to be up and about in the bright and early hours of the day, doesn't it? I've never been able to understand how people can lie in bed on a fine morning, sleeping away the best part of the day, just wasting time, wasting the golden hours and the glowing moments of life—oh, it's wicked, isn't it, to waste half your life in sleep?'

Here Cully put up two of his arms just in time to hide an enormous yawn—for he was feeling rather tired, as he often did—and Sam Sturgeon sat down on the rock beside him.

'The boys have volunteered,' said Sam.

'Yes,' said Cully, and looked more serious now. 'Yes, Gunner Boles told me they had. Well, I hope nothing happens to them. It's a great risk, a very great risk, but someone had to go, of course, and it was splendid of them to volunteer. Oh, splendid, splendid! And it will be a great experience for them—if they survive, that is, though if they don't survive, it won't be any good to them at all. That's the worst of experience, I always think: you never know whether it's going to be any good to you, because you never know if you're going to survive it! But we mustn't look

97

at the gloomy side, must we, especially on a fine morning like this. Oh, no, no! No, no, no! Most certainly not!'

Sam Sturgeon was silent while Cully talked. He was feeling very serious and not quite happy, because he did not like to think of Timothy and Hew setting out on their adventure without him to look after them. But Gunner Boles had said that he might be needed on Popinsay, just as much as the boys were needed to take a message to Davy Jones's Locker. He had to stay, and they would have to look after themselves as well as they could.

'Have you brought the oil?' asked Sam abruptly.

'There it is, in that little brass pot,' said Cully. 'Gunner Boles had it in his store.'

Sam Sturgeon unscrewed the lid of the pot and held it to his nose. He sniffed, and said, 'There's ambergris in this.'

'There are sixty-nine different ingredients in it,' said Cully, 'and ambergris is only one of them. There's cod-liver oil and halibut oil and dog-fish oil and flying-fish oil. There's essence of shrimp and essence of shark and sword-fish essence and sea-urchin essence and the essence of a perfectly horrible animal called a sea-cow. There's winkle jelly and skate jelly and conger-eel jelly and jellyfish jelly too. There's whale milk and pirate's blood and a spoonful of Davy Jones's own special rum and a drop of Stockholm tar. There are sixty-nine ingredients, all of them different, and I haven't told you a third of them yet. Now let me think. There's the yolk of turtle eggs and the white of sturgeon eggs—oh, I beg your pardon, Mr. Sturgeon, I wasn't referring to you, of course——'

'That's all right,' said Sam. 'It's a very good name, is Sturgeon, and a very fine fish it is too.'

He screwed the lid on the brass pot, and asked Cully about the other arrangements.

'Have you got the boys' chargers?'

'They're waiting under the west cliffs of the Calf,' said Cully, 'and there are two very clean and tidy little Powder Monkeys holding them. I can't say that I really know the boys—I don't pay much attention to them as a rule—but they look all right, and I am sure I hope they are.'

'What about their shoes?' asked Sam.

'They're behind that rock,' said Cully. 'I think they'll fit, but I can't be sure, of course. Gunner Boles will be very disappointed if they don't.'

Behind the rock to which Cully had pointed lay two pairs of the curious sort of shoes which Gunner Boles and the pirates wore. They had, indeed, been taken from the two men whom Sam had found in the wreck, and Gunner Boles had cut them down and remade them to fit Timothy and Hew.

'The boys will be here about half-past eight,' said Sam.

They sat together, not talking much, for a little longer, and then Sam looked at his watch and said, 'You'd better go down and warn him now. They ought to be here as soon as he is, if he starts at once.'

Cully sighed and said, 'How I wish I could stay in this pool all day! Just sun-bathing. I simply adore the sun, don't you, Mr. Sturgeon? Though too much of it isn't good for one, of course. It's very bad for the complexion, for one thing, and it may be quite dangerous if you have a delicate skin like mine.—Well, give my love to the boys, Mr. Sturgeon, and tell them I'll be waiting for them when they come back to Popinsay, and I'll look forward very much to hearing all their adventures.'

Cully hoisted himself out of the pool and hauled himself over the rocks to the seaweed at the water's edge. He looked round and cried, 'You'll take care of the oil, won't you?' And then he slid into the sea.

At Popinsay House Timothy and Hew had finished their breakfast and were standing at the front door. They were ready to go, but for a minute or two they could not make up their minds to start. It seemed to them, quite suddenly, that Popinsay was the pleasantest place in the world, and that it was quite foolish to go away and leave it. The sky was blue, the grass was green, there were seven white pigeons sitting on the garden wall, and a lark was singing high above the gooseberry bushes. The sun shone through the window of their father's study. A blackbird was chuckling on the lawn, and they had not made their beds—though they had promised Mrs. Matches that they would.

'Oh, come on,' said Timothy at last. 'Never mind about the beds, never mind about anything. If we start thinking we shan't want to go—and we do want to, don't we?'

'Yes, of course,' said Hew. 'Of course we do.'

But his voice was a little uncertain, and suddenly he bent down and picked up a stone and threw it at the blackbird.

'Shut up!' he shouted.

'Come on,' said Timothy again, and they set off together down the road to Inner Bay, and then across the sands to the Hen where Sam was waiting for them. They walked up the steep sloping turf, and clambered down the western cliffs. They came to the round pool where Cully had lately been singing, and at that moment the bald head and bright red whiskers of Gunner Boles appeared out of the sea, and he stumbled up the slippery rocks to greet them.

'Good morning to you, my fine young cocks!' he shouted, 'and how are you feeling this grand morning?'

100

'Very well, thank you,' said Timothy and Hew in their politest manner.

'And how are you, Sam? You're looking as worried as an old hen that's lost her chickens.'

'And that's what I feel like,' said Sam, 'when I think of the boys going off to sea without me to look after them.'

'They've got to set out on their own some day,' said Gunner Boles, 'and these two little game-cocks are ready for the fray—aren't you, my boys?'

Every now and then, as they walked across the sands, Timothy and Hew had looked over their shoulders at the green fields of Popinsay, and then looked wonderingly at the green sea that spread so far and lay so deeply to the west. They both felt a little frightened to be leaving the fields they knew for the deeps of the sea of which they knew nothing at all. But they felt excited too, and their voices were steady enough when they answered, 'Yes, we're ready.'

'You're good boys,' said Gunner Boles. 'You're like I was at your age, willing to go anywhere and set my hands to whatever was needed. And Lord Nelson himself, from all I've heard of him, was just such another when he was a boy.—You've got the oil, Sam, haven't you? And the shoes?'

'Here they are,' said Sam. 'Cully brought them.'

'Then the first thing we've got to do is to administer the oath.—You must promise, you see, that you won't ever tell, to anyone living on land, the mystery of those that live in the sea. For it's one of the great secrets of the world, and there'd be no peace in the ocean if it was commonly known. So stand side by side, and raise your right hands, and say after me the following words.'

Timothy and Hew stood together, facing Gunner Boles, who

recited in a very solemn voice these verses, which they repeated:

'By Rock, Salt, and Air,
By the Dog Star and Altair,
By the Seven Sisters and the Southern Cross,
And the Glittering Eye of an Albatross,
I, Timothy, do hereby swear,
And I, Hew, do swear also,
Never to tell, to friend or foe,
The Mystery of the Deep Green Sea
That the Shell will tell to me;

'By the Sea-Horse, and the Sea-Mare,
By Spindrift, Fog, and Ice-Glare,
By the Tropics of Cancer and Capricorn,
By the Cape of Good Hope and black Cape Horn,
I, Timothy, do hereby swear,
And I, Hew, do swear also,
Never to tell, to friend or foe,
The Mystery of the Deep Green Sea
That the Shell will tell to me;

'By Davy Jones's Stately Chair,
And his Cushion stuffed with Mermaids' Hair,
By Flying-Fish and the great White Whale,
And the Flying Dutchman's Fore-Topsail,
I, Timothy, do hereby swear,
And I, Hew, do swear also,
Never to tell, to friend or foe,
The Mystery of the Deep Green Sea
That the Shell will tell to me!'

'Now that's an oath that can never be broken,' said Gunner Boles, 'and very nicely you both said it. I've never heard it recited better in all my days.'

'But I don't understand the line about the Shell,' said Timothy.

'All in good time,' said Gunner Boles. 'You've got to be oiled first, and have your shoes fitted, and then you'll listen to the Shell.—Did you remember to make a brush, Sam?'

'Here it is,' said Sam, and held out a little brush he had made with sea-gulls' feathers. 'And here's the oil.—You'll have to take off your clothes, boys.'

Then Gunner Boles painted them all over with oil from the brass pot, and dropped a little into their eyes, and up their noses, and down their throats.

'That'll keep you warm,' he said, 'and after you've been told how to do it by the Shell, you'll be able to breathe, and see what's going on, and listen to such talk as there is on the bottom of the ocean, just as easy as you're breathing and looking round you at this very moment, on the Hen of Popinsay.'

But neither Timothy nor Hew found this as comforting as Gunner Boles supposed it would be. Their eyes were smarting, and they felt a little sick.

'It may be a useful kind of oil,' said Timothy, 'but I don't like the taste of it.'

'It tastes like toffee and sardines mixed up together,' said Hew.

'It's the best oil in the world,' said Gunner Boles. 'It's got sixty-nine ingredients, all different.'

'But it was a mistake to put both toffee *and* sardines in it,' said Hew.

'Not so much talk,' interrupted Sam, 'and put on your bathing-suits.'

He had brought the boys' bathing-drawers—which they very

rarely wore—and brushed them also with oil from the brass pot. Gunner Boles explained that he had been unable, in so short a time, to obtain suits such as he himself wore, but their own, he said, would be nearly as good now that they had been oiled. Then he helped the boys to put on the shoes that looked like great frog's feet; and they fitted very well.

'Now don't forget your oath,' he said, and from the pouch at his belt took a twisted Shell about four inches long. It was ridged with bright pink on the outside, but smooth inside and gleaming like a pearl. 'Put that to your ear,' he said to Timothy, 'and listen carefully.'

'I can hear the murmur of the sea,' said Timothy, 'but you can hear that in an ordinary shell.'

'So you can,' Gunner Boles agreed, 'but no one could say that this is an ordinary shell. So be patient, Timothy, and listen again, and maybe you'll hear something more.'

Then Timothy sat down on a ledge of rock, and held the Shell to his ear, and presently a look of wonderment appeared on his face as if, for the first time in the world, he was hearing the finest story in the world. For now, in the murmur of the sea, he could hear the tale of all who live in the sea. He was told about the mountains and the valleys on the floor of the sea, about coral reefs and the jungles in which great fishes lived. About old ships, all green with age, and the old sailors who looked after the huge cables that held the world together. About pearls and dolphins, and mermaids and Davy Jones's Locker. About the Powder Monkeys who were on the side of the loyal sailors, and the Cabin Boys who lived with the pirates. About the friendly creatures in the ocean, such as seals and herring and basking-sharks; and those that were unfriendly, such as skate and conger-eels and the Great Sea Serpent. About tides and forelands, and how to find his way from one part of the sea to another. About what to eat and how to breathe, about the speech of certain creatures that were able to speak, and where to sleep safely in the depths of the ocean. All this, and more besides, the Shell told him; and when he had heard enough, he gave it to Hew.

Then Hew sat with the Shell to his ear, and he was so delighted by what he heard that his eyes grew round as pennies, and his mouth was wide open, and every now and then he laughed aloud with sheer pleasure. But all this time Gunner Boles and Sam Sturgeon sat in utter silence by the side of the round pool where Cully had sung his song to the terns and the oyster-catchers. They sat cross-legged, with their elbows on their knees, and Gunner Boles smoked his pipe; but Sam Sturgeon wore a mournful look, which was most unusual for him, and once or twice he rubbed a tear from his eye.

When Hew had heard all that was necessary, he offered the Shell to Sam, but Sam looked doubtfully at Gunner Boles, and Gunner Boles shook his head.

'No, Sam,' he said, 'it's not for you. It's only those who must go down into the green deeps that can listen to the Shell; and your place, as we decided between ourselves, is here on Popinsay. I'm sorry, Sam, but orders are orders and you've got to abide by them.'

'That's true enough,' said Sam, but he looked longingly at the Shell as Gunner Boles took it from Hew and put it back into his pouch. Then Gunner Boles knocked out his pipe, and stood up and said, 'It's time to go, boys.'

Sam went with them to the edge of the sea, and knee-deep into the sea—they found it difficult to walk in their new frog-shoes—and as he said good-bye to them the tears were running down his face.

When they were thirty or forty yards from shore they looked back and saw him, still knee-deep in the water, and looking very lonely. They felt sad to be leaving him behind, and sorry because he was all alone; but they were too excited to think much about anything except their own adventure.

'He can talk to Mrs. Matches,' said Hew, 'and he'll have wonderful dinners when she's only got him to look after.'

Chapter Eleven

'And now,' said Gunner Boles, 'we'll go down to the bottom and see what it's like there.'

They were in calm water, about half-way between the Hen and the western cliffs of the Calf, and Timothy and Hew had already made several shallow dives, and found that they could swim comfortably under water for two or three minutes at a time. The shoes that made their feet look like frogs' feet were a great help, and the oil from the little brass pot kept them perfectly warm. But the thought of going down to the bottom of the sea was still rather alarming, and when Timothy looked at Hew, and Hew looked at Timothy, each of them thought how solemn the other was looking. But before they could think very much, Gunner Boles exclaimed, 'Here we go!' and turning himself upside-down like a swan feeding on water-weeds, swam straight down into the depths. Timothy and Hew followed him obediently, and presently they were all three sitting on a little patch of sand with a ledge of rock behind them and a tall hedge of seaweed wavering in front.

'And it's not half as bad as you thought it would be, now is it?' asked Gunner Boles.

'It's rather an unusual feeling,' said Timothy, as a large haddock swam out of the seaweed and looked them over, and swam back again. 'But it's not really uncomfortable.'

'I never thought we'd be able to see so well,' said Hew.

'It's the oil that does that,' said Gunner Boles. 'The oil with the sixty-nine ingredients that I dropped into your eyes, and down your throats though you didn't like the taste of it. And now let's go for a little walk, just to get accustomed to things, before we swim out and look for your chargers.'

He led them along the open sand that lay like a road beside the seaweed hedge, and then swam through the hedge, which easily divided to let them pass, and into a growth of taller weed that was rather like a little wood. Sometimes they walked and sometimes they swam, and when they came to a reef that stretched far out into the sea they clambered up the rock and down the other side. They remained on the bottom of the sea for about half an hour, and the boys were beginning to feel quite at home there when Gunner Boles said it was time to look for their chargers. Then they swam strongly through the middle depths of the sea towards the western cliffs of the Calf.

Presently through the green twilight of the water they saw the dark base of the cliffs, and felt the suck of the tide as it drew them to the north.

'There they are,' said Gunner Boles—and Timothy and Hew, in a sudden panic, headed for the surface and swam as hard as they could towards daylight and the shore. For what they had seen, at the very moment when Gunner Boles spoke, was a pair of enormous grey fish-like shapes in the water, about thirty feet long, which, they were sure, were sharks.

They were on the surface of the sea, and swimming furiously towards the cliffs, when Gunner Boles overtook them and demanded to know what had gone wrong.

'Sharks!' said Timothy. 'Didn't you see them?'

'Two enormous sharks,' said Hew.

'Sharks, my eye!' said Gunner Boles. 'They're your chargers, and they're what you're going to ride on to get to Davy Jones's Locker.'

The boys looked at him wide-eyed with astonishment, and Timothy said that he had never heard of anyone riding on a shark, and Hew added, 'But lots of people have been taken for a ride inside.'

'Now, now,' said Gunner Boles, 'don't waste my time with silly tales that you've learnt ashore. You've been given the freedom of the sea, and landlubbers' tales don't concern you now. And anyway, these sharks that you're frightened of are only basking-sharks, and no more dangerous than an old cow. So down you come again, and meet the boys who are looking after them. There's two Powder Monkeys down there, and they've had orders to go with you.'

Somewhat reluctantly Timothy and Hew followed Gunner Boles down to the bottom, and keeping very close to him swam towards the basking-sharks which lay side by side a few feet from the foot of the cliffs. They were huge creatures, but as the boys came nearer they could see that the sharks' expression was very gentle, and their little eyes were rather like the mild eyes of a cow, and when Gunner Boles patted their heads they quivered with pleasure and said 'Moo-oo!' just as a cow might have done.

Sitting on a shelf of rock were two boys, perhaps a little older than Timothy and Hew but no bigger, who held the sharks by long reins attached to whalebone rings that had been clipped into the creatures' noses—or where their noses might have been if they had had any. These boys were dressed in the same manner as Gunner Boles, and the nearer one wore on his vest the name of H.M.S. *Téméraire*, the other H.M.S. *Ajax*. They stood up and saluted, but not very smartly; for one of them yawned widely, and the other winked at Timothy.

'You miserable, naughty, uneducated, horrible little eelskin sacks of vice and idleness!' exclaimed the Gunner. 'Is that the way you've been taught to salute a superior officer, especially when he's coming aboard with a couple of distinguished visitors? Now stand still with your heels together, and your shoulders straight and a look of respect on your snub-nosed, pig-eyed faces and do it again—and again—and again!'

He made them salute seven times before he was satisfied, and then he told Timothy and Hew: 'Now these are two Powder Monkeys that I brought with me when I came into these latitudes, and they'll go with you to Davy Jones's Locker and look after your chargers. The one on the left is called William Button, and him on the right is Henry String. They're both of them the wilfullest, laziest, dirtiest Powder Monkeys I've ever known, but if you treat 'em badly and beat 'em twice a week they often behave like good boys who've been well brought up.—Isn't that so, William?'

'Yes, sir, I mean, no, sir,' said William Button.

'No, sir, I mean, yes, sir,' said Henry String.

'Well, they're your companions for the voyage,' said Gunner Boles, 'and I hope you'll get on together. Now saddle the chargers, boys, and look alive.'

William Button and Henry String set on the sharks' backs a pair of large boxes with seats in them, all made of whale-bone, and fastened them securely with strong girths of plaited strips of sealskin. These whale-bone saddles looked something like the howdahs that Indian elephants carry, and the passengers seated within them would be protected against the rush of water when the sharks swam swiftly through the sea.

While the Powder Monkeys were busy with the saddles, Gunner Boles took Timothy and Hew aside, and spoke to them very seriously.

'Now those two boys,' he said, 'are good boys, but like all the Powder Monkeys they're fond of mischief. They'd rather play than work, and you'll have to keep an eye on them and see they do as you tell them. That's the first thing to remember. And the second is this.—When you get to Davy Jones's Locker, you'll tell him that Gunner Boles, on duty at the Knot Latitude 59 North, Longitude 4 West, has got evidence of a dangerous conspiracy by the pirates Dan Scrumbril and Inky Poops to seize control of all cables north of Latitude 59 and between the coasts of Norway and America. You'll tell him that an attempt has already been made by the pirates to establish a base near the island of Popinsay, but that attempt was foiled by the prompt action of your friend, Mr. Sturgeon, late of the Royal Marines. You'll tell him that I, Gunner Boles, am so far in full control of the sea-floor round 59 North, 4 West, but have no reinforcements in case of a sudden attack. You'll give him my compliments and assure him of my loyal and faithful duty, and ask him to send help as quickly as he can because I don't like the look of things, and no more would Davy Jones himself if he was here in my place.—Now just say all that over again, so as I can be sure that you remember it.'

Timothy and Hew repeated what he had said, and by the time they were word-perfect the sharks had been saddled and William Button and Henry String were sitting in the howdahs with the reins in their hands. Timothy and Hew got in beside

111

them—Timothy with William Button and Hew with Henry String—and Gunner Boles shook hands with them and told the Powder Monkeys to be sure and behave themselves and waste no time. The sharks said 'Moo-oo-oo!' in a rather unhappy way as they felt the reins tighten on the rings in their noses—or where their noses might have been—and the Powder Monkeys pricked them two or three times with the short, slender lances which they carried. Then the sharks began to move at great speed, and the Powder Monkeys headed them to the south-west. The rush of water broke over the howdahs like enormous waterfalls, but Timothy and Hew were fairly comfortable inside them, and when they had become used to the rapid motion they began to enjoy their swift passage through the immense deeps of the sea, which grew lighter and brighter as the sharks rose towards the surface.

Gunner Boles swam with them for a little way, but the sharks were far swifter than he, and soon he was left behind in their bubbling wake. His last words, before he left them, were, 'The best of luck to you all—*and don't waste time!'*

The sharks were swimming just below the surface of the sea, and sometimes, when they broke the surface, the boys felt a rush of air and saw a curtain of spray flying over their heads, and their eyes, which had become used to the green light of the sea, were startled by the bright blue of the sky and white clouds shining in the sun.

William Button, sitting beside Timothy, said to him: 'You're green, aren't you?'

'I don't think so,' said Timothy stiffly.

'I mean,' said William, 'that this is the first time you've ever been down under. And that being so, you're green.'

'Well,' said Timothy, 'I've never been under the sea before, but I was once in a ship that was torpedoed, and my brother and I were on a raft in the South Atlantic for quite a long time.'

'That's nothing,' said William Button contemptuously. 'Nothing at all! Wrecks and rafts, they're as common as seaweed out here. Everyone's been wrecked sometime or other, I suppose. I was wrecked twice before I was twelve. But what counts is living down below. That's life, that is. You don't know what's worth while, you landlubbers that sit and toast your toes in front of a fire, and catch cold if you get wet! We'll show you how to live, now you've come to join us. But you've got to be careful, mind! You stick to us, and you'll be all right; but don't ever have nothing to do with those Cabin Boys, if you meet 'em. They're poison!'

William Button had a round rosy face, a snub nose, and hair that stood straight on end. Timothy felt a little disappointed when he was not impressed by the story of the raft, but he listened with great interest to William Button's tales of life under the sea—some of which he did not believe—and several hours passed pleasantly enough. Every now and then their shark would stop, and rise to the surface, and say 'Moo!' in a sleepy sort of voice. Then William would prick it with his lance to make it swim again.

'Fish,' he explained, 'are all the same, no matter what size they are. They're lazy, they're idle, they don't want to do nothing except eat, sleep, and take life easy. These basking-sharks, now, if they had their own way, wouldn't do a mortal thing but lie on top of the water and bask! That's what fish are like. There isn't one of them would know what it is to do an honest day's work, if it hadn't been for us sailors coming to teach them.'

'I suppose you have to work very hard,' said Timothy, 'to please Gunner Boles?'

'Me?' exclaimed William Button. 'Me work? Not blooming likely. Not if I can dodge it—and I'm pretty good at dodging, too. But for fish it's different, of course. They ought to work.'

On the other shark Hew and Henry String had sat for some time without speaking, because each was waiting for the other to begin. Henry String had a thin bony face and blue eyes and dark untidy hair; and every now and then he bent up his arms and looked at his muscles. At last he said to Hew, 'Have you ever been in any battles?'

'Not exactly,' said Hew. 'But I've often fought with my brother.'

'That's nothing,' said Henry String. 'Nothing at all! Everybody fights with his brother; that's natural. But I've been in proper battles. Naval battles. Guns firing right and left, cannon-balls cutting the rigging, masts coming down, the yards coming down, sailors falling dead and wounded, and all the deck covered with blood! I remember once, in a battle, there was only me and the Captain left alive, but we fought on, and after about seven hours the Frenchman struck his colours and we won. But if you'd been there, I don't suppose you'd have done any good at all.'

'I'd have been as good as you.'

'No, you wouldn't,' said Henry String.

'Yes, I would,' said Hew.

'You're a liar!'

'And you're another!'

'I'll knock your block off, if you say that!'

'I've said it!'

'Well, I'll knock your block off.'

'Try it and see,' said Hew.

Then they stood up in the swaying howdah on top of the shark, and Henry twirled his fists in front of his face in a very pugnacious manner. But Hew, pretending to punch with his left hand—as Sam Sturgeon had taught him—made Henry shift his guard to the right side of his head; whereupon Hew, very quickly, punched with his right hand and hit Henry so hard on the jaw that he fell overboard.

The shark, at the same moment, said 'Moo!' and decided to come up to the surface to bask. Henry was able to climb into the howdah again, and after pricking the shark to make it swim, said to Hew, 'That wasn't fair, that wasn't. You took me by surprise. So let's try again.'

'All right,' said Hew, and after two or three minutes Henry succeeded in hitting him on the cheek-bone, and knocked him out of the howdah. But quickly he stopped the shark and helped him to climb on again.

Hew stood up and was prepared to go on with the fight, but Henry appeared to be less eager. His nose was very red and one of his eyes was a little bruised.

'There's no need to fight any more,' he said. 'I'm satisfied now. I only wanted to see what you was made of, see? And now I know, see? You're not so bad, after all.'

'And I would have been quite useful in a naval battle, wouldn't I?' demanded Hew.

'Well, you might have been if you'd been properly brought up and got accustomed to it,' Henry admitted; and before Hew could think of a reply he pricked the shark deeply with his lance and said, 'Let's challenge the others to a race.'

William Button and Timothy were well pleased with the suggestion, and by and by the two sharks were racing through the water side by side at great speed. They swam just below the surface and tore through the sea under glittering curtains of spray. William Button shouted to Timothy, 'We're making thirty knots at least,' and at the same moment Henry String told Hew, 'The fastest I've ever gone before was forty knots, and that was one day when I was riding a sword-fish; but we're going just as fast now, I'm sure of it.'

They were undoubtedly travelling at great speed, and all afternoon the race went on, now with Timothy and William Button in the lead, and then with Hew and Henry String forging ahead and overtaking them. They rounded Cape Wrath, they raced through the North Minch, and swam swiftly down the Little Minch. They swept through the water when it was all golden in the rays of the setting sun, and then, when slowly it grew dark, they decided that they had had enough racing and that Timothy and William Button had won by half a length.

'And now,' said William Button, 'we'll go down and look for a sleeping-shell.'

'A sleeping-shell?' asked Timothy.

'You do sleep at night, don't you?' said William.

'Yes, of course,' said Timothy.

'Well, then, we'll have to find a sleeping-shell. That stands to reason, doesn't it?'

They dived steeply down, and for a little while swam slowly along the bottom of the sea until they came to an open stretch of sand about the size of a large field, with a thicket of tall weed growing at one side, and in the midst of the thicket there was a little lane with a notice board at the entrance which said: 'TO THE SLEEPING-SHELL.' They swam up the lane for about fifty yards, and then came into a smaller clearing in the middle of which an enormous shell lay on clean white sand with another notice board in front of it. On this notice board was printed:

NOTICE TO FISH

NO ADMISSION!
SAILORS ONLY

NOTICE TO SAILORS

YOU ARE WELCOME!
BUT NO FIGHTING
AND DON'T LEAVE
CRUMBS AND OLD
SHOES LYING ABOUT

'Well, here we are,' said William, and quickly he and Henry String unsaddled the sharks and tied them to two rings in a little ledge of rock behind the shell. Timothy and Hew went in—the opening of the shell was large enough for a full-grown man—and found inside it four bunks, made of whale-bone and filled with fine soft sand, which, they thought, would make very comfortable beds. The inner part of the shell grew narrower and narrower, and twisted round rather like a spiral staircase. There were several cupboards on the walls of this narrower part, on the doors of which were neatly printed notices that read: SHRIMP PASTE, BLOATER PASTE, LOBSTER PASTE, WHALE MILK, and RUM. They opened them and found that all the pastes were made up in neat little parcels, rather like small bricks, and the whale milk and the rum were in large old-fashioned bottles. William Button and Henry String came in and said, 'What's for dinner?'

'Shrimp paste, bloater paste, lobster paste, rum and whale's milk,' said Timothy.

'Just the usual old stuff,' said William. 'That's what you always find in these sleeping-shells.'

'And we're not allowed to drink the rum,' said Henry gloomily. 'It's only the grown-ups can drink rum, though some of those Cabin Boys sneak a cupful now and then, and start fighting and singing and showing off.'

Timothy and Hew each took one of the little bricks of shrimp paste, and found it more delicious than anything they had ever tasted on land. Then they had a brick of bloater paste, and another of lobster paste, and both were so good that they had second helpings of each. But they did not care for the whale milk, which had a slight flavour of castor-oil.

'You'll get used to it in time,' said William Button.

'And you'll get tired of shrimp paste too,' said Henry String. 'It's all right to begin with, but when you've been eating it for a hundred years or so you begin to think you'd like something else for a change.'

Timothy and Hew enjoyed their supper, however, and when they had eaten all they wanted, they lay down in two of the sandy bunks while William and Henry took those on the other side, and very soon they were all fast asleep.

They woke when morning came and went out for a little walk, and the first person they met was a very large and elderly Crab who spoke to them in a dignified voice.

'I hope,' he said, 'that you found everything to your satisfaction? This shell is widely known among travellers, and enjoys, I'm glad to say, a very fine reputation for comfort, cleanliness, good wholesome food, and beautiful surroundings.'

'Thank you,' said Timothy. 'We've been very comfortable here.'

'Is it your shell?' asked Hew.

'I am the caretaker, gentlemen,' said the Crab. 'Merely the humble caretaker, but, as you have doubtless seen for yourselves, I take a pride in my profession and endeavour to give the best possible service to all travellers who honour me with their company.'

William Button and Henry String now came out and joined in the conversation. They were not so much impressed by the Crab as Timothy and Hew had been, and William said to him quite rudely, 'Why weren't you here to meet us when we came in last night? What were you doing, you old skrimshanker, you? Sound asleep under the weeds, I suppose?'

'Not at all,' said the Crab. 'You misjudge me sorely, you do indeed. I had been summoned to the assistance of a neighbour of mine, who unhappily is in very indifferent health. I was sitting up all night, gentlemen, with a poor sick friend.'

'I don't believe a word of it,' said William.

'You were sleeping under the weeds,' said Henry.

'Gentlemen, gentlemen,' said the Crab reproachfully. 'You misjudge me sorely! There is no more honest, sober, hard-working, conscientious a crab in the Western Ocean than your humble servant. I have been in the public service for eighty-seven years———'

'And been asleep for eighty-five,' said William.

'Come on,' said Henry, 'we've got no time to listen to this old croaker.—Go in and get your breakfast, you two, and we'll saddle up.'

Timothy and Hew went in and made a good breakfast on shrimp paste and whale's milk, and talked politely to the Crab, whose feelings had been hurt by the rudeness of the Powder Monkeys. Then they made their beds, which didn't take long, and William and Henry came in and ate a large breakfast in a very short time. They said good-bye to the Crab, and remounting their sharks, began the second day of their voyage.

All day they swam swiftly to the south-west, and most of the time they travelled on the surface or just under it. But they kept a good look-out for ships and fishing-boats, and whenever they saw one in the distance they dived deeply and only came up again when they had made sure that there was no other vessel in sight.

That night they slept in a shell that lay on the bottom of the sea about forty miles from the west coast of Donegal, and the following morning they made another early start and in fine weather continued their journey.

'Gunner Boles,' said Timothy, 'told us not to waste time, and we certainly haven't wasted any yet.'

William Button yawned and said, 'Not half, we haven't.'

Timothy yawned too, for they were all getting a little tired of rushing through the bright water, and the sharks had to be pricked more and more often to keep them swimming.

Chapter Twelve

At midday they were moving just below the surface of a calm blue sea under an almost cloudless sky, and nobody had spoken for nearly an hour. They were going quite slowly now, and they all felt rather bored after sitting for two and a half days in their howdahs. But their attention was attracted by a school of porpoises which suddenly appeared not far in front, and with something like envy they watched them leaping out of the water, and diving and reappearing, in the liveliest way. The porpoises appeared to be enjoying themselves, and in comparison with their brisk and cheerful movement it seemed very dull to be sitting still in a whale-bone box on top of a basking-shark.

'I don't count this worth anything at all,' said William Button. 'Anyone can ride a shark, even old men like Gunner Boles. It takes something, though, to ride one of them porpoises. There's not many can do that.'

'Have you ever ridden one?' asked Timothy.

'Often,' said William. 'Often and often.'

On the other shark Henry String had said to Hew, 'I bet you couldn't sit on a porpoise for more than two minutes.'

'Could you?' asked Hew.

'Me?' said Henry. 'I've ridden them for years. But I've got a good seat, I've got good hands, and I understand them. Now you'd be thrown off before you knew where you were.'

'If you can ride them, I dare say I can too,' said Hew.

Henry String laughed scornfully and shouted to William Button, 'He thinks he could ride one of them porpoises.'

'That's what Timothy thinks too,' said William.

'Well, let 'em try,' said Henry, and standing up in his howdah he whistled to two porpoises who were swimming quite near them. They came alongside, and Henry gave each of them the half of a brick of shrimp paste which he had put in his satchel before leaving the shell in which they had slept.

'Whe-ooh, whe-ooh,' said the porpoises, and ate the shrimp paste with great pleasure.

'Now, there you are,' said Henry. 'There's two of the quietest, best-behaved porpoises in the Atlantic Ocean. If you can't ride them, you can't ride anything.'

When they considered the matter more closely, both Timothy and Hew were inclined to believe that it was quite impossible to sit on a porpoise; for there was nothing to hold. The creatures' dorsal fins were set so far back that it would be necessary to sit in front of them; and in front of the fin there was only a smooth slope down to the nose. The first time Timothy mounted his porpoise, he slid off immediately.

Then William Button said, 'Grip with your knees and use his breast-fins as stirrups.' So Timothy tried again, and setting his feet on the breast-fins—which were stiff and strong—he pressed his knees into the porpoise's side, which yielded like a rubber ball; and beneath his weight its back also sank a little, so that he was presently sitting quite comfortably in a small hollow. Then Hew, who had been watching him carefully, mounted the other porpoise and kept his seat without much difficulty.

The porpoises behaved very well. They swam slowly till Timothy and Hew had found their balance, and then they dived and came up, and dived again, in an easy movement like that of horses on a merry-go-round. It was very pleasant to be lifted from the sea into the bright summer air, and carried swiftly down through the sunlit water, and out again in wreaths of spray; and Hew and Timothy urged their mounts to swim more quickly. The other porpoises kept pace with them, and William Button and Henry String, on the basking-sharks, followed close behind.

But William Button and Henry String did not behave so well as the porpoises. After a few minutes William winked at Henry, and bringing their sharks alongside Timothy and Hew, as though to challenge them to a race, they leaned out and pricked the porpoises with their lances. The porpoises leapt wildly out of the water, then rushed through the sea at a furious pace. And now their movement, as they dived and came up again, was very violent indeed. They seemed to be running for their lives, and at the same time jumping over dreadful obstacles.

Timothy and Hew could do nothing but hold on with their legs as tightly as they were able, and try to keep their balance. They had no means of controlling the porpoises, and though they shouted 'Stop! Stop!' whenever their heads were above water, the porpoises paid no attention at all. After a little while the boys began to feel curiously tired, and rather dizzy, and very uncomfortable. They felt hot and nervous, they wanted to yawn and lie down. Timothy glanced at Hew, and saw that he was very pale; and Hew thought Timothy was looking green. They realised, then, what was the matter with them. They were both sea-sick.

Timothy was the first to fall off, and slowly he sank through the sea until he came to rest on a muddy bottom between two huge boulders. He lay there for a long time, and was very unhappy. He felt far too ill to wonder what had happened to Hew, or where William Button and Henry String had gone. He was all alone, he was lost on the bottom of the ocean; but he was too miserable to worry about that.

When at last he felt a little better he swam slowly here and there, hoping to meet someone. But in that part of the ocean, it seemed, he was the only living person. He could not find the Powder Monkeys, he could not find Hew, and for two or three hours he did not even meet a fish. He rose to the surface and swam to and fro in the evening light, but the surface of the sea was as empty as its depths. The sun was setting, and by now he was feeling not merely sad and lonely and a little frightened, but extremely hungry. So when the sun sank below the horizon he swam down to look for a sleeping-shell.

His luck changed, and after swimming rapidly for about half an hour he saw another notice board warning fishes to keep out, and beside it, in a pleasant little valley on the floor of the sea, the curving outline of a sleeping-shell. He looked both inside and out for the caretaker—every shell, he had learnt, was looked after by an elderly crab—but there was no one there. Crabs, he thought, did not make very conscientious caretakers, but perhaps they were the only creatures who would take on so dull a job. He was disappointed, however, that there was no one to talk to, and he was in a melancholy mood when he went to the cupboard to look for his supper. But he made a good meal of shrimp paste and bloater paste and lobster paste, and choosing a comfortable-looking bed in the innermost, narrow part of the shell he lay down and quickly fell asleep.

Some hours later he woke in a great fright, and heard voices at the entrance. There was a man's voice, loud and rough, and the voice of a whimpering little boy.

'Look alive, now,' the man was saying. 'Look alive, you miserable scrap of skin and bone, and find a couple of soft-heads and hang 'em up in the proper place. The Captain likes plenty of light, and you'd know that by now if you had any brain in that half-pint head of yours.'

'Yes, Mr. Kelly,' the boy's voice answered. 'Yes, I do remember. I've got the soft-heads here and I was just going to hang them up. I was, honestly I was.'

'Stow your gab,' said the man.

'Yes, Mr. Kelly,' said the boy, 'yes, I was just going to.'

A moment later the outer half of the shell was filled with a strange light and Timothy, peering cautiously from the narrow inner part that was still in darkness, saw that a wretched-looking little fellow—whom he took to be a Cabin Boy—had hung up a couple of fish of curious appearance that gave out a silvery light and served the purpose of a lamp. They were the soft-heads, he supposed, of which the man had spoken.

Then the man came in and Timothy saw, to his alarm, that he was dressed rather like the pirates whom Sam Sturgeon had discovered in the wreck. His vest was red—though not so red as theirs, but rather the colour of brick—and his trousers were dark brown with ragged edges. He was short and fat and very ugly, and looked as though, in private life, he might have been a hangman.

'Now bring the Captain's stool,' he said, 'and his own particular mug with the picture of roses on it, because I dare say he'll be tired after his long day's march.'

'Yes, Mr. Kelly,' said the boy in his whimpering voice, and at that moment another figure appeared at the entrance to the shell.

This was a tall, thin man with sloping shoulders like a bottle, and a long cruel face, the colour of cheese. He was dressed in the same colours as Mr. Kelly, but also wore, hanging from his shoulders, a short cloak that matched his vest, and a brass hilted cutlass dangled at his belt. As he came in, Mr. Kelly bowed to him in a very polite and humble manner, though he could not bow deeply, as his paunch prevented him.

The Cabin Boy brought a little three-legged stool made of whale-bone, and the newcomer sat down and said in a mournful voice, 'I haven't the strength I used to have, Darby, my dear. I'm not the man I was. I get tired too easily nowadays, and the doctor tells me that my vital organs are much impaired.'

'But your brain's as good as ever it was, Captain! You've still got the sharpest wits and the cunningest mind in the ocean. When it comes to a problem that no one else can solve, why, what do we all say? Send for Inky Poops, and he'll tell us what to do! That's what we say, Captain, and that's the truth of it.'

Timothy, watching them from the dark and narrow part of the shell, felt his heart beat quickly with fear and excitement. So this was Inky Poops! Here, within a few feet of him, was one of the pirate captains who were plotting to win control of the sea, and from the look of him he would not show much mercy to anyone he found spying on him. Timothy lay very quietly, keeping well within the darkness of the shell, and listened eagerly to all that was said, and tried not to think what might happen to him if he were caught.

Inky Poops was pleased by his lieutenant's flattery, and over his face that was the colour of cheese there spread a horrible expression which was probably meant to be a smile; and his mouth opened a little to disclose two long yellow teeth, one on either side of it.

'You're too kind, Darby, my dear,' he said, 'too kind by half, though what you say is true enough. I can still out-talk these dull, old timber-headed tarpaulins that we live among. I can outwit them, and out-smart them, as I always have out-smarted them from the first time I ever went to sea as a little boy helping the steward in a Bristol ship called the *Betsey Jane*. I started on the bottom rung, Darby, and I've worked my own way up the ladder. On that first voyage I spent all my time down in the bowels of the ship, in a little cock-pit that smelt of rancid butter and mouldy cheese, with a smoky lantern on the table in front of me, and a pen in my hand. I kept the steward's accounts, and kept them well; for he made a profit, and so did I.'

It was during this period of his life that Captain Poops acquired his yellow complexion and his nickname. After living for two or three years among bad cheese, his face had become the same colour; and because he was rather untidy in his habits, there was often more ink on his face and hands than there was upon his ledger, especially after rough weather. But Darby Kelly was not so tactless as to remind him of such vulgar details.

'It's an example to us all, is a life like yours,' he said, 'and it ought to fill any young boy with ambition to go and do likewise.—You, you miserable, pin-headed little squeaker, have you got the Captain's rum yet?' he shouted to the Cabin Boy.

'Yes, Mr. Kelly, sir, here it is.—It's your own special rum, Captain, in your own special mug.'

And he gave the Captain a large china mug which was very prettily decorated with red roses and forget-me-nots.

'A wonderful career,' repeated Darby Kelly, 'and all due to the sheer power of intellect.'

Captain Poops drank a little rum and said, 'But I've never got puffed-up with pride, have I, Darby? No, and I never shall, for pride is a great sin. I'll always remember that once upon a time I was just a miserable little boy, like this little boy here, that we call Dingy, because he looks as dirty as if he lived in a coal-mine and not in the nice clean sea.'—Captain Poops caught Dingy by his left ear and twisted it so hard that Dingy began to cry.—'Yes, that's how I began, and seven years later I was master of my own ship.'

'Having first persuaded the bo'sun to murder the captain and both the mates while they were fast asleep,' said Darby Kelly with an appreciative chuckle.

'He was a rough, brutal man, was the bo'sun,' said Captain Poops. 'I couldn't do such a thing myself. I can't bear the sight of blood, as you know. But when it so happened that the captain and his mates were no more, I had to take command of the ship for the sake of all the others who were aboard. They were simple souls, all of them, and I was the only one there with education. Education is a very useful thing, Darby, if you've got the brain to make use of it.'

'And what a brain yours is!' said Darby Kelly. 'Why, if it hadn't been for you, Captain, it wouldn't have been no use for Dan Scumbril to set himself up against Davy Jones. It was you that showed him the way, and I hope you'll remember that when he comes here to-night. I don't say nothing against Dan Scumbril. He was as good a pirate as ever strung up a ship's company to their own yard-arms, and he could drink more rum than any other sailorman from Barbados to the Dry Tortugas. But he hasn't the intellect that you've got, Captain Poops, and you ought to make that clear to him. You ought to make it clear that you're the senior officer in these operations, and Dan Scumbril ought to salute you when he comes aboard.'

Timothy nearly betrayed himself when he heard that Dan Scumbril was coming to the shell. He was suddenly breathless, and his knees felt weak and shaky; but he was so excited that he thrust his head beyond the shadow in which he lay to see how much room there was, and where Captain Scumbril would be likely to sit. By good fortune no one noticed him, and he quickly withdrew again. Both Darby Kelly and Captain Poops were now much occupied with their own thoughts, and Captain Poops appeared to be rather worried. He finished the rum in his rosy mug, and told Dingy to bring him some more.

'He's a rough man, a violent man, a man without any conscience,' he said solemnly. 'It won't do to offend Dan Scumbril, for he's not a man you can drive. He's got to be led. I'll have to use all my cleverness to-night, Darby. I'll have to be as cunning as a serpent, and as sweet as honey, and as gentle as my own mother. Oh, it does me good to think of her! I had the best mother in the world, Darby, and it was she that gave me the strength and ambition to pursue my great career. I owe everything to my mother.'

'I don't owe mine nothing but five shillings,' said Darby, 'which is what I stole from her purse when I ran away to sea.'

'That was very wrong of you, Darby, to steal from your mother. Very, very wrong of you! I never stole a penny from mine. When I was a little boy I never stole anything except from my poor old father. He was stone-blind, you see, and that made it easy.'

'You had all the advantages, Captain,' said Darby Kelly with a look of envy.

'But I had ideals too,' said Inky Poops, 'and I've got 'em still. I'm as full of ideals as a Christmas stocking's full of presents for the little ones. That's the sort of man I am: I'm a Christmas stocking for all humanity! And when I think of the way that things are mismanaged down here on the bottom of the sea, it makes me mad! To think of Davy Jones and all his wealth, and the fat mermaids that look after him, and the sailors that stand in long rows and salute him—oh! it fills my heart with bile just to imagine it! And those great clumsy knots that tie the Parallels of Latitude and Longitude together—why, they're all out of date, they're old-fashioned, they're no good in times like these, and we've got to change them. And we're going to change them, Darby. We're going to make fast the parallels with fine new modern knots of our own invention.'

'That's the spirit, Captain,' said Darby Kelly. 'I'm all for idealism too, because often it pays you better than anything else. But keep your eye on Dan Scumbril, and don't let him pretend that they're his ideals when in point of fact they're all your own; and you ought to get the profit from them.'

'I've made my plans, Darby, be sure of that, and by and large my plan's to send Dan Scumbril to the north while I go to the south and take possession of Davy Jones's Locker and Davy Jones himself. I've got three hundred good men here, well-armed and properly mounted. Dan Scumbril's coming with three hundred more and after we've conferred together in a friendly manner, as I hope, we up anchor and set out to win the sea. And that means, for a start, to get command of the northern parallels, and also to capture Davy Jones and the great treasure he carries with him.'

'If I know Dan Scumbril,' said Darby Kelly, 'he'll have an eye on the treasure.'

'I've got two eyes on it,' said Inky Poops. 'Wealth is the sinews of war, Darby, and very nice in many other ways as well, and I want Davy Jones himself because I've got some old scores to pay

130

back and I won't be happy till I've paid them. Now, from what I've heard he's only got a few men with him at his summer court—no more than a couple of score according to my information. And so I've come to the conclusion that we could serve our purpose best by splitting our forces, and I'll go south, as I said before, while Dan Scumbril takes a long voyage into high latitudes where it's likely to be rather cold and not very comfortable.'

'You won't find it easy to persuade him,' said Darby Kelly.

'I've got a silver tongue in my head,' said Inky Poops complacently, 'and I know how to use it.'

Dingy in his whimpering voice interrupted them. 'He's coming, sir. Here's Captain Scumbril now, sir.'

Chapter Thirteen

'Split my liver with a brass harpoon!' roared a fine brazen voice that echoed round the shell. 'What paltry sort of party is this? Here's parsimonious company! Why, a brace of pale, pettifogging parsons would do better than sit with one poor mug of rum between the pair of them, and a little boy to boot!—A little boy to boot! Ay, that's the word!'

Seizing poor Dingy by the scruff of the neck, Captain Scumbril kicked him out into the darkness and shouted after him: 'Quart cans and a puncheon of rum! There's a new brat of my own, skulking in the shadows there—take him to help you. I drink more rum than one small boy can carry.'

'Good evening, Dan,' said Inky Poops. 'I'm sorry if you're disappointed by these humble surroundings, but seeing as how we're met together for a great purpose, and difficult times lie ahead of us, I thought it would be out of place to sit down to a banquet as if I was the Lord Mayor of London and you were— well, you were a gentleman of almost equal importance coming to visit me. But I hope you've had a good voyage, Dan, and that all your preparations have been nice and tidily made, and that you yourself are in good health, Dan.'

'I heard a little word that I didn't much care for,' growled Scumbril. 'You used a little word, Inky, that I didn't like at all!'

'And what was that, Dan?'

'*Almost* is what you said, Inky. A visitor of *almost* equal importance is how you described me—and roast my pluck on a Guy Fawkes bonfire if I'll stand for that!'

'Now you don't mean to say, Dan, that you think I was trying to belittle you, surely? I'm the last man in the world to underrate your importance, Dan. Why, just before you came in, Darby Kelly and I were thinking of the old days on the Spanish Main, and talking about you, and saying as how there hadn't been a taller and handsomer pirate to be seen from Barbados to the Dry Tortugas.'

'True, true! That's very true,' said Scumbril.

'And if anybody had ever thought of giving a first prize for being ferocious, why, you'd have won it every year, Dan!'

'Many a time,' said Scumbril, 'have I dyed the whole sea scarlet, like a stormy sunset, with the bubbling blood of my vacillating victims! Ay, and made the Gulf Stream a stream of gore!'

'You were a terrible man, Captain Scumbril, there's no doubt of that,' said Darby Kelly.

'*Were!*' cried Scumbril. 'You pumpkin! You pot-bellied pompoleon, d'you say *were* to me? I *am* a terrible man!'

'Why, of course you are,' said Inky Poops. 'You're the most terrible man in the ocean. Oh dear, oh dear, shall I ever forget the sensation you made, that day in Campechy, when you came in with three-and-sixty Spanish sailors hanging from your yard-arms?'

''Twas a glorious sight, was it not? My ship looked like an orchard, so I thought—for at such moments, Inky, I am something of a poet, as you have no doubt perceived—an orchard heavy with ripe fruit. Ah, the good old days, the days of auld lang syne!'

All this time, in the dark part of the shell, Timothy had been lying very quiet and still, for no one who was not used to it could hear Dan Scumbril's voice without feeling extremely frightened. But now curiosity got the better of his fear, and he felt that he had to see what this man looked like, who talked so monstrously of blood and orchards. So, moving as softly as a cat stalking a blackbird, he crept forward till he could see the lighted part of the shell—the soft-heads were still glowing brightly—and there, sitting on Inky Poops's stool while Inky stood before him, was a tall broad-shouldered man with a great copper-coloured beak of a nose, a pair of black moustaches as big as bananas, and pale eyes like gooseberries under ragged brows. Like Inky Poops, Dan Scumbril wore a short cape, and across his knees he held a brass-hilted cutlass. His vest was crimson, his short trousers were purple with ragged edges, and on both hands he wore several large gold rings. He had dark curly hair, and his expression was both fierce and jocular. He looked much more dangerous than Inky Poops.

While Timothy watched them, they had a little argument— but in quite a friendly tone—about the most convenient way to deal with prisoners. Scumbril had always hanged them at the yard-arm, but Inky Poops had preferred to make them walk the plank. 'I used to enjoy waiting for the splash,' he said. 'To sit on deck, in the golden light of the setting sun, and hear them go *plop!* one after another, was quite a treat.'

Dingy returned with another stool for Captain Poops, and behind him came a boy who carried on his shoulder a small barrel of rum. Another Cabin Boy, thought Timothy, but as he came into the light he saw to his utmost astonishment that it was

134

Hew. He could by no means understand how his brother came to be in Captain Scumbril's company, nor why—as it appeared—he was in his service. For a moment he had the wild idea of rushing out and greeting Hew, for he was overjoyed to see him again. But quickly he realised how foolish that would be, and lay as still as he could. He saw that Hew had a black eye. He was so surprised, and his mind was so much occupied with the mystery of his brother's present employment, that for a moment or two he failed to realise that the pirates were talking about him. Captain Scumbril, it appeared, had found him lying asleep a few miles away, and had taken a fancy to him. But who he was he did not know and could not discover, because the boy, he said, was dumb.

'As dumb as a rock or a clod of earth,' he said, 'but what his tongue lacks he can make up for with his fists. I asked him if he could fight, and he understood me well enough; so I matched him with the Cabin Boy I had before—a rambling, shambling fellow I had grown tired of—and this dumb boy set about him like a master, and though he took some punishment, left the other lying like a wreck on a lee shore. So I brought him with me, and if he serves me well I'll keep him.'

Then Captain Scumbril drank a can of rum from the cask which Hew had brought, and, holding it out to be refilled, exclaimed, 'And now to work! What's your plan, Inky, for the conquest of the sea? My three hundred men are sleeping on the sand a cable's length away, and my lieutenant—if he's doing what I told him—is counting your company to make sure you brought the same and no more.'

'You never suspected that I'd deal unfairly, did you?' cried Inky Poops. 'I've never dealt unfairly in my life, and never shall! No, no, Dan, we must trust each other, and have no secrets from each other, and deal honestly in all things, for that's my nature, Dan, and I can't deal in any other way. We ought to be like brothers, and behave as such.'

'I had three brothers,' said Scumbril, 'and I behaved to all of them in the self-same way.'

'And how was that?' asked Inky Poops.

'I hanged them,' said Scumbril.

Ah, well,' said Inky, 'I've no doubt they deserved it. One's own family is often very trying. Very, very trying. I had an uncle, I remember—but no matter, he's of no importance now. He made a lovely *plop!* when he went in.—But we've no time to gossip, Dan, no time to talk about all those little details of domestic life that are so pleasant to remember in idle hours. No, no, we must be serious. We must discuss our plans. And here's what I suggest. We must divide our forces, Dan, for we have two objectives. We must take control of the Northern Parallels, and we must capture Davy Jones and all his court.'

'Agreed,' said Scumbril. 'So far we're in accord.'

'Now the important objective,' said Inky, 'by far the most important, the most dangerous, and the most difficult objective is, of course, the Northern Parallels; and though I don't distrust your ability, Dan, I think I had better look after that myself.'

Darby Kelly showed great surprise when he heard this, and Dan Scumbril immediately became most indignant.

'Mince my muscles for a sea-cook's pie!' he roared. 'If ever I saw an argument that came in like a man standing on his head, it's that argument of yours. *You'll* take the difficult task, you say, and leave the lesser task, the easy one, to *me*! You can pluck out my eyes and play marbles with them before I consent to that.'

'Now be reasonable, Dan,' said Inky Poops. 'Don't spoil discussion with a show of naughty temper like a little boy who can't get his own way——'

'I always get my own way,' interrupted Scumbril.

'And once or twice in your life,' said Inky Poops, 'you've wished that you had listened to others and taken their advice instead. Now I'm not arguing for my own sake, I'm arguing for the common cause that we're both interested in, and I've given this matter a lot of thought, Dan. It's very important—oh, it's very, very important!—that we should capture Davy Jones and take the treasure-chest that he never lets out of his possession. That's something we must do without delay, and make no mistake about it either. And it won't be a difficult thing to do. It's going to be quite an easy task, Dan, because I happen to know that at this very moment Davy Jones hasn't got more than two or three score of his own sailors to guard his court. And so I thought it would be a nice occupation for you, Dan——'

'For me!' shouted Scumbril. 'Am I a puppy dog in a basket? Am I an infant in pink ribbons and a perambulator that you think I want a toy to play with? Keep the little tasks and the easy ones for yourself, you lemon-coloured, limp and lackadaisical loblolly-boy! But if there's something hard and perilous to be done, why, that's my pigeon and none shall take it from me. I'll seize the Northern Parallels, and you'll look after Davy Jones!'

'It grieves me to hear you going on like that,' said Inky Poops, and shook his head as though he were the saddest pirate in the sea. But Timothy, watching from the inner part of the shell, saw him wink at Darby Kelly, and saw that Darby Kelly was now beginning to understand the means that Inky Poops was using to get his own way. For the more he protested that he must under-take the difficult adventure in the north, the more determined Dan Scumbril grew that that was the proper task for him; and after a great deal of argument Inky Poops at last gave in and said that he would make himself responsible for the capture of Davy Jones. Which was what he had intended to do from the beginning.

Timothy listened with great admiration to Inky Poops's cleverness, but it seemed to him that Scumbril had been clever too, in a way that Inky Poops did not suspect. For Scumbril said nothing about the pirates whom Sam Sturgeon had discovered in the wreck off Popinsay, though they were certainly two of Scumbril's men. He pulled a chart from the satchel at his belt, and unrolled it, and said that he had been studying the situation and had decided to start operations *there*.—'There,' he repeated, pointing to the chart with his blunt forefinger, 'by 59 North, 4 West, where there's an old wreck lying off the island of Popinsay, that'll serve me for my forward headquarters for a little while.'— But still he said nothing about the two pirates whom he had already sent to occupy the wreck.

'That'll be very convenient, Dan, my dear,' said Inky Poops in his softest voice. 'But how did you come to hear about the old ship that's lying there?'

'One of my men told me,' said Dan. 'An old lean scarecrow of a man who was carpenter aboard her when she struck upon a reef, and was lost on her way home after a seven years' voyage. And because she was a pirate ship he must have been a pirate too—and that's why I believe him, Inky, just the same as I believe you!'

'Ay, ay,' said Inky. 'It's a good thing to have friends you can trust. Oh, a very good thing! I was just wondering, Dan, if you'd made any other plans that you haven't yet told me about?'

'Stuff my gullet with hot buttered barnacles!' roared Scumbril. 'What do you hint at? Are you suspicious now? Do you insinuate? D'you think I'm working to windward of you?'

138

'I was just wondering,' said Inky.

'Then belay your wonder, for I'm an honest friend. As honest as you are, Inky, and there's my hand on it!'

'I'm very glad to hear it, Dan, for we couldn't get on without honesty, could we?'—But Inky was looking very thoughtful and rather worried as he took Dan Scumbril's hand in his, and pressed it affectionately.

Timothy, however, could watch them no longer; for he also was beginning to feel worried. Hew, in a very dignified and patient manner, was still standing beside Dan Scumbril and filling his can whenever Scumbril required him to do so; but Dingy, the Cabin Boy, had grown tired of so much talk, and was opening and examining the several cupboards on the walls of the shell, one after the other, and gradually he was coming nearer to the inner part where Timothy lay hidden. Now Timothy had to retreat again, and very carefully he crept backward a few inches at a time. He drew back a little more, wondering how far he could go—for he had not explored the narrowest part of the shell—when suddenly he felt a violent pain in the calf of his left leg, and before he could control himself, he uttered a shrill cry. The pirates stopped their argument and Inky Poops uneasily exclaimed, 'Now, what was that? Was that you screaming, Dingy?'

At the same moment Timothy heard beside him a grave voice whispering, 'My dear boy, I do apologise! It was quite by accident that I bit you—you startled me and without thinking I gave you a little nip—but there's no time for explanation. Come quickly, or you'll be discovered. No, don't turn round, I'll guide you—this way, this way—I'll let you out by the back door.'

Timothy had no idea who was speaking to him, but he obeyed the voice without hesitation, and a moment or two later wriggled feet first through a little opening in the shell that was just big enough to let him out. Beside him he saw a large and elderly Crab, who closed the door behind him and fastened it with a whale-bone latch.

'Now follow me into the weeds,' said the Crab, 'and there, I hope, we shall be fairly safe, and I can give you some very interesting news.'

About forty yards away the seaweed grew as thick as a jungle, and the Crab and Timothy, moving very quickly, were able to gain its shelter without being seen, though pirate sentries were guarding the shell on either side.

'And now,' said the Crab, 'let me apologise once again for hurting you. I really had no intention of doing such a thing, but, as I have already explained, you startled me, and before I realised what was happening, my claw, I'm afraid, gave you a little pinch on the leg. I hope you are no longer suffering?'

'Oh no,' said Timothy, 'at least not much.'

'It's a great relief to me to hear that,' said the Crab in his most serious voice. 'I am the caretaker of the sleeping-shell, and I was hurrying back to it in the expectation of company when I happened to meet a friend of mine, a most charming young female octopus called Miss Dildery Doldero Casadiplasadimolodyshenkendorf Rustiverolico Silverysplash.'

'An octopus?' demanded Timothy. 'And her name is Dildery—oh, I can't remember the rest of it?'

'Miss Dildery Doldero Casadiplasadimolodyshenkendorf Rustiverolico Silverysplash,' the Crab repeated.

'But I've heard about her!' said Timothy. 'She's a friend of a very great friend of mine called Cully. His proper name is Culliferdontofoscofolio Polydesteropouf, but we call him Cully.'

'So the lady is not entirely unknown to you?' said the Crab.

140

'That is interesting indeed, and she will be most gratified; for she has heard of you! Her friend, whom you call Cully, had told her quite a long time ago of his meeting with you and your brother in the South Atlantic Ocean, and when she encountered, earlier to-day, two Powder Monkeys who were searching for a couple of lost boys, and heard a description of their character, she at once decided they must be her friend Cully's old acquaintances; that they, in fact, must be *you.*'

'The two Powder Monkeys!' said Timothy. 'You mean William Button and Henry String? Are they here too?'

'They're not very far away,' said the Crab. 'They're in hiding, of course, because the pirates have assembled in great numbers, and if William and Henry were discovered, the consequences for them might be most unfortunate.'

'How did you know that I was in the sleeping-shell?' asked Timothy.

'Miss Dildery had learnt that too, from some small fish with whom she fell into conversation. She herself had been on her way to the shell to tell you where to find the Powder Monkeys, but Mr. Poops arrived before her, and she judged it best to wait for my return and let me convey her news.'

'My brother Hew is still there,' said Timothy. 'He must have been captured by Dan Scumbril.'

'How unfortunate,' said the Crab. 'How very unfortunate!'

'I don't know what to do,' said Timothy. 'I don't like to go away and leave him.'

For some minutes they sat together in the black shadow of the seaweed, and neither spoke. Timothy, thinking hard, was trying to make a plan to rescue Hew. But the Crab was no longer helpful. He was an amiable old crab, and his manners were perfect; but it was a long time since he had had any new ideas.

141

While Timothy was thinking, indeed, he fell fast asleep; and when Timothy suddenly discovered a brilliant device to save Hew, he had to shake the Crab quite hard to wake him up.

'How far away is Dildery?' he demanded.

'You mean Miss Dildery Doldero'—he yawned half-way through the name, but spoke it in full—'Casadiplasadimolodyshenkendorf Rustiverolico Silverysplash?'

'Of course, I do,' said Timothy.

'She likes to be treated with proper courtesy,' said the Crab. 'I advise you not to be too familiar with her.'

'Where is she?' demanded Timothy again.

'In her own home,' said the Crab, 'about two hundred yards from here. She has a very snug, secluded, and commodious little house, not easily found unless you know the way to it.'

'Can you take me there?' asked Timothy.

'Certainly, certainly,' said the Crab. 'Follow me closely, and if we keep within the shelter of the weed we shall avoid, I hope, all those detestable pirates. They're rude fellows, and I wish we were rid of them. Their manners when they come to my shell are often abominable, and they never remember to make their beds. Miss Dildery, who has been nurtured with the greatest care, cannot abide them.'

'I'm sure she can't,' said Timothy. 'But do let us hurry!'

Then the Crab set off by a path through the densely growing weed which only he could have discovered, and Timothy followed close behind.

Chapter Fourteen

When Hew, being sea-sick as a result of his wild ride on the porpoise, at last had fallen off, he had lain, like Timothy, on the floor of the sea feeling lost and bewildered and utterly wretched. Then he had risen to the surface to look for his friends, and after swimming for a long time and finding no one, he had grown tired and gone to sleep. He was lying afloat on the calm sea, fast asleep, when Dan Scumbril's pirate army came in from the west, on their way to the meeting with Inky Poops and his men. Scumbril's pirates were mounted on very large basking-sharks which they rode, not in howdahs, as Hew and Timothy had ridden, but on benches that looked rather like garden seats, and were lashed on either side of the sharks. Each shark carried ten men, five on the one side, five on the other. The pirates were well armed, and the sharks swam in good order in three long columns. The fleet was moving about six feet below the surface, and its centre column passed directly under Hew.

He was wakened roughly from sleep when a large hand grabbed him by the ankle and dragged him down. The pirates who had captured him wheeled about and headed back into the centre of the fleet, where Captain Scumbril sat in a large and

143

comfortable howdah on a shark driven by a tall, shambling, sulky-looking Cabin Boy with ginger hair and large red ears, who was called Foxy. Hew was thrown into Captain Scumbril's howdah, and the fleet continued on its way while Captain Scumbril asked him a great many questions and tried to find out who he was. But Hew would answer none of his questions. At first he did not reply because he could not decide what it would be safe to say; and then he decided that it would be best to say nothing at all. So he pretended to be dumb, and though Captain Scumbril pulled his nose and twisted his ears and pinched his cheeks he remained obstinately silent. But his expression showed that he was growing angry, and this surprised Captain Scumbril because very few people ever dared to become angry in his presence. So he said to Hew, 'I knew a pirate once who was as dumb as you, but his fists could play a very pretty tune. And yours, it may be, are also better than your tongue?'

Hew was so angry after having had his nose pulled and his ears twisted that he wanted very much to relieve his feelings by hitting somebody. So he nodded his head, and his eyes sparkled in a way that showed clearly what he was thinking. Then Captain Scumbril shouted loudly to the pirates on either side of him, and they passed on his orders to the whole fleet, which quickly halted and formed a great circle round their leader's shark; and Scumbril told them all that they were going to see some sport.

He had with him, he said, two of the liveliest little boxers on the bottom of the ocean, and they were going to fight to a finish for a prize of great value. On his left was Foxy the Cabin Boy, whom they all knew, and on his right there was someone whom none of them knew. The boy on his right was a stranger who could not speak, but looked as though he could fight. They could call him, said Scumbril, the Dumb Boy of Mystery! And as to the prize for which they were going to fight, he must admit that although Foxy knew how to use his fists, he was perhaps the worst Cabin Boy in the sea; and for a long time he had been looking for an excuse to get rid of him.

'But I've always been a kind-hearted man, and a generous master with a fine sense of justice,' said Scumbril—and here the pirates, sitting on their sharks, leant back and laughed uproariously—'and so I've decided to give poor Foxy one more chance. If he can beat the Dumb Boy of Mystery he will continue to serve me in his present honourable capacity. But if the Dumb Boy beats Foxy, then the Dumb Boy will become my Cabin Boy, and that's a prize to make any boy fight like a lion!'

While Scumbril had been talking the fleet had dropped down to the floor of the sea, and now on a level open space the pirates formed a ring, and Hew found himself in the middle of it with the tall, shambling Cabin Boy called Foxy. Foxy was a head taller than he, and in a very bad temper because Scumbril had spoken so unkindly of him. The pirates, pressed close together and eager for the fight, were shouting and cheering and making bets. Never in his life had Hew seen such a throng of cut-throats, and to be surrounded by them was rather like being in the middle of a pack of wolves. But he had no time, he realised, to worry about that, for Foxy was already squaring up to him and waving his fists about in a very threatening manner. So Hew stood on guard in the way Sam Sturgeon had taught him, and decided to do his best.

Foxy hit Hew on the forehead, and Hew hit Foxy twice on the ribs. Then Foxy rushed at him, and seizing him round the neck with his left hand began to punch very quickly with his right at whatever parts of Hew he could reach. It seemed to Hew that this was not the art of boxing as Sam Sturgeon had taught it, but

145

he realised that he could not complain because he was supposed to be dumb. So with all his strength he punched Foxy several times just under the ribs, and Foxy with a gasp released his hold and staggered back. Hew quickly followed him, and before Foxy could recover his balance, landed a very nice upper-cut on Foxy's chin. Foxy fell flat on his back, and half the pirates—those who had bet on the Dumb Boy—raised a great cheer, while the other half—those who had bet on Foxy—shouted angrily at Hew and still more angrily called on Foxy to get up and fight.

Foxy was in no hurry to rise, and when he did he hung his head and his guard was low and he looked very unhappy. Hew thought he was already beaten, and stepped rather carelessly towards him to punch him again. But Foxy was by no means beaten, and after retreating for two or three paces he suddenly leapt forward and hit Hew twice on the head. Now it was Hew's turn to lie on his back and hear half the pirates shouting at him, while the other half cheered Foxy. He got up with his head ringing, and defended himself against Foxy's furious attack. Because Foxy was so much taller Hew found it difficult to reach his chin, but punched steadily at his long thin body, and after some little time Foxy lost his temper and kicked. This was certainly not in the rules of boxing, but the pirates thought it funny and laughed; and Hew, of course, could not complain because he was supposed to be dumb. But the next time Foxy kicked, Hew was ready for him. Catching him by the heel, he tipped him off his balance, and jumping upon him before he could get up, sat on his chest. He came down so hard on Foxy's chest that he knocked all the breath out of him, and the Cabin Boy either could not or would not fight any more.

Now the pirates began to quarrel among themselves, for half

of them said that the Dumb Boy had won by a foul, while the other half said that to jump on your opponent's chest was no foul at all, but a very sensible thing to do. So to avoid a lot of trouble Dan Scumbril ordered them to remount their sharks, and then made a little speech in which he said that he knew more about fouls than anyone else in the sea, and the Dumb Boy had done nothing which he, Scumbril, would not also have done in the circumstances. And therefore the Dumb Boy was the winner, and henceforth would be his Cabin Boy.

Then the fleet moved forward again, and now Hew rode with Scumbril in the middle of it while Foxy sat unhappily on a shark crowded with pirates in the rear. It was fortunate that Scumbril's shark had been well trained, for Hew was not an experienced driver. More than once he pulled the reins in the wrong way, but the shark paid no attention, and they got on well enough.

Then they arrived at the sleeping-shell where Inky Poops was waiting for them, and Hew did just what he was told and brought Scumbril his rum, and refilled his can whenever it was empty, and all the time he listened carefully to what the pirates were saying, and tried not only to understand their plans but also to devise some means of escape from them. He had been wondering, while he was driving Scumbril's shark, what had happened to Timothy; and still with half his mind he wondered, while the other half listened so busily to the conversation. He could not guess that Timothy was lying hidden within a few feet of him, and it was a very good thing that he did not see Timothy peeping out from the darkness; for if he had, he might have forgotten that he was supposed to be dumb.

After the pirate captains had made their plans and Scumbril had drunk a great quantity of rum—and this was after Timothy had made his escape from the back door of the shell—Inky

147

Poops proposed a game of cards; and Scumbril said that nothing would please him better. Inky Poops had an old pack in his satchel, Dingy the Cabin Boy went to fetch another stool to serve as a table, and Darby Kelly, who was feeling sleepy, said good-night and went off to find a bed among the pirates outside. Dan Scumbril and Inky Poops began their game, and beside them stood Hew and Dingy ready to fill their cans as often as was necessary. Hew watched the cards with interest, for the pirate captains were playing a very simple game called Strip Jack Naked that he and Timothy had often played.

Scumbril had all the luck to begin with, but presently Inky Poops began to win, and once he had started to win it seemed that nothing could stop him. They were betting on the cards, and after a little while Inky had won all the fine handsome gold rings that Scumbril wore on his great thick fingers. When the last of them had gone Scumbril looked at his bare hands, and then at the little pile of gold and jewels on the other side of the stool, and began to curse and grumble and complain in a great rumbling voice that seemed to fill the shell with thunder.

Now for some time Inky Poops had been looking at Hew with great admiration, and regarding Dingy, his own Cabin Boy, with growing dislike. Hew was a very good-looking boy in spite of his black eye, and he appeared to be cleverer than Dingy although he was dumb. Inky Poops, who nearly always got his own way, had made up his mind to get Hew if he could. So now he proposed to bet all the rings he had won—and Dingy too, if Dan Scumbril wanted him—against the Dumb Boy. After a little hesitation Scumbril agreed, and they dealt again. But Inky still held the better cards, and Scumbril lost that game as he had lost the others. He lost Hew also, and Inky Poops rubbed his hands and chuckled with delight.

'Now you, my dear, must come and stand by me,' he said, 'and you, Dingy, can go and stand by Captain Scumbril. And see that you serve him well, and do as he tells you, and be a credit to me for all the training I've given you, that I couldn't have been more careful about if I'd been your own father!'

Hew had no cause to like Dan Scumbril, but he liked the look of Inky Poops even less, and it was with great reluctance that he changed places with Dingy. As for Dingy, he was so frightened at the prospect of becoming Dan Scumbril's Cabin Boy that he could scarcely move at all. Inky Poops was grinning and gurgling and cackling with delight, but no one else made even the smallest show of pleasure. Dan Scumbril was cursing again, and his deep voice was so very like thunder rumbling among distant hills that when it began to grow dark Hew wondered if a storm was blowing up; and thought there might soon be rain. But then he remembered they were on the bottom of the sea, where rain was quite unlikely and perhaps impossible.

It grew darker and darker, and Inky Poops said the soft-heads—the luminous fishes fastened to the roof of the shell—must be going out; and told his new Cabin Boy to find some more. Hew stepped outside, but was lost immediately in utter darkness, and now blackness filled the whole shell and put out the light of the soft-heads as though a tide of Indian ink had come flooding in. The pirates shouted at each other in terror and confusion, Dingy began to cry, and through the sooty darkness Hew heard a familiar voice.

'Hew, Hew!' it was calling. 'Where are you, Hew?'

It was Timothy's voice. He recognised it immediately, and turned back into the shell from whose inner parts the voice was coming. But in the darkness he ran into Inky Poops, who was fumbling and feeling his way out, and Inky seized him by the neck and dragged Hew with him. Somewhere in the gloom Dan Scumbril was bellowing and beating the wall of the shell with one of the whale-bone stools, but through the din Hew heard again his brother's voice crying, 'Where are you?' Then he heard Dingy screaming, but suddenly the scream was silenced as though some one had clapped a hand on Dingy's mouth.

Inky Poops, gripping his neck between bony fingers, thrust him ahead and Hew heard no more. A few yards from the shell the sea was no darker than usual, and to that sort of darkness Hew's eyes had become accustomed. But behind them the shell was hidden as if in a small cloud of impenetrable blackness. The pirates of both fleets, alarmed by the shouting, were hurrying towards them from their lines, and Inky Poops ordered some twenty or thirty of them to form a circle round the shell and see that no stranger came in and no stranger got out.

'For there may be strangers about,' he said to Darby Kelly who had wakened and come quickly at the sound of trouble. 'That was maybe an attempt upon our lives. It looked like a plot, Darby my dear. A plot against the lives of me and Captain Scumbril when we were in conference together. It may be that Davy Jones is cleverer than we think, and knows more than we suppose. His spies may be among us at this very moment!'

'There may be an easier explanation than that,' said Darby Kelly. 'That wasn't no plot, Captain Poops, at least not in my opinion. My own opinion—my humble opinion, if you think it's worth listening to, Captain—is that all that trouble was created by one of them there octopuses, which have the habit of squirting darkness into the sea if they feel so inclined. I wouldn't look for spies if I was you, I'd look for an octopus.'

Chapter Fifteen

Miss Dildery lived in a delightful little cave on the south-ward slope of a small hill that rose in a forest of seaweed from the floor of the sea. A narrow lane, twining and twisting through the weeds, led to the main entrance, beside which grew a charming pink and white bush, and above which, on a tablet of whale-bone, was the name *Coral Villa*. Over a very small opening on the left hand side of the cave was another notice which read: BEWARE OF THE DOG-FISH, and on a mat in front of the entrance was written, WIPE YOUR FINS. As Timothy and the Crab approached this very desirable residence, the Crab showed signs of nervousness and once again told Timothy that Miss Dildery was a person of considerable importance, that she had been very well brought up—and begged him to behave with all the politeness of which he was capable. Timothy assured him that he would say nothing improper, and do nothing unseemly; and after he had wiped himself all over on the door-mat, the Crab rang the bell and to the entrance of the cave came a large old female Cod, who rather surprisingly wore a cap and apron.

'Is Miss Dildery at home?' asked the Crab in a pompous voice.

'Perhaps she is, and perhaps she isn't,' said the Cod. 'It all depends on who wants to see her.'

'Please tell her,' said the Crab, 'that I have brought a very distinguished visitor; a young gentleman who actually lives upon dry land.'

The old Cod swam round Timothy to look at him from all sides, and then remarked, 'If everybody stayed in their own homes there'd be less trouble in the world, and I wouldn't be expected to answer the bell at all hours of the day and night.'

'Will you kindly deliver my message to your mistress?' asked the Crab; and behind his claw whispered to Timothy: 'An old family servant, you know. These old retainers are very independent, and sometimes even eccentric, as no doubt you are well aware.'

The old Cod, after staring at them for some time in a very disapproving manner, said grudgingly, 'Well, I suppose you can come in,' and then swam slowly round the corner to a farther part of the cave from which, after a few minutes, there emerged a creature of a very striking appearance. In a general way, of course, Miss Dildery resembled Timothy's old friend Cully, but she was far more delicately shaped, and to the eye of any good judge of an octopus, extremely beautiful. Her eyes were even larger than Cully's but her beak was much smaller—it was quite a dainty little beak—and it was so white that Timothy thought she must have powdered it. She held her eight arms close together and swam towards them with a graceful movement, as if she were wearing a long silk dress.

'How very, very kind of you to come and see me!' she exclaimed, and in the most elegant fashion offered Timothy the extreme tip of her nearest arm. 'But I feel we are old friends already, for I heard so much about you and your brother from a

152

very dear acquaintance of mine, Mr. Culliferdontofoscofolio Polydesteropouf.—And you have seen him quite recently, I believe? Do tell me how he is.'

'He was looking quite well when I saw him last,' said Timothy, 'and he knows a lot of very interesting songs.'

'He has a charming voice,' said Miss Dildery. 'I could listen to him for ever.—But please sit down and make yourself at home. Nowadays I live so retired and solitary a life that I have almost forgotten my manners, it seems. I have very few visitors, very few indeed. I am a very lonely person.'

Miss Dildery sighed, and blinked her enormous eyes, and then, as though she had just seen him, said, 'How do you do?' to the Crab in a rather cold and distant voice.

'I came to see you,' said Timothy, 'because Cully is a great friend of ours—of me and my brother, I mean—and he once spoke to us about you—'

'The dear fellow!' cried Miss Dildery. 'So he has not quite forgotten me?'

'And because you are a friend of his I thought you might help us,' said Timothy.

'But of course!' said Miss Dildery. 'I shall be only too delighted. You must consider this little house of mine as yours. Come here whenever you like. I shall always be pleased to see you.'

A sound of whispering, giggling, and sniggering from the inner part of the cave attracted their attention, and Timothy was surprised to see a whole family of little octopuses who seemed to be very much amused by his appearance, and were pushing each other, and pointing at him, like a lot of very badly behaved children. Miss Dildery was extremely displeased, and called sharply for the old Cod who was her maid.

'Take the children back to their nursery at once, Matilda,' she said, 'and keep them there! I have told you before that when I have visitors the children are to remain in their nursery unless I send for them!'

'I've got too much to do in this house,' said Matilda the Cod. 'What with sweeping and dusting and washing and cooking, I'm swum off my fins, I am, and how I'm to look after a whole pack of children as well I don't know, and I shouldn't be expected to.'

'Let us have no argument,' said Miss Dildery severely, 'but do as I tell you. Go with Matilda, children, and play quietly and try to be good little octopuses for my sake.—They're my poor sister's children,' she explained. 'She's a delicate creature and quite incapable of looking after them, and out of the kindness of my heart I offered to adopt them. But they're a great worry to me, a great worry indeed, especially as I have no one in the house to help me but poor old Matilda. I had to discharge my butler some time ago. He had very bad habits, poor fellow, but I miss him sorely—my father always kept a butler—and I am looking for another. It's so hard to find a good servant nowadays, isn't it?—But there, I mustn't bore you with family matters, must I? We all have our troubles, and really they are of no interest to anyone but ourselves. Do tell me what are your impressions of life under the sea?'

'Well,' said Timothy, 'the only impression I've got at the moment is that I must rescue my brother from the pirates.' And he told her, as briefly as he could, about his own misfortune and the capture of Hew by Dan Scumbril.

Miss Dildery listened very politely and agreed that the pirates were a most unpleasant lot of men and a danger to all respectable creatures in the sea. 'But what,' she asked, 'can I do to help you?'

'I've thought of a plan to rescue Hew,' said Timothy, 'but it depends on you. You can squirt ink, can't you? Well, I want you to come to the shell and fill it with ink, and when everything is dark inside I'll go in and fetch him out.'

To Timothy's great amazement Miss Dildery gave a little scream, closed her eyes, and blushed a deep coral pink. The Crab, coughing once or twice in an embarrassed manner, walked to the entrance of the cave and pretended to take no further interest in their conversation. Timothy could not understand how he had offended Miss Dildery, for he knew that octopuses were able to conceal themselves from their enemies by emitting a stream of inky fluid, and he thought it an extremely clever thing to do. Why Miss Dildery should be displeased by his referring to it he did not know, and he did not much care. All he was interested in was the rescue of his brother, and he described Hew's plight in such a moving way that presently Miss Dildery opened her eyes, and two small tears escaped from them, and ran down her carefully powdered beak. Then Timothy told her that they were on their way to Davy Jones's court to get help for Gunner Boles and Cully, his assistant; who were in great danger, he said. Gunner Boles and Cully were waiting very anxiously and impatiently for their return, he declared.

'Is Cullifer in danger?' asked Miss Dildery.

'Of course he is,' said Timothy. 'And if you help us you'll be helping him too.'

'Oh dear,' said Miss Dildery. 'I wish I could. I can't bear to think of dear Cullifer in danger.'

'Then come to the shell,' said Timothy, 'and do what I'm asking you to do.'

'But what a thing to ask a *lady* to do!' cried

Miss Dildery in great distress. 'To go alone among all those dreadful pirates, and then to—well, to call attention to myself by—by discharging some ink at them—oh, I couldn't do it!'

'I'm sure Cully would,' said Timothy.

'But he has always lived a daring life! He's been everywhere, he knows the world, he's quite an adventurer! I'm not like that at all. I am one of the shyest of creatures.'

'When he spoke to us about you,' said Timothy, 'he seemed to be very fond of you.'

Miss Dildery breathed deeply, and blushed again. She was so large—almost as big as Cully—that she blushed in many different colours in many different places: here the pink of a wild rose, there salmon-pink, then red as sealing-wax. And the shades of colour would alter and flow from one limb to another, now flushing darkly, now paling to the softest hues. It was fascinating to watch her, but Timothy wished she would make up her mind.

'There's my brother,' he said, 'there's Gunner Boles who is Cully's great friend, and there's Cully himself: all their lives may depend on you.'

Miss Dildery grew paler and paler till she looked like mother-of-pearl, and for more than a minute she said nothing at all. Then she opened her great eyes and gazed very solemnly at Timothy, and said, 'I will be brave! I will do what you ask me. Lead me to the pirates' den!'

Graceful as ever, she extended one of her several arms, and taking Timothy by the hand swept majestically out of the cave. The Crab looked at her reproachfully and said, 'I don't know what your mother would have thought, Miss Dildery, if she had lived to see this day. Your mother—'

'My mother,' interrupted Miss Dildery coldly, 'would have

known her duty as I know mine. Be so good as to direct me to your sleeping-shell.'

She knew the way as well as the Crab himself, but she insisted that he should accompany them. She held Timothy firmly by the hand, and listened attentively while he explained his plan. They reached the shell without being seen, and while Timothy went to the back door, Miss Dildery—who could assume almost any shape she liked—flattened herself beneath it and crept towards the front entrance. Timothy let himself in, very carefully, and waited in the darker part until he saw the light grow dim in the outer half. Then he moved slowly forward, ready to rush in and seize Hew as soon as the shell grew black. But Hew now stood on the far side of the pirates, and the blackness came so quickly, and was so impenetrable, that Timothy himself was lost in it; and though he shouted to Hew, Hew did not answer.

Then, in the inky darkness, he felt a boy's slim arm, and when the boy screamed he clapped a hand over his mouth and whispered, 'Be quiet, it's me! It's Timothy. Come this way, and come quickly.'

The boy resisted a little, but Timothy pulled him into the narrow part of the shell, and out of it by the back door where Miss Dildery and the Crab were waiting to guide him through the shadows. Not until they were several yards from the shell, and safely among the tall weed, did he discover that it was Dingy the Cabin Boy whom he had rescued.

Timothy and Miss Dildery were very depressed by the failure of their plan, and Dingy stood snivelling between them. The Crab said he had known all the time that no good would come of their scheme, and told Miss Dildery that it was time she went home. Slowly they returned to Coral Villa, taking Dingy with them because they did not know what else to do with him. Now, with all the pirates awake and alarmed, there was no hope at all for any further attempt to rescue Hew.

Timothy thanked Miss Dildery as warmly as he could for her help, and she said sadly that she had done her best and was sorry indeed for their ill fortune. She hoped they would meet again, she said. 'I feel our cause is not yet lost,' she added. 'I feel it *here!*—And she pointed with one of her long arms to what was presumably her heart.—'You must not despair, for I am sure that you and your brother will be reunited, and I even dare to hope that somewhere, and some day, I shall see Cullifer again.'

She blushed more deeply than ever, but at that moment her eight nephews and nieces rushed out to greet her, followed by the old Cod in her cap and apron, who had been trying without any success to put them to bed. So Timothy said goodnight, rather hurriedly, and persuaded the Crab to show him the way to the two Powder Monkeys' hiding-place. He took Dingy, because there was nowhere he could leave him.

They had a long way to go and Timothy was very tired, the Crab very sulky, and Dingy very tearful before they reached the dark uncomfortable cave, in a narrow ravine, where the Powder Monkeys and the two basking sharks lay all together in hiding. William Button and Henry String were overjoyed to see Timothy, and he was thankful to find them again. Even the sharks, who recognised him at once, said 'Moo-oo' in a very friendly way. The Crab fell fast asleep, without wasting any time, and Dingy crept into a corner and went to sleep too. But Timothy and the Powder Monkeys had a great deal to talk about. They had also plenty to eat, for William Button had robbed a sleeping-shell that morning, and Timothy, who was hungry, ate a hearty meal of shrimp paste and lobster paste and whale's milk.

He told the Powder Monkeys all he had learnt about the pirates' plans, and about his brother's capture, and his failure to rescue him. William Button and Henry String were by this time much more serious than they had been at the start of their voyage from Popinsay, for the disappearance of Timothy and Hew had frightened them badly and they bitterly regretted having dared them to ride the porpoises. They agreed that there was now more need than ever to hurry southward to Davy Jones's summer court, since Inky Poops was about to attack him; but they sympathised, too, with Timothy's reluctance to leave Hew in the hands of Dan Scumbril, who was preparing to voyage to the north.

'Your brother ain't going with Scumbril,' said a whimpering voice behind them, and looking round they saw the miserable face of Dingy the Cabin Boy. Dingy in his sleep had smelt shrimp paste, and being as hungry as Timothy he had wakened and come to see if he could beg some food. 'Give me a bite to eat and I'll tell you something interesting,' he said.

'If you know anything,' said William Button fiercely, 'you tell it now, or I'll give you punch-pudding!'

'No,' said Timothy. 'Let him have something to eat.'

Very unwillingly William Button obeyed him, and Dingy with his mouth full said, ''E knows better than you, Bill Button! 'E knows what pays in life, and that's kindness. If I'd ever been treated kindly——'

'You'd still be the same snivelling, sneaking little twister that you are now,' said Henry String.

'I ain't talking to you,' said Dingy. 'I'm talking to him, see? And give me another lump of shrimp or I won't talk to any of you.'

'Let him have it,' said Timothy.

'Thank you, mister. And maybe you'll give me something better when I've told you what I know about your brother?'

'What do you know?'

'He ain't going with Scumbril, he's going with Inky Poops. They were playing at cards for him, see? And Inky won because Inky knows how to deal, and Dan Scumbril don't.'

'If that's true,' said William Button, '—and if it isn't true I'll beat your ears off!—it means your brother will be there when Inky attacks Davy Jones's court. So perhaps we'll have a chance to take him prisoner.'

'If he's going the same way as we are, we might be able to rescue him before the battle,' said Timothy. 'How fast will Inky Poops travel?'

'A big fleet like his is always pretty slow,' said William.

'We could make double their speed, going on our own,' said Henry String.

'So we could afford to keep watch on them for a few hours at any rate,' said Timothy, 'and then, if there doesn't seem to be any chance of saving Hew, we'll put on speed and still be in time to warn Davy Jones.'

'It's risky,' said William Button.

'I think the risk is justified,' said Timothy in his most serious manner.

'Then we ought to get some sleep,' said Henry String, 'for Inky Poops may be making an early start.'

'Eight bells in the morning watch, that's when he's moving,' said Dingy. ''E never gets up earlier than that.—And wot about a reward for all the news I've given you, mister?'

'What do you want?' asked Timothy.

'A nice drop of rum,' said Dingy, swallowing the last of the shrimp paste and licking his thin lips.

'We haven't got any.'

'Ask 'im,' said Dingy, pointing to William Button. And William confessed that he had taken a bottle when he robbed the sleeping-shell, just in case it might be useful for bribing or cajoling a wandering pirate, if they should happen to meet one.

'But rum's against orders, isn't it?' asked Timothy.

'Orders!' said Dingy contemptuously. 'Wot 'ave we got to do with orders? There ain't no one 'ere to see wot we do.'

Timothy was still doubtful, but William Button took him aside and whispered, 'Give him a good dose of it, and it'll make him sleep. Otherwise, you see, we'll have to tie him or keep a watch on him to make sure he doesn't slip off and give information about us. A good dose of rum will save us a lot of trouble.'

'All right,' said Timothy, 'but don't give him enough to kill him.'

'Trust me,' said William, and went for the bottle he had hidden. He gave Dingy a good measure in a drinking-shell, and Dingy, with a hiccup and a wink and a wave of his hand, went off to sleep beside the basking sharks.

Henry String asked Timothy: 'What are we going to do with him to-morrow?'

'I've thought of that,' said Timothy. 'Miss Dildery—the octopus, you know—told me that she used to have a butler, and though she had to get rid of him because of his bad habits, she misses him dreadfully. The only maid she has now is an old Cod who wears a cap and apron, so I can't imagine what her butler was like. But she wants another, and I think we might give her Dingy. It will please her, and it will be promotion for him—from Cabin Boy to Butler is a tremendous step.'

William Button and Henry String began to laugh, and the

more they thought of Dingy's new occupation, the louder they laughed. They laughed so noisily that they woke the basking sharks, who complained like cows in summer when the milkmaid is late in coming. They woke Dingy too, and to celebrate his promotion they gave him a little more rum. Then they and Timothy went to their beds, and laughed more quietly till they fell asleep.

Chapter Sixteen

'We forgot all about the Crab!' said Timothy.

'I wouldn't worry about him,' said William Button, yawning and stretching himself. 'He'll sleep for forty-eight hours maybe, and then wake up and forget everything that's happened.'

They had risen in good time, and saddling their sharks, had taken Dingy to Coral Villa. Miss Dildery, though flustered by the arrival of visitors so very early in the morning, before she had powdered her beak, had been delighted to acquire a new butler. Dingy himself had not been much pleased by his promotion, but they paid no attention to him, and after a little polite conversation with Miss Dildery set off again with all possible speed. They showed proper caution, however, as they approached the outposts of the pirate armies.

There was no sign of movement yet in their lines, and Henry String took up a position high over Inky Poops's camp to keep watch, while William Button and Timothy rose above him to the surface to see what sort of a day it was. The sea was calm again, and lay like a great blue meadow stretching to a bright horizon, and the tall clear sky above them promised fair weather. They sat in the whale-bone howdah, and splashed their feet in the water,

163

as comfortably as if they were sitting on a ledge of rock on the Hen of Popinsay—and suddenly they remembered the Crab, whom they had left fast asleep in the dark cave where they had spent the night. But they forgot him again almost as soon as they had remembered him; for they had more important matters to occupy their thoughts.

Their intention was to swim southward on the flank of Inky Poops's fleet, and observe the manner in which it was ruled. If discipline was loose and the fleet moved in a scattered untidy fashion, they hoped there would be a chance to make a bold foray into the midst of it and snatch Hew from Inky Poops's howdah; in which, they thought, he was sure to be travelling. They had no great hope of success, and they could form no definite plan; but Timothy was very anxious to make one more effort to rescue his brother before the pirates joined battle with Davy Jones's loyal sailors.

The blue sea was all untenanted, there was no ship within its wide circumference, and for some time, while their shark had a morning nap, they kicked their feet in the clear water and tried to imagine the sort of opportunity they wanted, and the tactics they might use to save Hew from the enemy. Then, about half a mile away, the surface of the sea grew darker and was ruffled as though a breeze had suddenly sprung up. But there was no sign of wind elsewhere, and Timothy was puzzled by the patch of broken water until William Button told him there was a shoal of herring there.

'It must be a very big shoal,' said Timothy.

'Nothing like as big as sometimes they are,' said William. 'That one's no more than eighty yards across, by the look of it. I've seen 'em three or four times as broad.'

'How deep is the shoal?'

'I couldn't tell you that. I've never gone into the middle of one, and I don't think I'd like to, somehow.'

'It might be a good idea,' said Timothy, remembering that Gunner Boles's Shell had told him that herring were among the friendly creatures he could expect to meet. 'It might be a very good idea,' he repeated. 'But can they speak, or do they just make noises like a shark?'

'They speak all right,' said William, 'but not like you or me. They don't ever speak one at a time, and I don't think they can. But you'll hear a shoal of them chattering away like a lot of old women, though they're all saying the same thing, which isn't like a lot of old women after all. Let's go a bit nearer, if you want to hear them. They often have a sort of sing-song at this time of the morning, and the songs they sing are just what you'd expect from a lot of herring. Barmy, if you ask me.'

They woke the shark, and very slowly, so as not to alarm the herring, approached the Shoal, and presently they heard a soft and pleasant little tune that seemed to blow across the water like a summer breeze.

'We'll go down a fathom or two,' said William Button, 'and then you'll hear it clearer, and hear the words too.'

So they sank below the surface, and this is what they heard:

'Swift and soft and silent—*shoo!*
Shimmering, shivering—*whew, whew, whew!*
The Silver Shoal like a silver shade
Shows you a silvery sly charade—
What's the sense and significance
Of our slithery, slippery, silver dance?
　　　We seek a few
　　　Sweet shrimps—*hoo, hoo!*

For our supper, our supper, oh, what shall we do
If the shrimps have set sail for the South of Spain
And we never set eyes on a shrimp again?
   Swift and slim
   In a silver shoal
   We swoop and swim
   In search of our goal—
A sweet soft shrimp for our supper to-night
In the shimmering sheen of the silver light
Of a circlet of moon and the stars so bright—
Swift and soft and silent—*shoo!*
Shivering, quivering—*whew, whew, whew!*
Where the shallows skip on the saffron sand
   Or the surges sweep
   O'er the salt-sea deep—
To the scattering spray and the stormy strand
We whisper the secretest wish of our soul
In this silly sweet song of the Silver Shoal—
   Shoo, shoo,
    Shoo, shoo,
   Shoo, shoo, shoo!'

Then a great chattering broke out, and all the fishes in the
Shoal said to each other: 'How sweetly we sang! Oh, we sing
splendidly; that went with a bang! I'm sure there's no shoal in
the whole of the sea that rejoices in voices as choice as we!'

'Wait for me here,' said Timothy to William Button. 'I'm
going to talk to them.'

He jumped off the shark and swam towards the herring, and
when he was on the fringe of the Shoal he shouted in a friendly
way, 'Good morning, fishes!'

'Shining dawning!' they answered. 'And our best wishes!'

'I need help,' said Timothy, 'and I very much hope you'll do something for me.'

'Will it be stormy?' they asked.

'Well,' he said, 'there may be a little fighting.'

'But how exciting!' they replied. 'Swim in more approachably, and we'll share your story more sociably.'

A moment or two later, Timothy was entirely surrounded by thousands and tens of thousands of little glittering fish. They pressed closely against him, above and below, against his legs and his ribs. He could feel them under his feet and under his arms, and he hardly knew whether he was treading water or treading on the Shoal. Only round his head—and that was for politeness—did they leave a little clear space, and it was pinpointed with hundreds of gleaming eyes. For a minute or so the dazzle of light on silver scales bewildered him, and the pushing and prodding of a multitude of firm little heads—and the feathery stroking of a myriad brisk little tails—gave him an uncomfortable feeling that he was either going to be eaten alive or tickled to death. But the herring were so obviously friendly, and eager to help, that he soon forgot his discomfort, and in the simplest words he could find he began to explain the situation and tell them what he wanted them to do.

They listened closely, and whenever he mentioned the pirates they all hissed. Sometimes they found it difficult to understand him, and then the Shoal would exclaim: 'Softly, softly! Say it more slowly. Say it seven times slowly.' It was strange and a little confusing to listen to the voice of the Shoal—which was many thousands of voices all speaking together—for it came from under his toes and behind his ears, from the tips of his fingers and the back of his knees and beneath his chin; and because he had to repeat some parts of his story seven times, it took him a long time to tell it. But when at last he had finished, the herring spoke with a sudden rush, like a river running in spate.

'Full steam ahead!' they said. 'Smite and spare not! We'll slash 'em and smash 'em and smear 'em and smother 'em! Oh, steer us, dear boy, and we shall annoy Inky Poops with great joy. Every fish will do as you wish, and because our sense of solidarity is unerring, you can rely on us to the very last herring!'

Timothy was much encouraged by this quick and enthusiastic response, and he thanked the Shoal with all his heart.

'But please be patient,' he said, 'because we must wait till Inky Poops's fleet is moving, and then—well, we'll do what I suggested. So will you please swim in *that* direction as hard as you can'—he pointed south-south-west, which was the course that Inky Poops must take—'and William Button and I will join you as soon as we have made all our arrangements.'

'Sou'-sou'-west and we'll see you soon, and we'll save your brother before it's noon!' shouted the Shoal, and every fish immediately turned in that direction and swam so quickly away that in a few seconds Timothy was all alone again. The Shoal struck up a brisk and lively tune that sounded like a great yacht under full sail, heeling to the wind and cutting the pointed sea. It was evidently a marching-song, but Timothy could not stay and listen to it, because he had to hurry back to William Button.

William was waiting rather anxiously for him, though no warning had yet come from Henry String that Inky Poops was preparing to move. Timothy climbed into the howdah and carefully explained what he intended to do; and William Button was delighted by his plan and thought it had a good chance of being successful.

'I shall want you to come with me,' said Timothy, 'and you'd

168

better bring your lance, because that's the only weapon we have.'

William thrust at an imaginary enemy with the lance he used to spur the shark, and said, 'If I can tickle Inky Poops in the ribs with this, it'll be the happiest day I've had for many a year.'

'Do you think Henry String will be able to drive both the sharks?' asked Timothy.

'Easy,' said William. 'He's one of the best drivers in the sea.'

'Then let's go down and talk to him, and tell him the plan,' said Timothy.

They found Henry and the other shark floating in the middle depths of the sea, and far below they could just distinguish a busy movement in the pirates' lines.

'That's Inky Poops getting ready at last,' said Henry. 'Dan Scumbril went off an hour ago.'

'We're going to make an attack,' said Timothy, 'and this is how I think we should do it.'

Henry grumbled a little when he learnt that he was to play a less exciting part than William Button, but he agreed that he was a better driver than William, and therefore more capable of looking after the two sharks; as he might have to do for some considerable time. Then, when all the details of the plan had been settled, Timothy and William Button turned their shark to the south again and hurried after the herring, while Henry String remained to watch the pirates.

Timothy and William quickly overtook the Shoal, and encouraged it to keep swimming on a south-south-westerly course, while at the same time they kept a good look-out to the rear for Henry String. They had to wait for nearly an hour before they saw him and his shark break the surface. Then they stopped and waited for him, and the Shoal lay close beside them. Henry came up at high speed—'Doing thirty knots at the very least,' said

169

William—and told them that Inky Poops was under way at last.

'Well, it won't be long now,' said William, and passed his reins to Henry. Timothy and William jumped out of their howdah, and Henry a little jealously wished them luck. Then, with a firm grip on both sets of reins and the two sharks swimming side by side, he drove them westward, and presently turned north and went down. His part in the plan was to keep pace with the pirate fleet on its westerly flank: he had to avoid being seen himself, but watch carefully for what happened.

Timothy and William Button swam into the midst of the Shoal, and all the herring chattered, 'Screen 'em and cover 'em, hide 'em from sight; but careful, don't smother 'em, leave 'em some light.' They surrounded the two boys completely, in front and behind, above and below and on both sides, but beneath them the Shoal was more thinly packed so that Timothy and William could see between the herring into the sea below; and with their heads all pointing to the north, they waited for the pirates.

'I think,' said Timothy, 'you'd better sing something. If they hear you singing the pirates won't be suspicious.'

'Certainly, certainly,' said the herring and began to sing again the song that Timothy had first heard:

> 'Swift and soft and silent, *shoo,*
> Shimmering, shivering, *whew, whew, whew!'*

Presently they saw approaching the leading sharks of Inky Poops's fleet, who were travelling some three or four fathoms deeper in the sea.

'They're not in very good order, are they?' whispered Timothy.

'No discipline, that's what's wrong with them,' said William.

170

'They're out of line and out of column too.'

There were, indeed, wide gaps between many of the sharks, though here and there two or three swam close together. They were moving at a fair speed but in a very ragged untidy array, and the pirates paid no attention to the Shoal of herring singing above them. Nor, indeed, was there any reason why they should; for it appeared to be just the same as any other shoal, and its song was well known throughout the sea.

'Inky Poops is sure to be in the middle of the fleet, isn't he?' murmured Timothy.

'I don't know,' said William. 'He may be dawdling along behind it, and that'll be all the better for us—no, there he is! See him? There he is.'

'Down, down!' cried Timothy to the herring. 'Down and at them!'

'Smite and spare not!' shouted the herring. 'Slash 'em and smash 'em!' And in a great shining solid mass, all swimming swiftly together, with Timothy and William Button in the midst of them, the Shoal dived suddenly towards a shark in the middle of the fleet, in whose comfortable howdah, paying no attention to the danger above him, sat Inky Poops with Hew beside him.

Like a hail-storm glittering in the sun the Shoal burst upon the shark, and surrounded it and hid it from sight. Inky Poops howled in alarm, but his voice was quickly choked when a herring swam half way down his throat, and a thousand other fish so confused him and battered him that he fell out of the howdah, and William Button, striking shrewdly with his lance, managed to prick him as he fell. Timothy, in the meantime, had grappled Hew and lifted him from his seat, crying, 'You're all right now. Don't ask any questions, just swim—and swim hard!'

Hew was as much bewildered by the sudden bursting of the

171

Shoal as Inky Poops had been, but recognising Timothy's voice he obeyed him, and struck out strongly in the same direction.

The Shoal reformed, and now with three boys in its midst turned westward, while the nearer pirates steered their sharks hither and thither in great disorder. They had no idea what had happened, but some of them could see that their captain's howdah was empty, while others in the rear saw Inky Poops swimming round in circles, as though he were still trying to escape from the herring, which by now were two or three hundred yards to the west.

The Shoal swam on till it met Henry String, waiting with his pair of sharks, and there it stopped. There was no time for making long speeches, but Timothy told the herring how grateful he was, and promised to recommend them to Davy Jones for their splendid behaviour. The herring were so excited by the success of their manœuvre that for once they were unable to speak in chorus together, and though the sea was full of the whispering of innumerable voices, no one could understand what they were saying. But they were obviously delighted with themselves, for their eyes were glittering more brightly than ever, and their scales shone like silver new-minted and filled the sea with light. They remembered, moreover, what they had promised to do, and scattered right and left and up and down in a vast glimmering screen to cover the boys' escape.

Timothy mounted with William Button again, and Hew with Henry String, and pricking their sharks and waving good-bye to the herring they set off at their utmost speed. All day the sharks swam side by side, and when Hew saw Timothy riding within a few feet of him, and Timothy saw Hew no further away, they both felt as happy and as much at home again as if they were walking together on the beach of Inner Bay.

When night fell they went down and found a sleeping-shell without much difficulty, and saw, to their surprise, that the Crab who was its caretaker was actually on duty.

'How far is it from here to Davy Jones's summer court?' asked Timothy.

'The very same distance it is from Ushant to Scilly,' answered the Crab, and in an extraordinary voice like two stones being rubbed together, began to sing:

> 'Farewell and adieu to you, fine Spanish ladies,
> Farewell and adieu to you, ladies of Spain—'

'Oh, please don't bother to sing any more!' Timothy interrupted. 'I know the song quite well, and the distance is thirty-five leagues, isn't it?'

'It is, it is—or that's what it used to be when I was young,' said the Crab ill-temperedly; for singing was his only hobby, and not for many years had he found anyone who could bear to listen to him.

'And I don't suppose it's changed much: the distance from Ushant to Scilly, I mean?'

'Everything's changing,' said the Crab. 'Everything's getting worse and worse.'

'Not everything, surely?'

'Everything,' said the Crab firmly. 'Look at the shrimp paste they issue nowadays—'

'Yes, that's what I want,' said Timothy. 'Can you give us some food, please?'

'You'll get the usual food if you're going to spend the night here.'

'But we're not. We want to go on a little farther——'

173

'No refreshments can be served except on the premises,' said the Crab. 'That's orders, that is, and it serves you right for not letting me sing.'

They had decided that it would be dangerous to sleep in a shell, in case they were being pursued by any of Inky Poops's pirates. They had seen two of his sharks come through the herring-screen, searching vaguely for an enemy, and though they did not think they had been observed, they could not be sure; and they had judged it wiser to beg their supper, and then go on to find a hiding-place for the night. The Crab's refusal to give them food was annoying, and Timothy began to argue with him. His argument did no good, but he noticed, while he was talking, that William Button and Henry String were slipping in and out of the shell, behind the Crab's back, and helping themselves. So he went on talking until William signalled to him that they had got enough, and then he told the Crab how sorry he was to have troubled him; and said good-bye.

A couple of miles away, among little hillocks and ocean woods of tall weed, they made camp for the night, and Timothy and Hew went for a walk together while William and Henry were attending to the sharks. Hew said that Timothy had been very clever to rescue him from Inky Poops, and Timothy said that he had enjoyed doing it.

'Well, thank you very much,' said Hew.

'Did Dan Scumbril treat you badly?'

'Not very. He pulled my ears, and then I had a fight with a Cabin Boy.'

'Did you win?'

'Yes. He gave up.'

'That was good. Sam Sturgeon will be very pleased when you tell him that.'

Then they walked back and had supper with the two Powder Monkeys, and Hew told them a little more about his fight with Foxy.

'And I heard something very important from Dan Scumbril, while I was pretending to be dumb,' he said. 'He's going north, to take the northern parallels, and the first place he's making for is *our* wreck in North Bay. He's going to make it his forward headquarters.'

'I heard that too,' said Timothy. 'And it means that Gunner Boles, and Cully, and Sam too, I suppose, are in the most dangerous place of all.'

'Davy Jones will have to send them help as quickly as he can.'

'I'm not sure that he'll be able to. Inky Poops said that he had only a few men with him. Two or three score, I think.'

'Don't you worry about that,' said William Button. 'Davy Jones'll think of something all right. Davy Jones didn't get to the position he's in to-day without having brains in his head, and knowing how to use them too.'

'Who *is* Davy Jones?' asked Hew.

'He's the head man down here,' said Henry String.

'Yes, I know. But who is he?'

'There's some will tell you one thing, and some another,' said William Button, 'but there's one thing they're all agreed about, and that is that *Davy Jones* isn't his proper name. He just made it up, so as to keep his own name a secret.'

'And another thing is that he's been down here for a long time,' said Henry String, 'and for his first hundred years or so he had a very bad reputation. But then he settled down, and got respectable.'

'How long has he been here?' asked Timothy.

'Nearly four hundred years,' said William Button. 'At least

175

that's what they say. They say he was in the *Golden Hind* with Sir Francis Drake, when Drake went round the world. And he still talks in an old-fashioned way, so it may be true.'

'I've got an old-fashioned idea of going to bed,' said Henry String, yawning widely; and they all agreed that his idea was a good one, and lay down side by side in a patch of soft sand.

Timothy was half asleep when he woke again with a sudden thought, and pulling William Button's nearer arm, asked him, 'Is Drake himself down here?'

'No,' he answered, 'he isn't here. None of the admirals are down here.'

'What happened to them? Where did they go?'

'No one ever told me,' mumbled William, and when Timothy shook his arm again, he only snored.

Chapter Seventeen

Davy Jones's summer court was a great cavern, the entrance to which lay under a broad and massive arch of roughly shining stone that glimmered in the green sea like a rainbow of the moon. In front of it the ground had been levelled for nearly a mile, and here and there, like tall beeches in a deer-park, grew stately ocean-trees. Behind the cavern were stables for a hundred finback-whales to mount his sailors, and beyond the stables were great byres that housed two hundred milk-whales—and now, early in the morning, forty mermaids sitting on whalebone-stools were milking them into silver-gleaming nautilus-shells. For every morning, before breakfast, Davy Jones would drink a quart of whale's milk into which half a pint of the best Jamaica rum had been carefully stirred, and the milk had to be fresh. Most of his sailors began the day in the same manner, so a great deal of milk was required, and the milkmaids had to get up early.

But this morning—when Timothy and Hew and the two Powder Monkeys were swimming fast towards his court through the last thirty-five leagues of their voyage—this morning was no ordinary morning, as anyone could see for himself who happened to walk into the great hall of the cavern. For some eighteen or twenty mermaids were busily decorating its high stone walls with wreaths and sprays of seaweed, and branches of pink coral, and bright shells. At the back of the hall, on a dais, was Davy Jones's throne, which consisted of a huge plank of wood resting on two enormous barrels of rum. But though it was plain and homely to look at, it was in reality a most extraordinary and valuable throne; for the huge plank of wood was the original gangway of Noah's Ark, on which all the animals of the world had walked into the Ark before the Flood, and out of it again when the Ark grounded on Mount Ararat. And to make it more comfortable for Davy Jones to sit on, there was a fat cushion in the middle of it, stuffed with mermaids' hair.

Above the throne two mermaids had arranged some branches of coral in the handsomest style, and now, below the coral, they were hanging a long broad ribbon of pale blue on which, in darker letters, was written:

FLOREAT ETONA.

And in smaller letters below the motto—for the benefit of sailors who had forgotten their Latin—was the English translation: *Let Eton flourish.*

The two mermaids had just succeeded in hanging it to their liking, when into the hall came Davy Jones himself, and seeing the banner so prettily displayed he exclaimed in a rich rolling voice: "'Tis a rare device, is it not? And my old schoolmaster, Master Nicholas Udall, would rejoice to see it in this deep cavern of the sea, could he but come to visit us. But he's in a worse place, I fear, as many schoolmasters are, and their pupils also. It grieves me that in our celebrations to-day—this notable day, the Fourth of June—there will be none with whom I can sit and talk familiarly of schooldays and our youth. For I, my dainty maids, am the sole and solitary Old Etonian in all the ocean depths!'

The mermaids, who had all stopped work and begun to smile and curtsey when Davy Jones came in, made little cooing, soothing noises of sympathy; and after a moment or two of silent thought he spoke more cheerfully. 'Let us not give way to melancholy,' he said. 'A merry man lives as long as a sorry man, and a merry maid should live for ever. Let no wrinkle score your pretty brows to-day. No sighs, no pouting, no sad thoughts upon the Fourth of June! All must be gaiety and pride and gladness. I prithee, sweeting, fetch me my morning draught, a little rum and milk for my stomach's sake.'

The nearest mermaid curtsied deeply and swam to the dairy, while Davy Jones walked round his spacious hall to inspect the decorations, and out into the park where tables had been set up, and were being laid for a feast.

He was a man of huge girth and splendid appearance, and though, like the other sailors under the sea, he wore only a kind of bathing suit and a long blue cloak that hung from his shoulders, his air of majesty was undeniable. His forehead was broad and his fat cheeks shone like rubies. He had the brightest of blue eyes, and his hair, that grew thickly still, and his short beard were as white and curly as new-washed wool. His chest was as broad as a door, and his legs and thickly muscled arms looked as strong as oak trees.

He was not a young man, but age had not weakened him; and when he took from the mermaid whom he had sent for his morning draught a nautilus-shell brim-full of rum and milk, and drank it thirstily, it was fairly obvious that his appetite was

179

as good as ever it had been.

There were many stories told about him in the sea, but William Button had spoken the truth when he said that no one knew for a certainty what his real name was. He had been living on the bottom of the sea for a very long time, and it was known that he had been a sailor for many years before that. It was thought, by those who knew him best, that he had got into trouble when no more than a boy, and run away to sea. He was, he had told his friends, a man of middle age or rather more when he sailed with Drake in the *Golden Hind*, and his last voyage had been with Drake again, on Drake's last voyage, to the West Indies. But no one knew much more than that, however much they might guess. It was generally believed, for example, that he had gone to school at Eton, for he often spoke of his old schoolmaster and every year on the school Speech Day, the Fourth of June, he held a great celebration. But there were some who said that his schooldays had been very short, and that he had been expelled from Eton almost as soon as he went there.

He was still walking in the park when Timothy and Hew, and William Button and Henry String, came swimming down from the sea above. While the others remained beside a great tree on the fringe of the park, William Button approached him and saluted very smartly. There were two boys from the dry part of the world who had come to see him, he said, and they had news of great importance.

'They are most welcome,' said Davy Jones, 'and since they have come so far, there shall be no ceremony to delay their tidings. Bid them come hither, and I'll hear their story while we walk among the trees.'

Timothy and Hew were somewhat nervous at the prospect of

meeting Davy Jones face to face, but he received them very graciously, and invited them to walk with him. Then, pacing slowly in the park, they told their story and gave him Gunner Boles's message, and described all that happened to them, and all they had heard while they were in the company of Dan Scumbril and Inky Poops.

Davy Jones listened attentively, and asked shrewd questions. Sometimes he frowned and looked marvellously grim, and sometimes—had it not been for his questions—it almost seemed that his thoughts were far away and set on mild and pleasant things. But when he heard that Inky Poops, believing he had no more than three-score men to defend his court, was even now advancing to attack him, Davy Jones began to laugh. His great sides shook, his ruby cheeks were creased with laughter, and so ripe and jolly was the din he raised that Timothy and Hew were reminded of harvest-time and apples in October and April storms and Christmas pudding. But after he had laughed for several minutes he grew serious again, and said, 'I needs must call a council, and make due preparation. Come within, and while we talk you'll sit beside me on a right royal throne, a very sailor's throne.'

He shouted to a passing seaman, told him to summon his chamberlain, and led the boys into the cavern.

The chamberlain came—a stout, brown-bearded man—and Davy Jones asked him to be so kind as to order at once a meeting of the Privy Council. Then, pointing to his throne, he asked the boys if they liked the look of it.

'It's not the usual sort of throne, is it?' said Timothy.

'There was a day,' said Davy Jones, 'when it carried the whole breathing world. Those claw-marks there the Lion scratched, who roared and said there was no need to run away.

181

The Giraffe, stamping in pride, left there the drawing of his hoof. That splintered edge is the writing of an angry Crocodile. And there in the paint—for the paint was still wet when they went aboard—you can see the little footprint of the Dove. Now tell me whose plank it was in the beginning.'

'I'm afraid I'm not very good at riddles,' said Hew, and Timothy looked as if he would like to guess but dared not.

'''Twas Noah's gangway when he went into the Ark,' said Davy Jones, 'and there's the proof of it—that crack in the wood—if you disbelieve me. That crack was where old Mother Noah slipped and fell, for she was the heaviest burden of them all.'

Before they could decide whether this was a joke or not, twelve Councillors arrived, and Davy Jones took his seat on the cushion of mermaids' hair, and made the boys sit on either side of him.

They were very much impressed by the Councillors, who were all dignified and hardy-looking men: some of them handsome, and some not, some bearded and some clean-shaven. One of them—a thick-set man whose arms were tattooed from shoulder to wrist—wore his hair in a short pigtail.

Davy Jones told them all he had learnt of what was happening, and some of them growled like angry bears when they heard of the pirates' rebellion; but Davy Jones himself spoke calmly enough until he came to the end of his story, and then, when he told them that Inky Poops was even now on the way to attack them—because he expected to find no more than two or three score sailors at court—why, Davy Jones began to laugh again, and to the great surprise of Timothy and Hew, the Councillors laughed as heartily as he, ho-ho-ing and bellowing as if they had heard the greatest joke imaginable.

'O joyful day!' said Davy Jones at last. 'And the lesson for the day is that a merry man lives as long as a sorry man, as Nicholas Udall my old schoolmaster used to say when he flogged us; for he would laugh while we wept. And another lesson is that men are the better of a little education; for if Inky Poops had ever been to school himself, he would know better than to attack us on the Fourth of June, when six hundred of the tallest sailors in the sea are here on parade for the honour of Eton College!'

''Twill be as good a party as we have ever had,' said one of the Councillors. 'We shall know what games to play.'

'Kiss-in-the-ring!' cried another. 'With Inky Poops as the fair maiden, and all striving to embrace him!'

'We keep the sailors waiting,' said a third more gravely. 'They are ready to march past. I have but newly left them.'

'Then let them march,' said Davy Jones, 'and have their dinner too. And when they have fed, for better digestion they can fight! But we, at dinner-time, must think of strategy. There's Scumbril in the north, and we must plan our expedition. But come! The march, and then the feast. We've time for both, and I'll not spoil the Fourth of June for twenty Inky Poops!'

He led the way out of the cavern to where a platform had been erected in the park, and beckoned Timothy and Hew to follow him. A large crowd had gathered by now, of sailors who attended Davy Jones in his summer court, of mermaids who milked the whales and did the housework, and of fishes of all kinds from dolphins to sprats. They lined one side of the route along which the sailors would march, and opposite them was the platform for Davy Jones and his Councillors.

He made Timothy and Hew stand beside him, for they had done him great service, he said, in bringing the news from Popinsay; and they had doubled and redoubled its value by discovering, on their way through the sea, the pirates' plans.

'We should never have found our way here if it hadn't been for William Button and Henry String,' said Timothy.

'The Powder Monkeys? Where are they now?'

'Over there in the crowd,' said Hew.

'Let them stand beside us too,' said Davy Jones, and Hew went to fetch them; which made all the fishes and the mermaids and the old sailors wonder who they were, and what they had done, to entitle them to such an honour.

Davy Jones told the boys that it was his custom, every year, to celebrate the Fourth of June with a parade and feasting and games; but before he had said very much the crowd began to grow excited, and to lean forward, and to break out of line, for now in the distance the sailors could be seen marching towards them. Everyone on the platform stopped talking and stood at attention; and Davy Jones blew his nose on a large red pocket-handkerchief.

The sailors were marching six abreast in six companies of about a hundred each, and every man carried a cutlass stiffly upright in his right hand. Two officers marched in front of each company, and two behind; and the officer who led the whole parade was a little good-looking man with dark hair and a short pointed beard, whose appearance seemed oddly familiar to Timothy and Hew. But they had no time to think about that, for as the little officer came abreast of the platform, and swept down the point of his sword in salute, the sailors broke into their marching song:

'Out of Pompey and Plymouth we sailed, and our flag to
    the mast-head we nailed
When the enemy's topsails were hailed, and we mustered to
    quarters in haste;

From Wapping and Chatham we came, for rum we were
thirsty and fame,
Seafaring was our native game, and prize-money much to
our taste;
From the Solway to Pentland's rough firth we look back at
the lands of our birth,
But we scorned the green comforts of earth, and the desolate ocean we faced!

'When Drake, our good Captain of old, brought home
round the world a full hold
Of pearls and of ingots of gold, he raised up our hearts and
ambition—
So we fought with the French and the Dutch from the Skaw
to the Channel of Cutch,
Though we never knew why, but the touch of a cutlass
compelled the decision
To close them and grapple and board, in the smoke of a
broadside that roared
Like the ultimate wrath of the Lord, when their bulwarks
we rubbed in collision;
And after we'd practised our trade, and our seamen were
perfectly made,
Lord Nelson appeared on parade, and stopped Boney from
being so clever.

'So we steer by the light of his star to whatever new ventures
there are,
And our hands are callous'd with tar, but our spirits are
quick with endeavour;
And our guns are loaded again, with grape and with

round-shot and chain—

As we brought down the tall masts of Spain, we shall bring down all tyrants for ever!'

They made a gallant and a splendid sight, for they were all lively and stalwart men, though some were old and bearded; and some were bald, and some wore short thick pigtails. They marched with a slow rolling stride, but perfectly in time, and bold good humour kept company with broad shoulders and swinging arms. They wore on their vests the names of their old ships, and as they came marching past, rank after rank— bearded faces and brown faces, faces carved out of old oak and proud impatient faces—Timothy and Hew forgot they should be standing at attention, and in their excitement leaned forward to read the names of the ships and remember, if they could, the battles they had fought in. *Barfleur*, *Royal Sovereign*, and *Audacious*, they read. *Thunderer*, *Bellerophon*, *Invincible*, and *Agamemnon*. '*Agamemnon* was Nelson's ship,' whispered Timothy. 'I know,' said Hew, 'and *Barfleur* was Collingwood's, and there's a *Speedy!*'

'That was Cochrane's brig when he boarded the Spanish frigate,' said Timothy,' and look, there's a *Victory*, and a *Revenge*— he must be very old!' 'And an *Ark Raleigh*, said Hew, 'he's just as old.' 'And the *Triumph* was Frobisher's.' 'The *Jesus of Lubeck* was Hawkins'!' '*Breda* was Benbow's.' '*Shannon* was Broke's—and who had *Orion?*'

Memory stirred in their minds, and as, when a great tree is shaken by the wind, the sunlight sprinkles the grass below, so a light seemed to fall, quite suddenly and clearly, on all they had heard or read about the admirals who sailed with Nelson, and Queen Elizabeth's seamen, and frigates and line-of-battleships,

186

and voyages to the northern ice, and voyages to the Spice Islands, and capes and channels of the sea where battles had been fought; and history, which they had learnt from books, became a living thing as the sailors who had helped to make it marched past them with their swinging arms, and strong brown faces, and good humour in their eyes. And still they came—*Marlborough*, *Neptune*, *Euryalus*—with their rolling stride and cutlasses in their sturdy fists—*Arethusa*, *Thetis*, and *Blake*—chanting their song in voices like the north-east trades—*Boreas* and *Foudroyant*, *Goliath* and *Leander*, and last of all a sailor from the schooner *Pickle*, which had brought to England the news of Trafalgar and the death of Nelson.

And now, when the sailors all had passed, Davy Jones blew his nose again; and his twelve Councillors took out their handkerchiefs, and blew their noses with a noise like a bugle-band. For they had all been very deeply moved by the march-past, and the memories it awakened; and some of them, while they stood so straightly at attention, had been crying a little. And after they had blown their noses they all exclaimed, rather gruffly, 'A good show, wasn't it? They marched very well, I thought. Most creditable.'—So they congratulated Davy Jones on the parade, and he answered, 'Let us hope the dinner will be as good, and we must try to make it so. For we are the mess-men, Councillors, and the mariners are our guests.'

The sailors were already seated at the tables which had been set up, some little distance away, under the ocean trees; and as soon as Davy Jones and his Councillors, assisted by some fifty or sixty mermaids, had served everyone with a great helping of sea-pie—which had been specially made by an old mermaid who was the best cook in the whole Atlantic—and filled all their drinking-shells brim-full, the feast began. Always, on these occasions, Davy Jones and his Councillors waited on the sailors, and the sailors kept them busy; for they emptied their plates almost as quickly as they were filled, and waved their drinking-shells about and shouted for more.

The dinner went on for a long time, and one or two of the Councillors, thinking about Inky Poops, began to grow impatient. They suggested that Davy Jones should tell the sailors to hurry up, because they had to fight as well as eat. But Davy Jones said, 'They have time to eat their dinner and beat Inky Poops too. I will not hurry them.'

But when they had all finished, he stood up in the midst of them and made a speech. He said he was very glad to see them again, and they all cheered. He said he hoped they had had a good dinner, and they cheered again. He told them there would be no games that afternoon, as there usually were, because he had just learnt that a pirate fleet was on its way to attack them, and so instead of games they would have to fight a battle—and then the sailors all jumped to their feet, and climbed on to the tables, and cheered again and again.

They listened in a quiet and orderly fashion while he described what had happened, but when he told them of the manner in which he proposed to engage Inky Poops in battle, they laughed uproariously and cheered once more; and then they began to clear away the remains of the feast.

Half an hour later there was nothing to be seen in the great park in front of the cavern but two long tables, well supplied with food and drink, at which sat forty sailors eating and drinking. They had strict orders to go on eating and drinking—or pretend to—until Inky Poops and his three hundred mutineers should arrive. The rest of the sailors lay hidden in the cavern, or in the thickets of weed that surrounded the park.

188

Timothy and Hew, who had eaten their dinner with William Button and Henry String at a small table beside the sailors, now waited in the cavern, and one of the Councillors sat beside them to make sure that they kept out of the coming battle. They had to wait a long time, growing more and more restless and impatient. It was evening before Inky Poops arrived.

The light was beginning to go when one of the sailors, who were still sitting at the tables in the park, looked up and saw a dark shape overhead. 'That's them!' he said. 'That's their scouts, coming to see if we're all at home. Pass the rum, boys, and keep your cutlasses between your knees.'

None of the others looked up, but passed the rum from one to another, and pretended to be eating and drinking with as good an appetite as when they first sat down. Darby Kelly, who was on the shark overhead with five other pirates, swam slowly round and round, and counted the sailors who were having their supper, and satisfied himself that there was no one else in the park. Very cautiously he came down a little lower, and still could see no sign of life in the cavern. Then he returned to where Inky Poops and his fleet were waiting, and told them that, so far as he could make out, they had no more than forty sailors to deal with; though there might be some more inside, he said, who were probably sleeping.

'Well, isn't that splendid!' exclaimed Inky Poops, rubbing his hands together. 'Isn't that the nicest arrangement for a battle you could think of! And it's just what I expected! Well, Darby, my dear, you shall have the honour of leading my fleet into action. I'm not so young as I used to be, so I'll bring up the rear. Don't wait for me, Darby, but go ahead and start the battle as soon as you like.'

Darby Kelly, who was no coward, gave orders to the fleet to

189

attack in close formation, and placing himself in the centre and forefront of it, led the pirates in a long swift descent upon the forty sailormen at the supper-tables. The sailors made no move until the pirates were within fifty yards of them, when they leapt to their feet and stood on guard. At the same time Davy Jones led a hundred others from the cavern, in a headlong charge against the pirate fleet, while from the thickets on three sides of the park came the sailors, who had lain in ambush there, to join the battle or rise above it and cut off the enemy's retreat.

Some fifty or sixty of the pirates fought well, but the remainder, seeing themselves attacked from all sides, quickly lost heart and fled. Above and about the supper-tables there was some fierce fighting, but elsewhere the battle quickly became a chase through the darkening sea; and after Darby Kelly was made prisoner there was no more resistance. Darby Kelly had leapt from his shark on to one of the tables, and stood there waving his cutlass as if he were ready to engage a dozen enemies at least. But two of the sailors overturned the table, by pulling the legs from under it, and when Darby fell off, two others sat on him. Darby, in his own way, was an honest man, and truly devoted to Inky Poops. He looked so miserable, when he realised how overwhelmingly they had been defeated, that the sailor sitting on his chest felt sorry for him and gave him a shell of rum before taking him off to the stables behind the cavern, where prisoners were being collected and shut up.

More and more prisoners were brought in, and when they were counted, an hour later, they numbered a hundred and eighty-six. But Inky Poops was not among them. Inky Poops had not joined the attack. He had four well-armed pirates with him on his own shark, and two other sharks, fully manned, in attendance. They had waited above and behind the fleet to see how Darby Kelly fared, and when they saw that Darby had swum into an ambush they had not tried to help him, but turned and fled with all possible speed to the north.

Chapter Eighteen

Davy Jones wasted no time on celebrating his easy victory over Inky Poops, and by daybreak on the following morning he had made all preparation for a voyage to the north and battle against Dan Scumbril. His expeditionary force consisted of about five hundred men, well mounted on great finback-whales, which were faster by far than basking-sharks. The fleet was to move in five divisions and a supply-column, each under command of a Councillor. Each division would follow a given course, and in this way the whole fleet would cover a wide expanse of sea, and, it was hoped, pick up many stragglers from Inky Poops's army. All divisions had orders to assemble on the evening of the third day at North Rona, a small uninhabited island about fifty miles north of the Butt of Lewis. The supply-column carried a large quantity of rum and included a small flock of milk-whales; it would move more slowly than the others.

Timothy and Hew, and William Button and Henry String, were to travel in the same division, but the basking-sharks they had previously ridden were now added to the supply-column.

The boys stood together while the sailors were mounting, and the captains of each division went busily about to give their final orders, and those who were to remain behind to guard the cavern looked enviously at their more fortunate comrades. There was a good deal of noisy talking—especially from the mermaids, who were swimming to and fro and telling the sailors to be sure and remember them—and everything appeared to be in a state of great confusion. But quite suddenly, as it seemed, confusion vanished, and there was the fleet all trimly disposed and ready to move. Davy Jones, accompanied by several of his Councillors, inspected each division in turn while the mermaids, and the sailors who had to stay behind, and a great multitude of fishes, of all sorts and shapes and sizes, crowded together and watched in silence.

Davy Jones came to where the boys were standing, and called an officer of their division. This was the small good-looking man with dark hair and little pointed beard who yesterday had led the march-past. He saluted Davy Jones, and looked at Timothy and Hew with great curiosity and a very friendly smile.

'I take good care of my friends,' said Davy Jones, 'and lest you should be feeling lonely in this huge immensity of water, I have found one of your own family with whom you shall make the voyage. This gentleman, when I told him your names last night, and the name of your little island, interrupted our Council of War in the most unsailorly fashion by laying his head upon my shoulder and weeping down my neck.'

'But you forgave my emotion,' said the little officer, 'when you learnt the cause of it.'

'I would have forgiven ten times as much,' said Davy Jones, 'for it is not every day that we meet our great-great—but I have forgotten, Aaron, how many *greats* there are in it.'

'I do not know. Some eight or nine, perhaps.—But is it true, dear boys, that your name is Spens and you come from Popinsay?'

'It is,' said Timothy.

'We do,' said Hew.

'Then, there is little doubt of it, you are my great-great—oh! so many *greats*!—You're my great-grandchildren, and I am most heartily glad to meet you.'

'Are you Aaron Spens the pirate?' asked Timothy in great amazement.

'Dear me!' said the officer. 'Is that my reputation?'

'We've always been told that you were a pirate,' said Hew.

'You will have time to argue and clear your name upon the voyage,' said Davy Jones.—'I have found you an ancestor,' he told the boys, 'but whether he is a good one or a bad one you must discover for yourselves.'

'Come then, with your piratical great-grandfather,' said Aaron Spens, and led them to one of the largest and most powerful of the finback-whales, and helped them aboard. William Button and Henry String found room on the whale astern of them, and a minute or two later, with a cheer from the crowd, their division set off on its voyage.

All the sailors in Davy Jones's fleet were carried in long howdahs, cleverly made to fit the whales, and lashed securely on their backs. They sat three by three on low benches in the howdahs, a dozen or so on each whale. They travelled through the sea far faster than the basking-sharks could swim, and the rush of water was so loud and fierce that it was very difficult to carry on a conversation. Timothy and Hew sat on either side of Aaron Spens, and held themselves a little stiffly and doubtfully when he put his arms round their shoulders. It was extremely odd, they felt, to have discovered their very-great-grandfather on the bottom of the sea, and every now and then they turned and looked at him to see what he was really like. They discovered why his appearance in the march-past had seemed familiar, for in spite of his beard he was very like their father. He, looking down at them as often as they looked up at him, found it equally strange to have met his descendants in the depths of the Atlantic, and because he was grown-up he was much more deeply moved by their encounter than they were; but he could not tell them so because the rush of water prevented conversation. He wanted to ask them what they had heard about him, and whether they believed him to have been a very villainous and bloody sort of pirate.

Only once that day did they rise to the surface, and quickly they went down again to the calmer depths; for a gale was blowing from the west, and the sea rose in great humps and hillocks of green water, with ragged fringes, and the wind howled in the lurching valleys of the waves. But forty fathoms down it was still as a dew-pond on a fine morning, and they made such good speed to the north that they lay that night at the sleeping-shell where Inky Poops and Dan Scumbril had played at cards for Hew, and Timothy had failed to rescue him.

'Now tell me about Popinsay,' said Aaron Spens, while they sat at supper. 'Is the house I built still standing?'

'The house we live in is about two hundred and fifty years old,' said Timothy. 'So that's it, I suppose———'

'And it needs a lot of repair,' said Hew. 'The windows leak, and the doors don't fit very well, and there's dry-rot in some of the floors, and bees in the roof.'

'I built it in 1690,' said Aaron Spens, 'and lived in it for five years only. I married my cousin, and when my son was three years old I went back to sea. For seven years I traded a little, and fought rather more, in eastern waters; and when at last I sailed for home, meaning to grow old and die at home, my ship was wrecked under the west cliffs of Popinsay. So my homecoming was not what I expected.'

'But you were a pirate, weren't you?' asked Hew.

'I did not regard myself as one,' said Aaron Spens, 'and the manners of my crew were not piratical. They were good men, with two or three exceptions, of whom the carpenter was one: a villain indeed, but a very good carpenter. The others were well disciplined, and no one aboard my ship ever walked the plank or was hanged at the yard-arm.'

'But everyone who got ashore, when you lost your ship,' said Timothy, 'was made prisoner and hanged at Execution Dock.'

'So I heard, and I was very heartily sorry for them. But once I had a dear friend who choked on a fish-bone, and died of that: a man may die in many ways, and yet be a good man.—But tell me of Popinsay: do ospreys still breed upon the lake?'

'Not now,' said Timothy. 'My grandfather shot the last one, and had it stuffed. It's in a glass case in Father's study.'

'Your grandfather did that! 'cried Aaron Spens. 'My great-great-great-great-grandson! But the man was a scoundrel. He, not I, was the pirate in our family. To kill an osprey—oh, what wickedness!'

'Did you never kill anything?' asked Hew.

'Neither bird nor beast, and no men except such as chose to fight against me.'

'And who were they?' asked Timothy.

'When I was a young man,' said Aaron Spens, 'I made a voyage to Bantam, and became friendly with a Prince of Bantam. I lived in his country for several years, and traded with near-by states and islands. I made money enough to go home and build the house you live in and marry a wife; and then, in my own ship,

I went back to Bantam. But the Dutch, who were planting colonies there, had by then driven my friend from his dominion. I sought for him, and found him. He was eager to regain the land that had been his, and I, as I told you, was his friend. So I joined forces with him to make war against the Dutch, and sometimes we had the better luck, sometimes they. But we failed to regain his principality, and he at last was killed in battle for a ship we took. So I, with what wealth we found in the Dutchman, set sail for home; and was wrecked within sight of home. And because Holland and Britain were at that time in alliance—they shared, indeed, the same king—we were accounted pirates, though all I had been doing was to fight for my friend against those who had despoiled him. Your grandfather, my great-great-great-great grandson who shot the osprey, was a worse man by far.—But that's enough of an old story. Now tell me about Popinsay.'

So they talked till bed-time, and then slept soundly, and rose early in the morning. The boys were making their beds—that is to say, they were smoothing the sand on which they had lain—when the caretaker of the shell, the elderly Crab, came in very importantly, and said there was a lady in the weeds outside who would like to speak to them.

'It must be Miss Dildery!' said Timothy. 'Hurry up, Hew, because we've only got a few minutes to spare.'

They found Miss Dildery hiding in the seaweed about forty yards away—she was too shy to come nearer—and Timothy introduced Hew to her. He said how glad he was to see her again, and added, with regret, that they were rather in a hurry.

'Oh, I know,' said Miss Dildery. 'You must be in a great hurry, and perhaps I shouldn't have come to see you at all, because I'm only interrupting you, and keeping you from doing other things that you must want to do far more than stay and talk to me. But

I did want to see you, just for a minute, because I couldn't let you pass without saying how grateful I am to you for finding me such a wonderful butler!'

'Do you mean Dingy?' asked Timothy in great surprise.

'His real name is Horace,' said Miss Dildery, 'and that is what I call him. Oh, he's such a nice boy, and so good with the children! We're going to be very happy together. He tells me that never in his life until now has he been treated kindly. But I, of course, am kind to everyone, and Horace in particular deserves to be well treated. He has great gifts.'

'Dingy has?' asked Timothy again.

Horace,' said Miss Dildery firmly. 'Yes, he is a most talented boy. He is an artist! And that is another reason why I came to see you. Because he has drawn a picture of me. He found a little piece of whalebone, and carved my portrait with a knife, and then—well, then I gave him some ink, and he inked it in—and here it is.'

She held out a little disk of bone, about the size of a large medal, on which her portrait had been drawn with some skill; and as Timothy took it, wondering why she should give it to him, he heard Aaron Spens calling for them loudly and impatiently.

'I want you,' said Miss Dildery, in a great hurry, and blushing rose-pink all over, 'I want you to give it to Cullifer.'

'Oh, I see!' said Timothy. 'Yes, Cully will be very glad to have it, I'm sure.'

'And say,' said Miss Dildery, hanging her beak and looking extremely shy, 'say that I sent it with—with—with my love.'

Her rose-pink blush deepened to scarlet, and with a sudden movement she disappeared among the seaweed.

'I don't suppose Cully wants her picture,' said Hew.

'You never know,' said Timothy, and together they ran to

Aaron Spens's whale, and climbed aboard.

Another day's swift voyaging brought them to a sleeping-shell off the west coast of the Island of Mull, where again they talked of Popinsay and Aaron Spens's adventures in Bantam; but only for an hour or so, because they were tired and sleepy. And then, in the evening of the third day, they came to North Rona, and went ashore on the east side of its northerly point, where a flight of steps in the rock led to green turf and the ruins of a little house; but the island was uninhabited except by grey seals and puffins and guillemots and starlings.

Davy Jones and two of his Councillors had arrived before them, and another came in not long after, who, on the second day of the voyage, had captured nearly thirty of Inky Poops's men, and sent them back under escort to the cavern.

Davy Jones called a Council of War, but Timothy and Hew and William Button and Henry String were sent to bed. He was going to ask them to get up very early in the morning, said Davy Jones, to undertake a task which they could do better than anyone else.

Chapter Nineteen

The morning was grey and windless. The sun had risen, but it was hidden by a great bank of cloud that filled the eastern sky when three divisions of Davy Jones's fleet set out from North Rona. Popinsay lay about sixty miles to the east, and Davy Jones's plan was to surround it and so make sure of capturing both Dan Scumbril and Inky Poops; for he guessed that Inky Poops, when he fled from the battle at his summer court, had hurried north to join his bad companion. The three divisions that were now moving off were to station themselves to the north and east and south of Popinsay, but at some considerable distance from the island. A much smaller force, of three whales only and their crews, had already left to take up positions close inshore, and at the proper time Davy Jones himself, with the two divisions that remained, would come in from the west and compel the pirates to give battle within the double ring that he had drawn round their headquarters.

Timothy and Hew and the two Powder Monkeys had gone with the small force that was the first to leave, and which Aaron Spens commanded. It was very early when they started, and the morning twilight was cold and cheerless. The boys were sleepy and in no mood for adventure. They would have much preferred to stay comfortably in bed on the sea-sand at the bottom of the little cave under the cliffs of North Rona where they had slept, but Davy Jones had asked them to undertake an important task and go ashore on Popinsay to see Sam Sturgeon, and find out if he had any fresh news from Gunner Boles. They had readily agreed to do this, and now, when the time came, they had to keep their promise in spite of the cold and the cheerless sky and the fact that they were only half awake. But they sat rather glumly beside Aaron Spens in the howdah on his whale, and none of them spoke very much until they approached the island, and, rising cautiously to the surface, saw its pale shape lying against the western sky. They had come round about the south end of Popinsay, and were going to land on the long beach on its east side. One of the three whales under Aaron Spens's command remained near the skerries off Fishing Hope, to watch the southerly part of the island, and another had gone to the north end to lie close under the northern cliffs. Aaron Spens himself, after he had landed the boys, would watch the east coast.

Very slowly they approached the land, and now the boys grew wide awake and eager to go ashore. They pointed to farm-houses and fields and the low hills of the island, and recognised them as gladly as if they had been away from home for several years. They told Aaron Spens the names of the houses and the names of the fields, and some of them he remembered though he had not heard them for more than two hundred years. They saw too—and this at the moment was more important—that all the farmers, and their wives and their children, were still in bed. There was no smoke rising from the chimneys, and no one stirring in the fields, though the cattle which lay out all night were already feeding, and here and there young horses rolled upon their backs, waving their great hooves in the air, then rose and shook themselves in readiness for another day.

The whale grounded on the sand, and the boys, after repeating their instructions to Aaron Spens, slid into the water, swam a few yards, and then waded ashore. A seal raised its head from the pale green sea to watch them. Some oyster-catchers screamed excitedly, and a flock of dunlin and ringed-plover rose from the sand and fled before them. They took off their frog-like shoes, and Timothy led them in single file across the fields and past the lake to Popinsay House. Hew and the two Powder Monkeys lay hidden in the little wood that grew behind it, while Timothy went in alone to rouse Sam Sturgeon. They never locked their doors on Popinsay, so he had no trouble in getting in. But Sam Sturgeon's room was empty, and the door of Mrs. Matches' room above the kitchen stood open, and it was empty too. Timothy, bewildered and feeling a little frightened, did not wait to search the rest of the house, but hurried back to Hew and the Powder Monkeys.

For a minute or two they could not decide what should be done next. Then Hew very sensibly proposed a thorough search of the whole house, to make sure there was no one there, and they went in, all four of them, walking very quietly as if they were anxious not to disturb anyone. They looked into every room in turn, and still found no one. They went downstairs again to the hall, and stood there, very puzzled and somewhat alarmed.

'But where can they have gone?' said Hew. 'What can they be doing?'

'It isn't likely that the pirates would come ashore, is it?' asked Timothy.

'No,' said William Button, shaking his head. 'No, they wouldn't do that, not if they could help it.'

202

'The pirates!' said Timothy again. 'I'd forgotten all about them. I mean the pirates in the cellar.—The two pirates Sam Sturgeon found in the wreck,' he explained to the Powder Monkeys. 'We brought them here, and tied them up, and locked them in the cellar.'

'We'd better see if they're still there,' said Hew.

'I suppose we had,' said Timothy, a little reluctantly, and opened a door above the stone steps that went curving down to the cellars. The others followed him, tiptoe and silent.

There was a main cellar, and two smaller ones leading off it. It was in one of these that the pirates had been imprisoned, but now the door stood as wide open as the door of Mrs. Matches' bedroom, and there was nothing inside but a few blankets, a couple of dirty plates, a newspaper, and some ragged, tattered pieces of rope.

'They've got away again,' said Hew, and hurriedly they ran upstairs and out into the garden. In the open air they all felt more comfortable, for the empty house was rather eerie, and though they had searched it thoroughly they still thought it possible that the pirates were hiding somewhere. They told each other that it was all very odd, and very strange and mysterious, and they repeated these observations several times without feeling any the wiser.

Then Timothy said, 'Well, there's no use standing here talking. We'd better go down and see if *Endeavour's* at the pier. If Old Mattoo and James William Cordiall are aboard, perhaps they can tell us something.'

They were all pleased with Timothy's suggestion, and ran down to Inner Bay as quickly as they could. But the *Endeavour* was not at the pier, and the whole beach was empty. Again they stood, unhappy and perplexed, but now Hew said, 'Come on, let's go over to the Hen. We may find Cully there. Or perhaps *Endeavour* went out early, and we'll see her in North Bay.'

The tide was at half-ebb, and most of the sand between Popinsay and the Hen was covered. They had to swim for about twenty yards, and then splashing through the shallows they waded ashore and ran across the turf towards the northern cliffs. They had not gone very far when a most unexpected figure—a tall, lean figure in black—appeared on the skyline in front of them, and they stopped abruptly.

'It's Mrs. Matches,' said Hew. 'What's she doing here?'

'The tide's going out, so she must have been here for a long time,' said Timothy. 'Unless she swam, and that's not likely.— Wait here,' he said to the Powder Monkeys, 'and we'll go and talk to her.'

With Hew beside him he ran uphill, and when they were about fifty yards from her, they began shouting, 'Mrs. Matches! Mrs. Matches!'

She turned and threw up her arms in astonishment when she recognised them, and hurried to meet them.

'You bad things!' she cried. 'You bad, worthless, runaway things! Where have you been all this time? What do you mean by going off and leaving me when I was in charge of you, without so much as a word to say where you were going? And what have you done with all your clothes? You'll catch your death of cold coming out half-naked at this time of the morning!'

Timothy and Hew were rather taken aback, for they had quite forgotten that they had gone to sea without asking her permission, and indeed without her knowledge. She would, they had thought, be delighted to see them, and it was a nuisance having to explain what they had been doing when they wanted to know what Sam was doing.

'We've been very busy,' said Timothy. 'We had to go somewhere, and take a message, and—well, now we've come back again, and we can tell you all about it some other time. But where is Sam?'

'Where indeed?' exclaimed Mrs. Matches. 'Your father goes off, and you go off, and Sam goes off, and I'm left behind with never a word of explanation. And old Mattoo and James William Cordiall went off in the *Endeavour* just after dinnertime yesterday, and they've been out all night.'

'Is *Endeavour* in North Bay now?' asked Timothy.

'They've been there all night, I'm telling you,' said Mrs. Matches.

'And is Sam aboard?'

'He went away with her and he's never come back, so he must be aboard unless he's drowned by this time. It was the thought of them out there, all night long, and me alone in that great house, that brought me here and kept me here, when I should have been sleeping peacefully in my bed like any other Christian woman. And here I've been, all night, waving to them and crying to them, and never a bit of notice will they take.'

They had never before heard Mrs. Matches talking so excitedly, or looking so wild and worried, and Timothy thought he had better try to soothe and comfort her. So he said, 'Well, we've come back again, and that ought to please you. You won't need to worry about us any more.'

'But where have you been?' she demanded. 'That's what I want to know.'

'Oh, never mind about that,' said Hew. 'When did the pirates escape?'

Mrs. Matches' jaw dropped. She breathed deeply and stood gaping at them.

'The pirates in the cellar,' Hew explained. 'The ones you hit on the head with a poker.'

'They've gone?' she asked.

'The door's open, and there's no sign of them except some bits of the rope they were tied up with,' said Timothy.

'And me all alone in the house!' said Mrs. Matches. 'I might have been murdered in my sleep!'

'Not if you had your poker beside you,' said Hew.

'You probably weren't there when they got out,' said Timothy. 'Wait here, will you, till I've had a look at *Endeavour?*'

He ran uphill to the top of the cliff and saw the fishing-boat lying at anchor in North Bay, in the position where she had been when Sam first went down to look for the wreck. But there was no sign of life aboard her, and after shouting once or twice he ran back to Hew and Mrs. Matches, and said to Hew, 'I think we ought to find out what's happening, and William Button and Henry String can go for help in case it's needed.'

'That's a good idea,' said Hew.

'Where are you going now?' asked Mrs. Matches.

'Out to the boat,' said Timothy.

'I'll not stay here all by myself,' cried Mrs. Matches, 'for I left my poker behind me, and those two men may be hiding anywhere!'

'We're going to send for help,' said Timothy. 'We've got two friends here, and a lot of friends not very far away.'

'What sort of friends?' asked Mrs. Matches.

'Come and see them,' said Timothy.

They walked down to the lower part of the island, where the Powder Monkeys were waiting for them, and Timothy said, 'This is William Button, and this is Henry String.'

'Where do you come from?' asked Mrs. Matches.

'That's telling,' said Henry String.

'No names, no punishment-drill,' said William Button. 'We're not allowed to say, ma'am.'

'Whoever it was that sent you might have given you some clothes to wear,' said Mrs. Matches. 'Are you not starving with the cold?'

'No, ma'am, we're pretty comfortable,' said William Button.

'We're used to it, you see,' said Henry String.

'We want you to get help,' said Timothy, 'as quickly as you can. One of you had better go to the north cliffs and the other to the skerries, and say that there seems to be some trouble in North Bay. Hew and I are going out to see what's wrong, and it would be a good thing if a few sailors could come too. There's a fishing-boat at anchor there, and the wreck lies about fifty yards inshore from her.'

'That's clear enough,' said William Button.

'We can do that,' said Henry String.

'It's rather a long way to the skerries,' said Hew.

'I know,' said Timothy, 'and I thought that Mrs. Matches might take Henry as far as Fishing Hope on her bicycle.'

Mrs. Matches had listened to their conversation with much bewilderment and a little hope. Timothy's voice was fairly confident, and he seemed to know what he was talking about.

'Is it real help they're going for,' she asked, 'or just some more naked boys like yourselves?'

'Real help,' said Timothy.

'Sailors,' explained Hew, 'like Gunner Boles.'

'Then I'll do what you want,' she said, 'if these two boys will come with me as far as the house to get my bicycle. For I'm not going back there alone.'

'They'll do that,' said Timothy, 'and if you take Henry to the shore above the skerries, you can stay in Fishing Hope; though I don't suppose there's anyone up yet. But please don't tell anyone what's happening here.'

'They'd think I was mad if I did,' she answered, and they went with her to the beach.

She and the two Powder Monkeys waded across the channel, where the water was now quite shallow, and hurried back to Popinsay House. Mrs. Matches kept her bicycle in the stable, and they got it without seeing anything of the two pirates. Then William Button set off to the north cliffs, and Mrs. Matches rode as quickly as she could, with Henry String sitting on her handle-bars, to Fishing Hope. They presented rather a curious sight, but fortunately there was no one to see them.

Timothy and Hew, in the meantime, were swimming out to the *Endeavour*. They swam round her, and saw no one on deck. Then they climbed aboard, and looking through the window of the little wheel-house saw James William Cordiall and Old Mattoo asleep in opposite corners. They looked very uncomfort-able, for there was no room to lie down and scarcely room to stretch their legs; but in spite of that they were sleeping soundly. Timothy opened the door and Hew shouted, 'Wake up! Wake up!'

They started up, and rubbed their eyes, and looked with amazement at the two boys.

'And where have you been all this time?' asked Old Mattoo hoarsely.

'Never mind about that,' said Timothy. 'Where's Sam?'

'He went down to the wreck,' said Old Mattoo, 'and he never came back.'

'We have been waiting for him all night,' said James William Cordiall. 'Keeping watch through the night, and waiting for him to return.'

'When did he go down?' asked Timothy.

'He was diving all through the afternoon,' said Old Mattoo, 'and he found two more of those green skulls.—They are over there, James William.'

James William picked up two green-stained skulls that lay in his corner of the wheel-house, and shook them. They rattled like money-boxes, and he said, 'That's eighteen of them altogether that he has brought up.'

'When did you see him last?' asked Timothy.

'It would be at the back of eight o'clock, or maybe it was nearer nine,' said Old Mattoo. 'There's not much darkness at this time of year, and he was working late.'

'But there's no breast-line over the side,' said Hew. 'There's no air-line. How is he diving without your help?'

'He doesn't use those things nowadays,' said Old Mattoo. 'He has given up the diving-suit.'

'It was two days ago that he went down without it for the first time,' said James William. 'He came aboard in his bathing-suit, smelling as if he had been washing himself with fancy soap; or had put something on his hair that the barber gave him. He was wearing big black slippers that made his feet look like frogs' feet, and he said he had learnt a new way of going down and wouldn't be needing the suit any more.'

'Gunner Boles must have told him the secret,' whispered Timothy to Hew.

'He must have listened to the Shell,' said Hew; and Timothy nodded and asked Old Mattoo, 'Have you seen Cully again?'

'Not for three days,' answered Old Mattoo. 'He has been aboard us twice since you went away, and had his tea with us. But the last time was three days ago.'

'And a right good tea he took,' said James William Cordiall, 'for we had plenty of jam aboard and a dozen eggs too, that we had taken just in case we should see him.'

'Well,' said Timothy, 'I think we should go down and look for Sam.'

'That's the thing to do,' said Hew, and sat down to tie his frog-shoes more tightly.

Old Mattoo and James William Cordiall watched them with the look of men who could no longer be surprised by anything that happened. They had seen many strange sights in the last week or two—they had grown friendly with an octopus, and entertained it to tea—and now they took for granted the most unlikely and curious events, and were quite untroubled by them.

'And what do you want us to do?' asked Old Mattoo.

'Just stay here till we come back,' said Timothy, and he and Hew dived neatly over the side.

Chapter Twenty

'There she is,' said Hew, and pointed to a kind of hump on the bottom of the sea, that looked at first sight more like an outcrop of rock, all draped in weed, than the wreck of a ship.

'We'd better go carefully,' said Timothy. 'We don't know who's aboard.'

They swam forward another few yards, close to the bottom as though they were a pair of flounders. The pirate ship lay half-buried in a patch of sand. Her masts and spars had long since gone by the board and been carried away, but a little hummock, forward of the larger mass, might show where a broken yard, now covered by a curtain of seaweed, lay across her main deck. It was her great high poop that rose above the sand, and though the weed hung thickly from its sides the deck seemed to be fairly clear, and a little breadth of the main deck in front of it, under the break of the poop, had been swept clean. On the far side of the poop, at the extreme stern of the ship, there was something which they could not distinguish—a mere darkness in the shadows of the sea—until it moved, and separated, and came forward; and then they realised that two men had been standing there, close together.

'They may be Sam and Gunner Boles,' said Hew.

'And they may not,' said Timothy.

Very cautiously they swam a little nearer and then, some thirty feet from the wreck, lay still behind a great boulder when the two men turned and walked slowly to the near side of the ship. Now the boys could see who they were, and they got no comfort from what they saw. For the two men were Dan Scumbril and Inky Poops.

'What shall we do now?' whispered Hew.

'I think we ought to wait till the sailors come,' said Timothy.

'Well, perhaps,' said Hew, 'and perhaps not.'

Dan Scumbril and Inky Poops were walking up and down, as captains do aboard their ships, and when they turned away again Hew said, 'We listened to them once before when they were talking, and we heard a lot of interesting things. We might hear some more.'

'We might,' said Timothy. 'I don't think it's very sensible, but—oh, well, let's try.'

They waited until the two pirate captains were on the far side of the poop, and then, moving as swiftly as they could, but still like flounders close to the bottom, they swam towards the sunken bow of the ship. They lay still when the pirates turned towards them, and swam quickly when they turned away; and presently they were creeping towards the curtain of weed that hung across the main deck, where perhaps a broken spar had fallen, and from there they could hear most of the pirates' conversation. They could hear Dan Scumbril quite easily; for, in his usual manner, he was shouting.

'Slice my sirloin with a rusty razor!' they heard him exclaim. 'I'm in command here now. You were caught like a rat in a trap, Inky. Your fleet was defeated, and you came running north to

212

seek refuge with me. I'm master now, and you're nobody! But if you behave yourself, if you're sensible and modest, I'll give you employment, and you can be my lieutenant.'

'Now do be reasonable, Dan my dear,' said Inky Poops. 'Don't let's quarrel, for I hate quarrelling, and it won't do us any good, will it? If you'd only look at things in the proper way, like I look at them, you'd realise that you owe me a great deal.'

'I owe you nothing,' roared Scumbril. 'Crunch my bones in Mother Bunch's coffee-mill if I owe you as much as the dirt in my finger nails!'

'And that would be quite a lot if you weighed it,' said Inky Poops. 'But you owe me more than that, Dan my dear. For what did I do? First of all, I took on Davy Jones in battle, though he had twice as many men as I had—but I was always unselfish, and it was for your sake I did it, Dan—and then, after we'd fought for nearly half a day, I broke out of the fight and came here as quickly as ever I could, just to let you know what was happening. We swam day and night, Dan, we gave ourselves no rest at all, and now when I've given you this valuable information, all you do is to say that you're the captain, and I've got to salute you when I come aboard. Oh, it breaks my heart, Dan, to see you so ungrateful!'

'You were caught in a trap,' said Scumbril again. 'You were defeated and you ran away. That's the truth of it.'

'Well, even if it is, Dan—but I'm not admitting it, oh, I'm not admitting it, no, not for a moment—but even if it was the truth, you couldn't do without me, could you now? Who's going to make the speech, for example, when we cut the knot? I am, and you know it; because I've got the speech all written out here in my satchel.'

'D'you think I can't make a speech as well as you?' shouted Dan.

'I know you can't,' said Inky. 'You're pretty good when it comes to fighting, but I've got the better brains and the better tongue, and I'm the speech-maker. You can't do without me, Dan.'

Pressed close against the curtain of seaweed, Timothy and Hew lay and listened to the pirates with great interest. They were so interested that they quite forgot they were in a rather dangerous position, and they jumped with surprise—like flounders that had been speared—when they heard behind them a slow, thick, rumbling voice say quietly, 'I hope you're enjoying the conversation, little boys?'

They turned swiftly and tried to escape, but the voice said, 'Oh, no, you don't!' And the pirate to whom it belonged grabbed Timothy by his right ankle, and Hew by his left arm, and carried them like that, both struggling wildly, to the break of the poop. He was a huge man with shoulders like an ox, and hands as rough as a bear's claws, and they were quite helpless in his grasp.

'Look what I've found, Cap'n,' he said to Dan Scumbril. 'They were lying behind that seaweed there, a-listening to you and Cap'n Poops. I saw them come aboard, and I've been watching them ever since.'

'Why, tap my napper with a blacksmith's hammer,' roared Scumbril, 'if it's not the Dumb Boy of Mystery, my lost Cabin Boy!'

'*My* Cabin Boy,' said Inky Poops, 'that I won from you, Dan, in a game of Strip Jack Naked. But who's the other young fellow? I'll play you a game for him, Dan, when we've time for a little rest and relaxation.'

Then they leapt down to the main deck, and Dan Scumbril pulled Timothy's ears and twisted his nose.

'Are you dumb too?' he demanded.

Timothy, with tears in his eyes, thought he could not do better than follow Hew's example, and made no reply.

'Well, now,' said Inky Poops, 'and isn't that a very sad and curious thing, to be sure? Here we've got three strangers aboard our ship, and none of them able to speak! Oh, isn't it sad? It's very, very sad!—And you, you creeping, crawling, spying little boys, you'll be the saddest of all unless you find your tongues and tell us who sent you here!—They're spies, Dan, they're all spies, him in the sail-locker, and these two creeping, crawling little boys. But I'll chop their toes and fingers off if they won't speak!'

'Spies they may be,' growled Dan, 'but what harm can they do us now? I'm in command, my men are at the knot, and we'll have control of all the Northern Parallels before Davy Jones can muster a force against us.'

'I don't like it, Dan, I don't like it at all!'

'There's a hundred things that I dislike,' said Scumbril, 'but none of them keeps me awake at night.—Throw them into the sail-locker with the others, Hatch,' he told the big pirate, 'and I'll deal with them when we come back.—My men are ready, Inky, and it's time to cut the knot. Get your speech ready, and be ready to read it quick. I'll waste no more time on talk.—Away with them, Hatch.'

'Ay, ay, sir,' said the big pirate, and tucking both Timothy and Hew under one arm, carried them through a door in the break of the poop, and opening another door threw them into a room in which the weed grew so thickly from the bulkheads, and the deck above and the deck below, that at first they did not see the two figures who lay side by side in a far corner. Dan Scumbril and Inky Poops stood in the door-way, and Scumbril said, 'Tie them up, Hatch, and tie them tight. Captain Poops and I have a ceremony to perform, and we leave you in charge. They're your prisoners till we return. Are the men ready to move?'

'Your own crew, Cap'n? They're down in the hold, sir, taking their ease till they're called.'

'I'll leave you half a dozen, Hatch, and you must keep them on deck in case more visitors appear. But we'll make haste with the ceremony—cut down your speech, Inky, cut it by half—and we'll come back within the hour. Now bar the door, Hatch.'

'Ay, ay, sir,' said Hatch, and the boys, now tightly bound, heard a heavy bar fall into place on the other side of the door. They heard the pirates' voices talking still, but growing fainter, and some shouting from the forward part of the ship. Then there was silence till one of the other prisoners in the sail-locker said quietly, 'Are you all right, boys? Tell me how you got on.'

'Sam!' they exclaimed. 'Oh, Sam!'

'We couldn't see who you were,' said Timothy.

'Is that Gunner Boles beside you?' asked Hew.

'Boles is the name,' said the Gunner sadly, 'and both of us tied up like a couple of parcels in string and brown paper.'

'They took me last night,' said Sam, 'after I'd been diving for a couple of days without interference. They tried to make me speak but I told them nothing. And then they brought Gunner Boles in half an hour later.'

'A score of Dan Scumbril's men came down on me from all sides when I was sitting by the knot,' said Gunner Boles. 'I left my mark on some of them, but I hadn't a chance. Not a chance. And how did you get on, my young cocks? Did you find your way to Davy Jones?'

'We did better than that,' said Timothy. 'We brought him back

216

with us. We all lay at North Rona last night, and he must be on his way here now.'

'In force?' asked Gunner Boles.

'He's got about five hundred men,' said Timothy.

'They could save the knot then,' said Sam, 'if they come in time, and know where to come. But we won't see nothing of the fighting. We'll be lying here till it's all over.'

'That won't matter if they save the knot,' said Gunner Boles.

'We may get out sooner than you think,' said Timothy, and told them about the Powder Monkeys who had gone for help, and about the little force of Davy Jones's men who lay in the inner ring round Popinsay.

'You've done well, boys, you've done very well,' said Sam, 'but you shouldn't have come down here. That was too risky by half. You should have waited safe on shore till it was all over.'

'How did you get on with Davy Jones?' asked Gunner Boles.

The boys began to tell the story of their long voyage. They interrupted each other, and boasted a little, and were so eager to tell all that had happened that they were quite incapable of telling it in any sort of order. But in the excitement of their story they, and Sam Sturgeon and Gunner Boles too, almost forgot the discomfort of lying tightly bound in a small dark room full of seaweed that hung like ragged curtains from the deck above and grew like a jungle from the deck below. They could move neither hand nor foot, but their tongues were free; and while Sam and Gunner Boles listened with one ear to the boys' story, they listened with the other for the coming of a rescue party.

They had not long to wait, and while the boys were describing their meeting with Aaron Spens they were interrupted by a great clamour above them, by shouting and the sound of heavy blows and heavy bodies falling, and then they and Gunner Boles and

Sam Sturgeon all shouted together to let their rescuers know where they were. The door was unbarred, and a couple of Davy Jones's sailors came in.

'Who's here?' they asked. 'And what are you, friends or foes?'

'Is that Bill Nye?' asked Gunner Boles.

'It is,' said one of the sailors. 'But who's speaking? I can't see the cut of your jib in the shrubbery there.'

'Boles is the name,' said Gunner Boles, 'and I'll be much obliged if you'll cut these lashings.'

Within a minute they were all freed from their bonds, and standing up they rubbed their wrists and ankles. Sam Sturgeon led the boys into the saloon, where there was better light and he could see them properly, and stood looking at them as if he was surprised to find them just the same as they had been when they first set out from Popinsay. Gunner Boles went with Bill Nye to see what had happened, and found that Hatch and his fellow pirates had all been overpowered. William Button, who was looking very pleased with himself, had led six men from the patrol under the north cliffs, who, by the suddenness and determination of their attack, had given the pirates little chance to defend themselves. And now that he was free, Gunner Boles had only one thought in his mind, and that was to return to the knot he guarded. So, without waste of time, the pirates were tied up and thrown into the saillocker, and Gunner Boles led all the others westward through the sea.

Chapter Twenty-One

Timothy and Hew thought they had learnt to swim very well by this time, but they were no match for the sailors. The sailors, swimming at full speed, would soon have left them far behind, so Timothy got on the back of one, Hew on another; and now Sam Sturgeon lagged in the rear. It was only a few days since Gunner Boles had decided that Sam should be told the secret of the Shell, and oiled with the oil that smelt of ambergris and contained sixty-nine ingredients; and Sam, though a good swimmer in the ordinary way, could not compare with the sailors who lived under the sea. But he did his best, and groaned with the effort he was making, and Gunner Boles took him by the arm and helped him. They all swam close together, and after what seemed a long time—for they were impatient to reach the knot— they came to a long dark reef that rose from the bottom in a broadening ridge, and Gunner Boles led the way into a small cave. At first it was no bigger than a tunnel through which they could crawl, one at a time. But the tunnel led through the rock, and became broader and higher, and at last it opened like a great window under a heavy fringe of seaweed. And there, looking out, they saw below them the huge knot which tied together, where they crossed, the 59th Parallel of North Latitude and the 4th Parallel of West Longitude. To the east of the knot, only forty yards below their rock-window, stood three or four hundred pirates, with Inky Poops and Dan Scumbril out in front of them.

In this part of the ocean the bottom of the sea was an ugly muddy plain on which great boulders were scattered, some of them almost as big as a cottage. Lying on the mud the two thick cables ran north and south, and east and west. Here and there grew clumps of seaweed like low bushes—there was a growth like a little shrubbery quite close to the knot itself—but the cables had been kept clean, and no weed covered them.

Between Dan Scumbril and Inky Poops and the pirate army that stood facing them lay a vast coil of new rope that looked very clean and white against the muddy floor. Inky Poops was making a speech, and several times he pointed to this new rope, and spoke of it with pride and pleasure. They would splice it to the old cables, he said, and with it tie a new and splendid knot, a knot that he and Dan Scumbril had invented. It would be far better than the old knot, he said. It would be stronger, it would look nicer, and because they would all help to tie it, they would all feel very proud of it.

He also spoke about Davy Jones, and called him a great tyrant, and said he had no right to be so wealthy. It would be much better for everybody, he said, if he and Dan Scumbril took possession of Davy Jones's wealth, because they, being honest pirates, would never put it to any bad use. They would buy new rope with it, he declared, and tie new knots all over the world. The pirates cheered him loudly, whenever he stopped for breath, but he never explained why the new knots would be better than the old ones, and Timothy and Hew thought he was talking a lot of nonsense. The sailors and Sam

Sturgeon, however, were very worried indeed, because four tall pirates, with axes in their hands, stood on each side of the knot that Gunner Boles had kept, ready to cut the old cables when Inky Poops or Dan Scumbril gave the word.

'And they'll spring apart!' muttered Gunner Boles. 'We're done for if they cut them. They can't ever hold them. If the knot goes, the cables go, and they can't hold them, I tell you!'

'But what can we do to stop them?' asked Sam. 'There's eight of us, and three little boys, against more than three hundred of them. We can't do nothing.'

'Nothing,' said Gunner Boles, 'except hope that Davy Jones will come in time.'

Inky Poops was nearing the end of his speech. He was talking so quickly and so excitedly, and the pirates were cheering so often, that they could not hear what he was saying; but they could see that the four men who were to cut the cables now stood with their axes raised aloft.

'Where's Cully? 'asked Sam Sturgeon. 'Was he off duty when you got taken prisoner?'

'I let him off for an hour or two,' said Gunner Boles, 'because he was feeling sleepy, he said. That octopus sleeps more than anyone I've ever known. But I told him not to go far away.'

'He ought to be here,' said Sam. 'He ought to be at the knot.'

'I'm going down!' cried Gunner Boles. 'I can't sit here, doing nothing, and see the cables cut. I'm going down!'

'Stay where you are,' said Sam. 'You couldn't do any good.'

He took Gunner Boles by the arm, and two of the sailors helped to hold him. It would have been sheer folly for one man, or even eight, to attack the pirate army, but Gunner Boles could not bear to see the destruction of his knot—and now Dan Scumbril, turning to the four tall pirates who stood with axes aloft, shouted, 'Cut!'

They hewed at the cables, and strand after strand of the stout rope parted under their blows. Gunner Boles struggled with the sailors, and shouted to them to let him go; but the pirates were cheering so loudly that there was little danger of their hearing him. Timothy and Hew could see that the cables were beginning to yield and strain and tear apart under the blows of the axe-men, and they wondered fearfully what would happen when they parted. But now, in the water above the knot, a shadow appeared and slowly spread. The water grew darker and darker, till only the heads and arms and shoulders of the axe-men could be seen; for their legs were invisible in a black pool, and the knot was out of sight. But still they struck at the cables they could no longer see.

'It's Cully!' cried Timothy. 'He must be in the seaweed there!'

'Cully's been hiding there all the time!' exclaimed Hew.

The darkness in the water grew larger, like a thundercloud rising behind a hill, and the axe-men fled from it while Inky Poops and Dan Scumbril stood perplexed, not knowing what to do, and all the pirates shouted and growled and chattered with wrath. Sam Sturgeon and Gunner Boles, and the sailors and the three boys, stood up in the window of their cave, careless now of being seen—and then Timothy cried, 'Look! Look! They're coming!'

Down through the green sea, diving steeply, came ten, twelve, fifteen great whales of Davy Jones's fleet. Straight for the pirate army they dived, and the sailors in their howdahs rose for the attack, and the voice of Davy Jones, like a great bell tolling, resounded in the depths: 'Out cutlasses and board!'

Chapter Twenty-Two

The charge of the finback-whales broke the pirates' array, and the sailors' sudden descent scattered them far and wide. But Dan Scumbril's men had stout hearts, and here and there, in small groups, they fought fiercely though they had small hope of winning.

'Now you can take a hand if you like,' said Sam Sturgeon to Gunner Boles, 'but I'm staying to look after the boys. They're not going to get mixed up in this, not if I can help it.' And with a nimble movement he sat on William Button, seized Timothy firmly in the one hand, and Hew in the other.

Gunner Boles and the sailors, diving from the cave, attacked three or four pirates who stood below. The pirates fled from this unexpected assault, and for a few minutes there was little to be seen. Most of the fighting seemed to be taking place on the far side of the knot. But then a dozen pirates swam into sight, followed by five sailors, and made a stand against the rock-face under the cave. The sailors attacked without hesitation, though the odds against them were heavy, and very quickly it became apparent that they were going to get the worse of it. Sam decided that he could not sit quietly by and see them beaten; so he said to the boys, 'Now, you stay here till I come back, and don't you move an inch, or I'll give each of you a clip over the ear that you won't forget in a hurry!'

Then he leapt down and clouted one of the sturdiest pirates on the head, and threw another into the mud. This broke up their defence, and the others scattered, pursued by the sailors. Sam fought with the man whose head he had punched, and the pirate whom he had thrown, rising to his knees, found his cutlass and waited for a chance to cut Sam's legs from under him.

But Hew said, 'This is our chance!'—Timothy said, 'Come on!'—And William Button said, 'What are we waiting for anyway?'

Then, close together, they dived down on the kneeling pirate, and felled him, and pushed his face into the mud again. Hew sat on his head, Timothy sat on his back, and William Button sat on his legs. Sam swung a tremendous punch to the other man's jaw, and laid him flat on his back. He looked round for a new opponent, and when he saw a pirate swimming overhead, leapt up to grapple with him.

'It's Inky Poops!' cried William Button, and leaving their former enemy in the mud, the boys followed Sam, who was now wrestling with Inky some forty feet above them. Hew and William Button seized the pirate captain by his ankles, and Timothy embraced his left leg. But suddenly, as if a whirlwind or a bull or a battering-ram had suddenly struck them, they were swept away, and Sam, who had been kicked on the head, came drifting down in the midst of them.

'Now who was that?' he asked. 'Something hit me before I could get a chance to see it, and it felt like fifteen pirates all together, or else a ton of rock.'

'I *think* it was Dan Scumbril,' said Hew. 'He'd very hairy legs.'

'Then he and Inky Poops have both got away,' said Timothy.

The fighting had become more and more distant, and now there were no pirates near the knot except some twenty or thirty prisoners who stood like a herd of cattle under their guard. The darkness over the knot was growing paler. The blackness was fading, and Gunner Boles, with a score of sailors whom he had summoned to help him, was already splicing the new rope, which the pirates had brought, into the old cables. The cables seemed to be holding still, for they had not sprung apart; but they could not see what damage had been done to the knot till the water cleared, nor could they see what had become of Cully. The sailors worked hard, and spliced the new rope in on all four sides of the knot, and brought the ends together ready to be tied.

The shadow in the water was now no darker than the shadow of a cloud, and presently a little current, or eddy on the bottom of the sea, swept it away. And then, where the knot had been, they saw Cully. But Cully was pale as death, and his eyes were closed. Two of his arms were twisted firmly about the cable that ran to the north, and two about the southward cable; two held the cable to the east and two the cable to the west. Whether he was alive or dead, they did not know, but he had held the great parallels together when the knot was cut, and he held them still. For the last strokes of the axe-men had severed the cables, and the knot that had bound them lay in the mud like the core cut out of an apple.

'Make haste now, make haste,' cried Gunner Boles, 'and take the strain off him! Come over with that end and under with this, then over again and under in a Carrick bend, and a couple of stops will hold it it till we can make a proper job of it. And hurry, hurry!'

So they tied the knot anew, and carefully and tenderly

released Cully's hold on the cables which had been cut. His long arms lay limp and useless, but when they no longer felt the strain a tremor went through them, and his body moved a little, as if in relief. He began to breathe again, and in a minute or two he opened his eyes. He saw Gunner Boles leaning over him, and Timothy and Hew.

'Oh dear, oh dear!' he said, in a voice so faint they could scarcely hear him. 'What a very horrible experience, to be sure! But I held on, didn't I?—I told you that was my job,' he said to Timothy and Hew, 'and a most important job it is—and very, very painful.'

Then he closed his eyes again, and Gunner Boles, with the most mournful expression on his face, said, 'He's saved us all, poor Cully has, and whether we'll save him there's no one can tell. He looks mortal bad now, doesn't he?—You'd better take him ashore, lads,' he told the sailors. 'There's a little island called the Hen over there, and a pool in the rocks below it where he used to lie whenever he had the chance. Take him there and let him rest.—But he'll never be the same octopus again, Sam. He's stretched himself too much.'

Four of the sailors swam with Cully towards the Hen, and Sam Sturgeon and the boys went with them to show them Cully's pool. But Gunner Boles stayed by the knot to put more stops on the new rope and make sure it would stand the strain.

The battle was over, and Davy Jones, sitting on the poop of Aaron Spens's old ship with Aaron Spens and two of his Councillors beside him, was counting his prisoners. All the pirates who had been captured were being carried or driven to the wreck, and thrown into the hold; which Dan Scumbril, with a great deal of labour, had cleared for his own purposes. Nearly two hundred prisoners had already been brought in, and many more, who had fled north and south and beyond Popinsay to the east, were in the hands of the sailors who had lain far out in a broad ring to watch for runaways. But neither Dan Scumbril nor Inky Poops had been caught, and the frown on Davy Jones's forehead deepened as he waited for them to be brought before him, and waited in vain.

On the surface of the sea, above the wreck, the *Endeavour* lay; and Old Mattoo and James William Cordiall were drinking a cup of tea and eating some bread and cheese.

'The boys have been gone for a long time,' said Old Mattoo.

'And Sam Sturgeon has been away for much longer than that,' said James William.

'They told us to wait for them,' said Old Mattoo, 'but how long have we got to wait? That is what I should like to know.'

'There are many things that I want to know,' said James William. 'I want to know what has been going on, here in Popinsay, for the last two weeks or more. But I do not suppose they will ever tell me.'

'Perhaps you would not understand them if they did.'

'Then they needn't bother, if that is the sort of things they are. For it is just a nuisance listening to what you cannot understand.—Is there any more tea in the pot?'

'Not very much,' said Old Mattoo, 'but listen, James William! Do you hear anything?'

'Is it someone shouting, do you think?'

'It may be. But he has a very weak voice, or else he is very far away.'

'I'll take a look,' said James William, and coming out of the little wheel-house he stared north and east and west before he thought of looking south. And then, on the cliffs of the Hen, he saw Sam Sturgeon waving, and the boys beside him.

'It is Sam,' he said, 'and the boys are with him. They have all gone ashore.'

'Then we need not wait any longer, so start up your engine, and I will see to the anchor.'

Old Mattoo put his cup on the deck, and the last of the bread and cheese in his mouth, and went slowly forward while James William went down into the little engine-room. And a few minutes later the *Endeavour* was peacefully on her way home.

Chapter Twenty-Three

Among the disadvantages of Popinsay House—such as doors that did not fit and windows that leaked, dry rot in the floors and bees in the roof—there were also mice and rats. Every night rats could be heard running over the ceilings, and in every room mice would come out from the wainscot and scamper across the carpet. In the attics and the cellars the mice used to stroll about as boldly as people walk in the park on a Saturday afternoon.

The two pirates whom Sam Sturgeon had found in the wreck, and who had been imprisoned in one of the cellars, took a great deal of interest in the mice, for it was a long time since they had seen any. They would lie still while the mice walked over them, and after the first day or two of their imprisonment the mice became quite used to them, and would walk over them merely to save the trouble of walking round them. One of the pirates, whose name was Pott, was a sullen, silent sort of man who did not much mind being in prison; but the other—the one with triangular teeth—was active and talkative, and he would have disliked it extremely had he not been so interested in the mice. His name was Kettle.

Until he was captured by Inky Poops and Dan Scumbril in the

wreck, Sam Sturgeon had looked after Pott and Kettle very well. He went in to see them every morning, and after untying the ropes round their ankles would take them out for an hour's exercise in the garden. Then he would tie their ankles again, and take the lashings off their wrists, and give them their breakfast. He brought them a newspaper every day, and in the evening untied their wrists so that they could take their supper. And then, with their ankles free, they went for a little walk before bedtime. But when Sam was taken prisoner, Pott and Kettle got no supper, and they lay in the cellar, with the mice walking over them, and felt very hungry and discontented.

The mice were hungry too, and one of them, almost by accident, discovered that the rope which bound Kettle's wrists had a very pleasant taste. Kettle, while he was living under the sea, had oiled himself every couple of weeks with the oil that smelt of ambergris and contained sixty-nine ingredients; and the rope round his wrists and ankles had become oily too, and in the opinion of the mouse who happened to taste it, it tasted like the sponge-cake in a good trifle, though it was a lot drier, of course. The mouse quickly told all his friends of his discovery, and within a couple of minutes at least fifty mice were enjoying an unexpected feast of oily rope. Five minutes later, their bonds bitten through, Pott and Kettle stood up and shook hands. They were almost free men. Only the bolted door now kept them prisoner.

'Butt it,' said Kettle. 'Break it open with your head. Your head's solid bone, so it won't hurt you.'

Pott had a skull as thick as a bison's, and he was very proud of it. So he nodded, and bent down, and charged like a bison at the door. Three times he rammed it, and the fourth time it fell open, and the pirates walked out.

Mrs. Matches had by this time left the house, and gone over to the Hen to look for Sam Sturgeon. So the pirates found no one in the kitchen, and ate the supper which Mrs. Matches had cooked for Sam. Then they went out, and in the darkness walked down to Inner Bay, and waded into the sea. They swam for a few yards, and dived—and quickly came up again.

'I'm drowning!' cried Kettle, and seized Pott round the neck.

'So am I,' growled Pott. 'Let go!'

They sank again, and came up struggling, and in great alarm headed for the beach. They were glad to reach shore, but when they stood ankle-deep at the edge of the sea they stopped and looked at each other in perplexity, and Kettle asked, 'What can we do now?'

'Nothing,' said Pott.

'We're sunk,' said Kettle.

'We should be,' said Pott, 'if we went in again.'

They had realised that they would not be able to swim so well without their frog-like slippers—which Gunner Boles had taken to makes shoes for Timothy and Hew—but what they had not known was that most of the oil on their skin, the ambergris oil that contained sixty-nine ingredients, had dried up while they were ashore, and was no longer any use. They had felt the coldness of the sea, but that was not very serious. What really mattered was that now they could not breathe under water; and when they dived, they had had to come up again very quickly or they would have drowned.

'If we can't go to sea, we can't escape,' said Kettle.

'That's so,' said Pott.

'Well, what can we do?' asked Kettle again.

'Hide,' said Pott.

Then Kettle had a good idea, and walking back to Popinsay House they went quietly in with the intention of stealing some clothes. For it had occurred to Kettle that if they were dressed in the ordinary way they could walk about like other people, and no one would pay any attention to them.

They found the door of Mrs. Matches' room standing open, and going from room to room they soon discovered that the house was empty but for themselves. They had no need to hurry, and they could look for the clothes they wanted without being disturbed. But there was not much to choose from, for Captain Spens's suits, of which they found several in a large wardrobe, were far too small for them, and Sam Sturgeon only had the clothes he wore on week-days and a best suit for Sundays. His week-day clothes were in the *Endeavour*, for he had changed into his bathing-drawers aboard the boat; and when Kettle found his Sunday suit, he claimed it for himself. So Pott was left with nothing to wear.

'Unless,' said Kettle, 'you wear a dress. There's plenty of dresses in the woman's room, and you might look very nice if you choose a smart one.'

'Liar,' said Pott, and sat glumly on Sam's bed.

Kettle found a shirt and a tie, and dressed himself in Sam's blue serge suit. He looked even more villainous than before, and he still had to go barefoot because there were no shoes in the house big enough to fit him. But he stood in front of a looking-glass, smiling hideously, and felt very pleased with himself.

'I'm all right now,' he said to Pott, 'but if you're seen in daylight, looking like that, they'll set about you with sticks and stones as if you were a rat.'

Pott sat on Sam's bed, thinking. Then, without saying a word, he went into Mrs. Matches' room and looked for some clothes. He found a tartan skirt, a blue woollen jersey, and a very old bonnet that Mrs. Matches kept in a cardboard box because it had belonged to her mother. But Mrs. Matches was a thin woman, though tall, and her skirt would not meet round Pott's waist; so he had to keep it up with an old cricket-belt that Kettle found in Sam's room. The blue woollen jersey had been knitted by Mrs. Matches herself, and it stretched. But it did not stretch enough, and when it split over one shoulder, Pott decided to wear a grey shawl as well. He had no difficulty with the old-fashioned bonnet, which had long black ribbons that he tied under his ear.

Even Kettle, who had not seen a woman for a hundred and fifty years, could not say that Pott looked really attractive. The bonnet hardly suited him, and though they could think of no way in which to improve it, his costume did not seem to be quite complete. The effect was spoiled, perhaps, by his bare feet; which were very large and red.

They both felt satisfied, however, that they had properly disguised themselves, and that no one could now recognise them as pirates. So they went out to explore the island and find, if they could, a deserted lonely cottage in which to live.

It was by now three o'clock in the morning; and sixty miles to the eastward Timothy and Hew and Aaron Spens had just set out from North Rona. On the Hen of Popinsay Mrs. Matches was walking about, looking for Sam Sturgeon; and Sam and Gunner Boles were prisoners in the wreck. The morning was cold and desolate, but not dark; for in the latitude of Popinsay there is very little darkness in June. Pott and Kettle walked quickly, and when they came to a small house, stopped to look at it. But when two dogs, that were tied in a shed, began to bark loudly, they hurried on again.

They went from house to house, over all the northern and the middle parts of the island, but in every house there was a dog, and whenever they stopped, the dogs smelt them and began to bark. They could not find an empty cottage, because there were no empty cottages on Popinsay, and at last, feeling very downhearted, they walked back towards Inner Bay. As they were passing a farm near Popinsay House, a boy came out and saw them. He had got up early to go and look at some rabbit-snares he had set; but when he saw Pott and Kettle he let out a wild, chattering cry of fear and ran home again.

Pott and Kettle were even more alarmed than the boy. They could not think why their appearance had frightened him, and they looked at each other closely and carefully, and walked round each other, to see what was wrong. But nothing at all was wrong with them, so far as they could discover, and they grew very worried indeed. They realised that if everybody screamed at the mere sight of them, and all the dogs barked when they smelt them, they could not go about like ordinary people, as they had planned. They had hoped to avoid attention, but instead of that, it seemed, they were going to attract attention. And that would not suit them at all.

They stood on the beach at Inner Bay, and Kettle said, 'We've got to think hard, and make new plans, and that's going to take some time. We've got to find a good hiding-place, and where are we going to look for it now?'

'There,' said Pott, and pointed to the pier.

The pier, where the *Endeavour* often lay, was built on wooden piles, and at high-water, when there were spring-tides, the sea came in almost to its landward end. The wooden piles were covered with barnacles and seaweed, and weed hung thickly down from the underside of the pier. The pebble-stones beneath

234

it were always slippery and wet, and below the innermost part of the pier it was as dark as a cave. It was by no means a comfortable hiding-place, but it was certainly useful, and Pott and Kettle lay there all day and no one saw them.

In the evening the *Endeavour* came in, and tied up at the end of the pier, and Old Mattoo and James William Cordiall went ashore. Pott and Kettle lay quietly and listened to them talking, and the slow tread of their boots on the planking overhead. When darkness came, said Kettle, they might be able to steal the boat, and escape to sea. But Pott reminded him that they knew nothing about engines, which had not been invented in their time, so Kettle had to give up his idea and try to think of something else.

Between midnight and one o'clock in the morning, when the night was as dark as it would ever be at that time of year, he was still trying to think of a plan when he heard a little noise, as of someone splashing at the edge of the sea. Then a voice, a low muttering voice that said: 'Under the pier! It looks nice and dark in there, let's go under the pier.'

Kettle and Pott, in the darkest part of all, where there was little room between the pebble-stones and the boards above, lay quietly and listened nervously and peered through the shadows. They saw, but dimly as if they were darker shadows, two figures stooping and bending in the outer twilight, and then there was a little noise like a cricket-bat blocking a fast straight ball. One of the figures had knocked his head on the pier—and immediately he let out a great roar: 'Fry my fingers with bacon and tomatoes! Who hit me? Was it you, Inky?'

'It's the Captain!' cried Kettle and Pott together, and in a great hurry to meet him, rose too quickly and knocked their heads on the pier.

'Who's there?' shouted Scumbril. 'Friend or foe? Come out and be recognised—and do you, Inky, stand behind me and guard my back.'

But Inky was waist-deep in the sea again, and would not come ashore until he was quite certain that it was safe to do so. Then he joined the others, and they all sat down beneath the pier to discuss the situation.

Kettle and Pott, who had been very pleased to see their Captain again, listened gloomily to the news of his defeat. But Scumbril and Inky Poops, who had had a hundred narrow escapes before they got ashore, were so pleased with themselves, and so happy to have eluded capture, that they hardly gave a thought to the fate of their men; and were indeed already thinking of ways and means to raise a new force and try their luck in another battle.

'We're safe enough here,' said Scumbril. 'They'll never look for us ashore. Davy Jones hasn't come aland for four hundred years, and has forgot there is dry land. His head looks like a field of cotton by Savannah, but his thoughts are hung with seaweed like this pier.'

'True enough, Dan my dear,' said Inky Poops. 'That's true enough, but don't forget whose plan it was to come ashore. Give credit where credit is due, Dan, for it was me that thought of it. It was my plan, not yours.'

'And forty times I saved you from the enemy to bring you ashore,' replied Scumbril. 'You'd be Davy Jones's captive now— ay! taken forty times over!—had it not been for me.'

'You're very useful in your own rough way, Dan, I've never denied that,' said Inky. 'But I've got the brains, Dan, and brains are more important than brawn, especially now when you've lost all your men, and you're all alone in the world.'

'Not yet!' said Scumbril. 'With Pott and Kettle here, I've two good friends that I can count upon. And that's two more than you can find!'

'If they were friends of mine,' said Inky, 'I'd ask them what they mean by dressing-up in that curious way.'

'Tell us,' said Scumbril, 'and give us the tale entire. I sent you north to occupy the wreck and clear a cabin for my headquarters. What happened next?'

Pott said never a word while Kettle told the story of their capture by Sam Sturgeon and Cully, their imprisonment in Popinsay House, and their escape from it. The pirate captains were astonished to hear that Timothy and Hew had been aboard the *Endeavour* when Pott and Kettle were hauled out of the deep; and Inky sadly shook his head when he learnt that Hew was not really dumb.

'Oh, what deceit!' he said. 'To think a young boy like that could be so deceitful! It takes away all your faith in human nature, doesn't it, Dan?'

But Scumbril wanted to know more about the boys. 'Who are they?' he demanded.

'They live in the house where we was imprisoned,' said Kettle, 'and so does the cove with the big ears that found us in the wreck: Sturgeon, they call him.'

'Then hang my tripes on a dirty clothes-line,' roared Scumbril, 'if we're safe after all! Your plan's worth nothing, Inky. You've brought me to an island where I'm known! The Dumb Boy, who is not dumb, he knows me well. The other boy has seen me, and so has the man called Sturgeon. And they're in league with Davy Jones, so if I'm found, I'm lost!'

'And so am I, Dan, so am I. We're all in the same boat,' said Inky. 'And talking of boats, the two little boys and the man called

237

Sturgeon may still be safe and snug in the sail-locker where we left them.'

'Build no hopes on that,' said Scumbril. 'Davy Jones or his men will have found them by now, and set them free.'

'Then we must go into hiding for a little while, until the hue and cry dies down. Davy Jones will go south again, to his summer court, and when he's withdrawn his men, we shall escape to sea and look for new friends—and with my silver tongue, Dan, I'll never fail to make friends!'

'But you'll fail to find anywhere to hide,' said Kettle. 'There's no hiding-place, not except this, in all the island.' And he described how he and Pott had looked for an empty cottage, and how the dogs had barked at them, and a boy had been frightened by their appearance. 'There's nowhere to lie-up, and it doesn't do no good to disguise yourself,' he concluded.

'So there's the problem, Inky,' said Scumbril, 'and you're the man with the brain and the silver tongue, so you can wrestle with it and tell us the answer. And tell us quickly, for I'm losing patience with you!'

'All in good time, Dan my dear. There's an answer to everything, if you can find it.'

'Pott and Kettle were looking for a house, and couldn't find one.'

'I wonder if they found a church?' asked Inky.

'There's one down about the middle of the island,' said Kettle.

'And what good will it do us?' asked Scumbril.

'When I was a little boy,' said Inky, 'I had a favourite uncle, who was a smuggler. He used to smuggle brandy and tobacco, and he always tried to bring in his cargoes early on a Monday morning, because where he used to hide them was the parish church. Well, if he got in on a Monday, he had six clear days to dispose of his cargo, and his brandy and tobacco, which would fill the whole pulpit sometimes, was as safe as if he'd locked it up in the Bank of England. Because no one—at least no true-born Englishman—would ever dream of going to church on Monday, Tuesday, Wednesday, Thursday, Friday, or Saturday: now would he?'

'True, true,' said Scumbril. 'We're famous for propriety, we Englishmen.'

'Well then' said Inky, 'if brandy can lie safe and undisturbed in the pulpit of a parish church, so can we.'

'Boil my brisket and serve it up with dumplings and spring carrots,' roared Scumbril in high delight, 'if you're not the greatest genius that ever lived in salt water! I take back all the abuse I've given you. You're a better man than I am, Inky Poops! Your tongue is silver, and your brain's pure gold! To sleep in the pulpit—oh, it's the prettiest plan I ever heard!'

'I've always been good at making plans,' said Inky, smiling complacently, 'and I flatter myself that this is one of the best of them. We've got somewhere now where we can sleep all day in perfect safety, and at night we can go out and look for our vittles.—You can always rob a hen-roost in the country: that's why so many people live in the country.—But before taking up our new quarters, we've got to make sure of one thing first. We've got to find out what day of the week it is, so as to be sure it isn't Sunday to-morrow.'

'To-day, you mean,' said Scumbril. 'It's after midnight now.'

'Quite right, Dan, you're quite right. Well, what day is it to-day?'

There was silence for a long minute, and then Pott, speaking almost for the first time, exclaimed, 'Wednesday.'

'How do you know that?' asked Scumbril.

'Newspaper,' said Pott.

'That's right!' said Kettle. 'I remember seeing it too.—That man Sturgeon,' he explained, 'used to bring us a newspaper every day, and the last time we saw him, this being the early morning, was the day before yesterday. And it was Monday's paper he brought us then, so to-day's Wednesday, and Pott's right.'

'Then we have four days to lie in peace,' said Scumbril, 'and already I feel a kind of yearning for sleep. To sleep in church, as I used to do when I was a little boy! To the pulpit! Come!'

They set out, down the beach and over the fields, and soon found a hen-roost from which they took a dozen new-laid eggs. Then they walked quickly past sleeping houses and drowsy cattle, and did not stop again until they stood by the door of the parish church. The church stood on a little round hillock, and the nearest house was a quarter of a mile away. Inky Poops lifted the great iron latch, and the door opened; but before going in he said to Scumbril, 'I've thought of something else, Dan my dear.'

'Let's hear it,' said Scumbril, 'for you're a man whose thoughts are valuable.'

'True, Dan, very true,' said Inky, 'and what I've thought of now is that you and I would be safer still if we were disguised. Because we'll have to venture out by night, you see, to look for our vittles, and we might happen to meet someone who was going home rather later than usual.'

'Well thought of,' said Scumbril, 'and my good friends Pott and Kettle have provided our disguise already.—Off with those clothes, my lads. Your captain needs them, and you can raid a sleepy house and find some more.'

Pott and Kettle grumbled a little, but Scumbril made them take off their borrowed clothes, and he put on Sam Sturgeon's

240

blue suit—and split the jacket up the back—while Inky dressed himself in Mrs. Matches' tartan skirt, her blue jersey and her grey shawl, and her mother's bonnet.

In a corner of the graveyard there was a little shed where the gravedigger kept his tools, and it was decided that Pott and Kettle should lie there. And having seen that they were comfortable, Dan Scumbril and Inky Poops went to sleep in the pulpit.

Chapter Twenty-Four

'**A** little farther,' said Cully. 'Move it *that* way a little.—No, no, you silly boy, the *other* way!'

Cully lay in the rock-pool under the west cliffs of the Hen, and William Button and Henry String were looking after him. He was a difficult patient, and kept them busy. His eight long arms had been so badly strained by his heroic determination to hold the severed cables together, that he had lost all power in them. The dreadful strain had pulled them out to twice their ordinary length, and they were quite limp and useless. He could not lift them, nor hold on with them, because there was no strength in them. But otherwise he seemed to be in fairly good health, and he had recovered his spirits.

He had thought of a very ingenious way in which to lie comfortably in his pool, and that was to fasten each of his arms to a large stone which would serve as an anchor. He had told William Button and Henry String to find eight suitable stones, and tie them to the tips of his arms, and now he was instructing them where to place the stones so that he could lie exactly in the position he wanted. He was very particular, and every stone had to be moved a dozen times at least before he was satisfied. But he decided at last that he was as comfortable as he could be, and after giving the Powder Monkeys a little good advice about things in general, he fell asleep.

William Button and Henry String sat down and talked about the great battle of the day before. William boasted of having led the rescue party to the wreck in North Bay, and then of seizing Inky Poops by the leg and very nearly taking him prisoner. Henry String, after an interesting ride on the handle-bars of Mrs. Matches' bicycle, had had some difficulty in finding the patrol that lay near the skerries; but later on, he said, they had performed remarkable feats and captured seven pirates. They both agreed that, had it not been for them, the battle would not have been so successful.

Then Cully woke up and complained that the sun was in his eyes. The day, indeed, was very fine and warm, and the sun shone from a clear blue sky. There was no shade near the pool, and William Button offered to move the anchor-stones nearer to the edge of it, so that Cully could sink to the bottom. But that was not what Cully wanted. He wanted to float and he wanted a sunshade.

'That's it!' he exclaimed. 'That's what I need—a sunshade! And if you haven't got such a thing with you, I can tell you where to find one. Go and look for Timothy or Hew. They're both extremely nice boys, and they're sure to have a sunshade in their house.'

The Powder Monkeys had been forbidden to leave the Hen, but rather than argue with Cully, William set off to see if the boys were down at the pier, and met them walking across the sand. Timothy had a basket of new-made scones and a pot of jam for Cully, and while Hew returned to look for a sunshade, he and William Button went on to the pool.

'You never expected to see me like this, did you? ' said Cully in his most mournful voice. 'A poor old worn-out octopus, no good to anyone! Just a bit of wreckage on the sea of life. Ah me, ah me!—But what have you got in that basket, Timothy?'

'Some scones that Mrs. Matches baked.'

'Scones! Oh, I'm very fond of scones!'

'And there's some butter and a pot of jam.'

'What sort of jam?'

'Black currant,' said Timothy.

'Black currant!' cried Cully. 'Why that's absolutely and completely and far-away my favourite jam of all!—Well, what are we waiting for, Timothy? Don't waste time, you foolish boy.'

So Timothy began to spread the scones with butter and black-currant jam, and leaning over the pool placed them one by one in Cully's beak. And while he was so engaged he told Cully how proud of him they were, and said they all owed him more than they could ever repay: 'Sam Sturgeon says that to hold on like that, when you must have thought you were going to be torn apart, was the bravest thing he ever heard of.'

'Duty, duty,' said Cully with his mouth full. 'All I did was done in the way of duty.—Another scone, please.—It was my job to hold on when required, and when the need arose—there wasn't enough jam on that last one—I held on. It wasn't pleasant, and I didn't like it.—Another, please.—It was, as a matter of fact, extremely painful, but when you've been brought up to do your duty—they *are* good scones! And it's so nice to get really fresh butter—well, you just do it. Though I must say that I hope I shan't ever have to do it again.—Well, one more, if you insist.'

'And I've got something else to give you,' said Timothy. 'When we were on our voyage to Davy Jones's court, we met a friend of yours: Miss Dildery.'

'That lovely creature!' exclaimed Cully. 'Tell me how she is!'

'She's very well, I think. She came to see us when we were on our way home again, and sent you her portrait. Here it is.'

Timothy showed him the drawing that Dingy the Cabin Boy had made on a round piece of whalebone, and Cully exclaimed, 'What a delightful picture! And so like her, isn't it? Dear Dildery!'

'She sent a message too,' said Timothy. 'She asked me to give you her love.'

Very sadly Cully shook his beak and said, 'Too late, too late! That lovely young creature could not love a poor old cripple like me. There was a time—but not now. Oh no! No, no, no! Love comes too late. Ah me!'

He looked inexpressibly sad, and on the lower rim of his saucer-like eyes there hovered two large tears. Timothy felt very embarrassed and hardly knew what to say next; but Hew appeared, just at the proper time, with a yellow sunshade that had belonged to their mother, and gave Cully something else to think about.

'What a handsome sunshade!' he cried. 'It's exactly what I had hoped for. Thank you very much for bringing it! And now give it to William Button, please, and he'll hold it over my head.—Hold it higher, William, and move a little to that side. No, the *other* side, you silly boy!—There, that's better. That's very comfortable. Now put Miss Dildery's portrait on that little ledge of rock, Timothy, where I can see it. That's right!'

Cully shone like a great buttercup under the yellow sunshade, and with his eight arms securely anchored, and four boys to attend to him, he looked very comfortable indeed.

'There's something to be said for *not* being able to work,' he admitted. 'For work is a great nuisance, the greatest nuisance in the world, and if you're a cripple no one expects you to work, and you haven't got to dodge it, so to speak. Hold the sunshade a little higher, William.'

But William Button had closed the sunshade and tucked it under his left arm. He and Henry String stood straightly at attention, and faced the sea. Knee-deep in the water stood Davy Jones himself, with Aaron Spens and Gunner Boles close behind him. Timothy and Hew ran to meet them, and Davy Jones came majestically ashore.

'For more than three hundred years,' he said, 'I had never left the green sea and its deep caverns, to walk upon the land, till I set foot, two nights ago, on the little island of North Rona. And now already—so quick is the heart to find new moorings—I feel a kind of love for sun-warmed rock and the soft turf.'

'I hope you'll come ashore often,' said Timothy politely.

'Come and stay with us,' said Hew.

Davy Jones laughed and said, 'Your many-times-great-grandfather has a great longing to visit the house he built, and to please him, and please myself too, I have promised to bear him company and drink a pint of wine with you—or rum if you have not wine, or ale if you have not rum. But we must wait, I said, for your invitation.'

'But of course you're invited,' said Timothy. 'It will be a great honour for us.'

'Come now,' said Hew. 'Come and have lunch.'

Davy Jones laughed again. 'I must not be seen beyond the frontiers of my own kingdom, for we break the rules when we step ashore. But when it's dark a broken rule's not easy to be seen, so you can look for us at night.—Now take me to the octopus, for I have come to thank him for yesterday's good deed.'

'He's lying there in the pool,' said Timothy.

Davy Jones stood facing Cully, with Aaron Spens and Gunner

246

Boles beside him, and the four boys stood behind Cully. The sun was shining brightly, and William Button put up the sunshade again. Cully, who was deeply embarrassed, said nothing, but floated on the water like a great buttercup, and blinked his big eyes.

Davy Jones made a little speech in which he praised Cully's bravery, and on behalf of all the sailors in the sea thanked him for holding the cables together with such heroic determination and disregard of his own safety. Then he took a large silver medal, on a loop of blue ribbon, from his satchel; and kneeling down, hung it over Cully's beak, for there was nowhere else to hang it.

Cully was so overcome by this honour that he could only murmur, 'Too kind! Too kind!'

Davy Jones sat down to talk to him, and the others moved away, except William Button who stayed to hold the sunshade. Gunner Boles was very cheerful, because Cully, though he would always be a cripple, was certainly not going to die; and because the knot was safe again. He and a score of sailors had worked all night, for Davy Jones's supply-column had now arrived, bringing new cables, and these had been spliced into the old ones, instead of the pirates' rope—which no one trusted—and the knot had been tied again in the old way.

It was well guarded, for not all the pirates had yet been captured, and Inky Poops and Dan Scumbril were still at large. But they would be taken before long, thought Gunner Boles, and Aaron Spens described how all the near-by sea was being searched for them. The sailors had entirely surrounded Popinsay, and search-parties were hunting everywhere within the ring they made. They were sure that Scumbril and Inky Poops were somewhere inside the circle, and Davy Jones would not leave Popinsay till he had found them.

'My old ship,' said Aaron Spens, 'is again in service, and has become our prison. There's a full cargo in her hold, and we have made her saloon the guard-room.'

'We've been rather disappointed by your ship,' said Timothy. 'We hoped to find enough treasure in her to repair our house.'

'It needs a lot of repair,' said Hew. 'The windows leak, the doors don't fit, there's dry rot in the floors, and bees in the roof, and the rain comes through it too, and the chimneys smoke, and it hasn't been painted for years, and half the ceiling in our room fell on us last year when we were fast asleep.'

'There'll be a heavy bill to pay, if all that's to be done,' said Aaron Spens. 'But there's enough money in the ship to meet it, unless others have been there before you. How much have you found?'

'Sam Sturgeon brought up eighteen money-boxes, and Father found one on the beach a long time ago,' said Timothy. 'Sam says that he made a thorough search before he was captured, and he doesn't think there are any more. And none of the money-boxes had more than fifteen gold coins in it.'

'And some of the coins were very small,' said Hew.

'And in any case,' said Timothy, 'the money isn't ours any longer.—It's yours, isn't it?'

'The money in the ship,' said Aaron Spens, 'belonged to me and to my crew. We had earned a little by hard work, and more by hard fighting. We had, moreover, all the same intention: to spend our money in Popinsay, to build and beautify our houses, plant gardens, fence fields, buy sheep and cattle, and give presents to our wives and children. That was our purpose, and that is how the money should be used. And perhaps there is more in the ship than Sam Sturgeon found.'

Now Davy Jones came to them and said it was time to go back to sea; but he and Aaron Spens would visit them at night.

'And Gunner Boles too,' said Timothy. 'Sam Sturgeon would be very disappointed if Gunner Boles didn't come, and so should we.'

'Gunner Boles will be our guide,' said Davy Jones, and having told the two Powder Monkeys to take good care of Cully, he stalked majestically into the sea, and quickly disappeared.

'Until to-night,' said Aaron Spens, and followed him.

'Give my regards to Sam,' said Gunner Boles, and he went in too.

Then Timothy and Hew said good-bye to William Button and Henry String, and promised to bring some more scones to Cully, and went home.

Mrs. Matches was unusually quiet and subdued, for Sam had been talking to her very seriously, and she knew now that Timothy and Hew had been taking part in affairs of great importance. Previously, of course, she had supposed that they were only getting into mischief, and what had upset her most of all was that she could not imagine what sort of mischief it was. But now, having learnt that they had been helping to defeat a great plot against the government of the sea, she did not want to know any more about it; because keeping house for Captain Spens gave her quite enough worry, and she did not want to worry about plots as well. So she asked the boys no difficult questions, but only such simple things as whether they had had enough to eat, and if they had got their feet wet. They answered 'Yes,' and Mrs. Matches said they ought to be thankful to be safe at home again.

After supper Sam told her, very politely but quite firmly, that he hoped she would go to bed early and sleep soundly; and if she heard any strange noises during the night, she wasn't to be alarmed, he said, and on no account was she to get up to see what was the matter. Mrs. Matches, being determined to have nothing to do with plots, said she knew how to mind her own business and didn't need Sam to tell her; and went to bed at half-past nine.

'That means we shan't be disturbed when Davy Jones is here,' said Sam, and busily began to mix an enormous bowl of rum-punch.

They had to wait until after midnight, however, before Davy Jones and his companions arrived, and Sam and the boys were all asleep—Timothy and Hew on the sofa and Sam in the big chair in their father's study—when Gunner Boles tapped on the window. *Tap, tap*, they heard in their dreams, and half-woke up. *Tap, tap*, again; and then a hoarse whisper, 'Ahoy, there, Sam! Show a leg, will you? The Admiral's coming aboard!'

'They're here!' cried Timothy, and ran to the door while Hew straightened the cushions and Sam put a kettle on the fire, and drew the curtains close.

The mighty figure of Davy Jones stood in the hall, and though he had looked great and majestic in the ocean and on the seashore, he now seemed larger and more kingly than ever. Aaron Spens stood at his side, and Gunner Boles came in behind them and softly shut the front door, which had been left open for their arrival. Timothy bowed politely.

'Not for three and a half centuries,' said Davy Jones, 'have I entered a house built upon dry land—but I was born in a house, and I feel as if I were coming home!'

'I wish you were,' said Timothy. 'It would be very nice if you

250

decided to live in Popinsay.'

'That's prettily said!' exclaimed Aaron Spens. 'It makes me very happy to see such good manners in my great-great-grandchild!'

'It wasn't good manners,' said Timothy. 'I was speaking the truth.'

'And that, Aaron, should make you happier still,' said Davy Jones; and seeing that Sam was holding the door of the study open, went in. Hew, who was standing in front of the fire, bowed as politely as Timothy had done, and said, 'Won't you sit down, sir?'

But Davy Jones wanted to look at the painting of a ship-of-the-line that hung over the chimney-piece; and then at photographs of cruisers and destroyers; and at Captain Spens's books, some of which were very old; and at the globe of the world, which stood in a corner of the study; and at two old-fashioned swords which lay on a table; and at the Captain's medals in a glass-case; and at the model of a frigate carved in bone by a French prisoner in Napoleon's time; and then at the bowl of rum-punch which Sam Sturgeon was mixing. For it was so long since he had been in a house that everything he saw was full of interest.

To Aaron Spens, of course, the whole house was interesting, because he had built it; and presently he asked Timothy to let him see over it. So Timothy took a lamp from a table in the hall, and led his great-great-very-great-grandfather from room to room; and Aaron Spens said that he remembered them all, and agreed with Timothy that they would all be the better of being plastered and painted and papered. Then they came to Mrs. Spens's room, which had not been used for a long time, because Mrs. Spens had been away from home for several years; and

Aaron Spens said that he would like to be left alone there for a little while, because it had been his own wife's room when the house was newly built and he had lived in Popinsay for a few years between his voyages to the South Sea.

Timothy waited for him, and after about five minutes Aaron Spens came out looking very sad; and he wanted to see no more of the house. So they went back to the study, and Aaron Spens had a glass of rum-punch and grew quite cheerful again. But Gunner Boles was saying that he had enjoyed himself far more on his previous visit when, because it was his birthday, he had been invited to lie in the softest, handsomest, and most commodious bed he had ever seen. A big four-poster bed, he explained, and the pillows were stuffed with little clouds, and the sheets were as smooth as the Indian Ocean, and the mattress as soft as cream and as firm as jelly. Now when Davy Jones heard about the Captain's bed, nothing would satisfy him but to spend the rest of the night in the comfort that Gunner Boles had enjoyed— and to cap it all, said the Gunner, he had worn a suit of pyjamas the colour of an oriental sunset.

'I'll wear them too!' cried Davy Jones. 'It's three and a half centuries since I slept in a mortal bed, and never yet have I slept in the colours of a sunset. What riches they enjoy who live ashore!'

'It was my father's bed,' said Aaron Spens. 'He had it built of Spanish mahogany that he took from a ship wrecked on the skerries off Fishing Hope.'

'Then you have the better right to it,' said Davy Jones. 'You will go first to bed, and I shall humbly follow.'

Then Sam took the lamp from the study, and Gunner Boles carried the punch-bowl, and they all went upstairs to Captain Spens's bedroom. Sam found the Captain's red silk pyjamas, which Davy Jones put on over his bathing-suit, and another pair of sea-green silk for Aaron Spens. They lay back against the pillows with a look of perfect happiness on their faces, and Gunner Boles refilled their glasses. Timothy and Hew sat cross-legged at the foot of the bed, and Sam closed the window; for the wind was rising and the rain was coming in. The wind, indeed, was blowing half a gale and getting worse. It howled in the chimney and the rain beat upon the window-panes, but no one paid much attention for everyone was listening to Davy Jones, who was telling the story of his last voyage with Drake. Then Aaron Spens told them a tale of the Prince of Bantam and the great island of Java, and when he had finished Gunner Boles began to talk about the battle of Trafalgar. Sam Sturgeon said that he knew some good stories too, but the best he had ever heard was what the Shell had told him when Gunner Boles was preparing him for service under the sea.

'I wish I could listen to the Shell again,' said Timothy.

'So do I,' said Hew. 'Have you got it with you?'

Gunner Boles looked inquiringly at Davy Jones, who nodded and said, 'Let them hear it and remember if they can.'

Gunner Boles took the Shell from his satchel and gave it to Timothy, who held it close to his ear. For a little while no one spoke, and while Timothy listened to the story of the sea the others listened to the wild song of the wind as it beat upon the roof. Then Gunner Boles, sitting comfortably in an armchair, gave a little jump and looked up at the ceiling. A drop of water had fallen on his bald head, and another drop was about to follow. It fell before he could avoid it, and Sam got up to give him an umbrella that stood in a corner of the room.

'On a bad day,' he said, 'when it's raining hard, I've always got to hold it over the Captain while he's dressing himself.'

'Our house,' said Hew, 'does need repairing, doesn't it? And we didn't find nearly enough treasure in the wreck to do everything that should be done.'

'How much did you recover?' asked Aaron Spens.

'Eighteen skulls in all,' said Sam, 'and the most that any of them held was fifteen gold coins, some of them small.'

'You would have done better if you had looked in the proper place,' said Aaron Spens; and then asked Gunner Boles, 'Where did you leave them?'

'Downstairs,' said the Gunner. 'Shall I bring 'em up?'

'If you please,' said Aaron Spens; and explained that he himself had visited the wreck after hearing of their ill-success, and found what Sam had failed to find. Gunner Boles came back with a canvas bag out of which he took three skulls, as green in colour as the others, but much heavier. He gave one of them to Sam and one to Hew, and the third to Timothy, who had laid the Shell on the bed.

'Now lift the tops,' said Aaron Spens, 'and look inside.'

The top of each skull had been neatly cut—as if it were the top of an egg—and cleverly fitted again with a small hinge at the back, so that it could be lifted like a lid; and inside lay a little parcel wrapped in thin lead.

'Lead is soft,' said Aaron Spens. 'If you have a knife you can cut it.'

Sam Sturgeon took out his pocket-knife, and slitting the three lead parcels, poured on to the quilt three little streams of marvellously coloured jewels that winked and sparkled in the lamplight. There were diamonds and sapphires and rubies and emeralds, white and green and blue and crimson, and they lay on the Captain's bed in a glittering pool while the rain made another

254

pool on the faded carpet beside it.

'Is that enough to repair your house?' asked Aaron Spens.

'There's enough to build a palace,' said Timothy.

'Hardly, hardly,' said Aaron Spens. 'It would be a very small palace, I fear, and not all that's there belongs to your father. Each of my crew kept his own money-box, some of which you have found, and I kept for them as well a certain share in the profits of the voyage. Now there upon the bed are all the profits, and here in your island there must be descendants of my crew. Before I go I shall tell Sam Sturgeon the names of those who sailed with me, and the shares they were entitled to. Then when your father returns he can divide that little treasure as I should have divided it, had I, more than two hundred years ago, come safely home— and his own share, I think, will be more than enough to mend his roof and paint his walls.'

Timothy and Hew were admiring the jewels and letting them trickle through their fingers. But Sam spoke sharply, after watching them for a little while, and said, 'Now take care what you're doing, or before you know what's happened you'll have lost half of them. You give them to me and I'll put them in a safe place till the Captain comes back.'

He took from a drawer the round leather box in which the Captain kept his collars, and gathering up the diamonds and the rubies, the emeralds and the sapphires, dropped them in and put the box in its proper place between the Captain's neckties and a pile of handkerchiefs. Then he set the three skulls on the chimney-piece, and tidily dropped the lead wrappings into a waste-paper basket.

'Thank you very much indeed, sir,' he said to Aaron Spens. 'The Captain will be most grateful, I'm sure, and I only wish he was here himself to say so.'

Gunner Boles stirred the rum-punch, and having filled every-one's glass again said in a husky voice, 'About this time o' night, being in good company among cheerful friends and with a glass in my hand, I've always felt much inclined to raise my voice in song. It would be an honour, sir'—he bowed to Davy Jones— 'and a pleasure too, if you would give us a lead, and we'll bring in the chorus.'

'I know two hundred songs,' said Davy Jones. 'Which one do you want?'

'It comes into my mind, sir, seeing how snug you are, that you couldn't do better than to start off with *The Big Four-Poster Bed.*'

'As you will,' said Davy Jones, and having cleared his throat with a noise like a clap of thunder, began to sing in a voice like the rolling sea:

> 'To Cadiz in a galleon,
>   To Yarmouth in a smack,
> To Galway Bay with a load of hay
>   And donkeys coming back—
> I've sailed the Arctic ocean
>   Where the sun is white as lead,
> But the finest ship for a midnight trip
>   Is a Big Four-poster Bed!'

Aaron Spens sang the next verse:

> 'In a sloop to St. Helena,
>   To Java by canoe,
> I've fished for skate in the Denmark Strait
>   To sell in Timbuctoo;
> I've sailed from the Roaring Forties

By the Cape to Beachy Head,
But the finest ship for a midnight trip
Is a Big Four-poster Bed!'

Then it was Gunner Boles's turn:

'To Ushant in a frigate,
    Bermuda in a brig,
At Trinidad when quite a lad
    I didn't care a fig!
I've loaded a Maltese bumboat
    With butter and eggs and bread,
But the finest ship for a midnight trip
    Is a Big Four-poster Bed!'

Sam Sturgeon stood up and shut his eyes, for that was always
the way he sang:

'To Rio in a cruiser,
    Manila in a junk,
I caught a seal at gay Deauville
    And kept it in my bunk.
The sea's bright blue at Chios,
    At Mocha it is Red,
And the very best ship for a midnight trip
    Is a Big Four-poster Bed!'

Then, all together, as loud as a gale of wind, they sang the chorus:

'Oh, haul your night-shirt down, sir!
    The sheet is trimly spread,

The King's took off his crown, sir,
  And he's called the Queen to bed—
Hear 'em snore!
    Hear 'em snore!
Hear 'em snoring like the roaring
  Of the waves upon the shore!'

'Thank you kindly, sir,' said Gunner Boles, bowing again to Davy Jones. 'You're in very good voice, if I may say so. And what shall we have next?'

'Before we have anything next,' said Sam, 'I'm going to take the boys to bed. They're dropping off to sleep already.'

'We're not!' said Timothy.

'We're wide awake!' said Hew.

'You won't be so wide awake at breakfast-time,' said Sam, 'and that's what I'm thinking of. So just you say good-night to the Admiral and your great-granddad, and come along with me and let's have no argument about it.'

Davy Jones, in his most solemn voice, assured them that when he was their age he had never been allowed to stay up late, and Timothy and Hew, after saying good-night all round, went off unwillingly to their own room. They were very tired, and in the morning, when Mrs. Matches came in to wake them, they still felt tired; for they had been dreaming of gales and storms and hurricanes.

Mrs. Matches herself looked tired, for she had slept badly too. Davy Jones and his companions had sung a lot of songs, and they believed in singing loudly.

Chapter Twenty-Five

Captain Spens and Mrs. Spens were flying home from South Africa. They were sitting side by side in the aeroplane, for in spite of all his doubts and fears he had found it very easy to persuade her to come back with him; it had been quite unnecessary to say anything about the sack that he had brought in case she was obstinate. The truth of it was that Mrs. Spens had been thinking so much about hats that she had almost forgotten how very fond of her husband she really was; but when she saw him again, it all came back to her. She realised, too, that he must be very fond of her, or he would not have gone to so much trouble and expense to bring her home; and that pleased her so much that she agreed almost at once to return to Popinsay. But neither of them was enjoying the journey, because flying made Mrs. Spens feel sick, and the Captain had caught a cold.

They arrived in London, and spent a day there. Mrs. Spens went shopping, and the Captain, whose cold was rather worse, began to feel seriously ill; for everything in the shops was very expensive indeed. On the following day they went aboard another aeroplane to fly to the north of Scotland, and landed on an airfield between a little town and an angry sea that broke against tall grey cliffs. From there they drove to a near-by harbour and went aboard the small steamer that crossed every day to Popinsay. The steamer looked even smaller than usual, for the sea was extremely rough: it was the day on which Timothy and Hew and Mrs. Matches all felt tired when they woke up, and though the gale that had been blowing the night before was wearing off, the sea was still running high and the waves were grey-bearded like old bad-tempered giants.

Mrs. Spens, who felt sick even before she went aboard, lay down at once in the only cabin and said she was going to be very ill indeed; but Captain Spens walked about the deck and said that a good fresh gale was exactly what he needed to cure his cold. They had a very rough crossing, and when they reached Fishing Hope, Mrs. Spens had to be helped ashore. Sam and Timothy and Hew were there to meet them with the old shooting-brake, for Captain Spens had sent them a telegram before leaving London. The boys were delighted to see their mother again, and she was very pleased to see them, but asked them not to talk much until the following day; when she hoped she would feel better.

As soon as they reached Popinsay House she went to bed in her room that had originally been Aaron Spens's wife's room. Mrs. Matches had lighted a fire, which was smoking badly, but Mrs. Spens said that a little smoke could not make her more miserable than she was already. So she drank a cup of tea, swallowed two large white pills, and went to sleep.

Captain Spens, in the meantime, was listening with great excitement to a story that Sam Sturgeon was telling him. Sam and the boys had been taken completely by surprise when they received the telegram that said he would be home again within a few hours. They had not expected him for several weeks. They had, indeed, been so fully occupied with the war between the pirates and Davy Jones that they had scarcely given him a thought; and now, without warning and with very little time to spare, they had to decide what to tell him. They had recovered the treasure from the wreck, but they had recovered it only with the help of Aaron Spens; and they could not tell him about Aaron Spens without also telling him about Gunner Boles and Cully and Dan Scumbril and Inky Poops and Davy Jones himself. About these people, however, and about all the life that went on under the sea, they had been pledged to secrecy. They could not tell him of the cutting of the knot, nor of the boys' journey to Davy Jones's summer court. They could tell him nothing of all the great and momentous events in which they had been taking part except one thing only: and that was that they had found the treasure. But even to tell him that they could not tell the truth. They were sadly worried by the problem, and it seemed more difficult still because the boys were so tired that morning, and Sam himself, who had sat up very late with Davy Jones and Aaron Spens and Gunner Boles, was not feeling very well. After a great deal of discussion, however, they decided to pretend that Sam had found the wreck all by himself, after a long search for it, and diving steadily, day after day, had recovered eighteen skulls that held gold coins and three more valuable skulls that were packed full of jewels. They would say nothing about the help they had received, nothing at all about Cully and Davy Jones and the pirates.

This, then, was the story that Sam was telling, and Timothy and Hew sat beside him in the study and watched their father closely to see if he would be satisfied by it. They had warned Mrs. Matches and Old Mattoo and James William Cordiall to keep quiet about all the strange sights they had seen, and they hoped that their father would be so pleased by the recovery of the treasure that he would not bother to ask many questions. Captain Spens, however, wanted to know everything that had happened, and every detail of the search. Sam Sturgeon had to invent the details and tell a great many lies, but he was very good at making up stories, and he had no trouble at all until the Captain exclaimed, 'But where are the jewels?'

He had examined the eighteen skulls which had been used as money-boxes with great interest and pleasure, and congratulated Sam on his good work. Now, quite naturally, he wanted to see the diamonds and the rubies—and Sam, for the moment, could not remember where he had put them.

'In the collar-box,' said Timothy.

'Why, of course,' said Sam. 'That's where they are, sir. I put them in your collar-box.'

'What for?' asked the Captain.

'Well, sir,' said Sam, 'I wanted to put them somewhere safe, and it seemed to me that your collar-box was the very place; because there's nobody here except yourself that's going to bother about looking for a clean collar, now is there?'

'You may be right,' said the Captain. 'Well, go and get them, will you?'

Then Sam went upstairs and brought down the collar-box, and tipped out the jewels on the Captain's desk. The Captain felt them and weighed them and counted them, and divided the diamonds from the rubies, and the sapphires from the emeralds, and sat looking at them in great wonder and delight. But then he sneezed so violently that he blew half a dozen emeralds on to the floor, and sneezed again and again, and scattered rubies and diamonds all over the carpet.

Sam and the boys went down on their hands and knees to

gather them up again, and the Captain, wiping his eyes, declared that his cold was getting worse and he must go to bed.

'My room's ready for me, I suppose?' he asked.

'Yes, sir,' said Sam, and Timothy and Hew looked at him rather doubtfully. They remembered that Davy Jones and Aaron Spens had spent the night in their father's bed, and they wondered if Sam had removed all the traces of their party. Sam, however, appeared to be quite confident, and when the jewels had been found and put back in the collar-box, the Captain took it and walked to the door, where he stood for a moment and sneezed again.

'Bring me some hot toddy in half an hour's time,' he said, 'and tell Mrs. Matches that I only want a very light supper. Then I'll have another glass of toddy, and that will cure this confounded cold of mine. To-morrow's Sunday, isn't it? Your mother will be better too, I hope, and we'll all go to church together; the whole family together for the first time in many years.'

'Good night, Father,' said Timothy and Hew, and the Captain went upstairs.

'Did you tidy his room properly?' asked Timothy as soon as he had gone.

'It's all right,' said Sam. 'We put everything shipshape and in good order before we left. We pulled the sheets up, smoothed the pillows, straightened the quilt, took away the glasses, and left the room looking as neat as a row of new pins. Don't you worry yourselves about that.'

He went out to make the Captain's toddy, and Timothy told Hew, and Hew told Timothy, that their story had gone very well. Their father, they thought, would probably not bother to ask many more questions, and that was very satisfactory; though it was disappointing, of course, that they could not tell him about their adventures under the sea. They sat for a little while thinking of Cully and the battle with the pirates, and then they were startled by an old familiar noise—a noise they had not heard for some time. Their father was shouting.

'Sam!' he roared. 'Sam Sturgeon, you villain, you miscreant! Come here at once. Come here, I say!'

They heard Sam running, and following him upstairs saw their father standing at his bedroom door. He had undressed, he was ready for bed—he had taken out his glass eye, he had taken off his artificial foot and his artificial hand—he was wearing his red silk pyjamas, and he was in such a flaming temper that anyone who did not know him would have thought that he and his pyjamas were all on fire and burning together.

'Come in here!' he shouted. 'Come in here and tell me what's the meaning of this!'

They followed him into the room, and saw that he had pulled down the bed-clothes and discovered in his bed something which they would have great difficulty in explaining. On the under-sheet there lay a long piece of seaweed, now almost dry, and one of the frog-like shoes which were worn by the sailors under the sea.

'What sort of a mess is that?' demanded the Captain. 'I go away from home on most urgent business, and when I come back I find my bed looking like Brighton beach at the last of the ebb, littered with seaweed and old boots. What is that fantastic object, and how did it get here?'

'Well, sir,' said Sam, scratching his head and looking very unhappy, 'I never did expect to see that there. I give you my word, sir, it's almost as big a surprise to me as it is to you. We've had some difficult times here, with very heavy weather while you were away——'

'Heavy weather, my wooden foot!' roared the Captain. 'Do you tell me the tide came in through the upper windows of Popinsay House and covered my bed with seaweed? Is that your story, you dog, you renegade, you scorpion?'

'No, sir,' said Sam, 'that's not what I was trying to say. I was just trying to explain that there's some things which can't be explained, and perhaps didn't ought to be, and when a gentleman comes home from abroad and finds his collar-box stuffed full of rubies and diamonds, perhaps he ought to be satisfied with that and not ask questions which only embarrass those who are called on to answer them.'

'So that's your point of view, is it?' asked the Captain. 'You refuse to answer me, do you? And you know what that means, don't you? That means mutiny!'

'I think Sam is perfectly right,' said Timothy.

'So do I,' said Hew.

'Shut the door,' said the Captain. 'Shut it quietly so as not to wake your mother. Now stand over there, all three of you. This is mutiny beyond a doubt of it, and as such requires serious consideration, careful treatment, and in all probability very heavy punishment.—Be quiet, Timothy! If you have anything to say, I shall listen to you at the proper time. But say nothing until I give you permission.'

On the opposite side of the room to that where the three mutineers were standing there was a small writing-table, and the Captain, hopping towards it, pulled a chair into a convenient position and sat down beside it. On the table were a blotting-pad, a silver inkpot, a pen-tray, and a visitors' book bound in red leather. The visitors' book had not been much used for several years, but the Captain valued it highly because he had had it ever since he first commanded a ship, and many distinguished people and nearly all his friends had at one time or another written their names in it. Now he saw that someone had recently been handling it, and handling it carelessly; for a pen from the pen-tray had been left between its leaves.

'Who's been tampering with my visitors' book?' he demanded, and opening it where the pen stuck out as a marker, shouted, 'What's the meaning of this?'

Nervously the three mutineers approached him, and looking over his shoulder saw written on a clean page of the book three names, one below the other:

Davy Jones
Aaron Spens
Gunner Boles

'Who wrote that?' demanded the Captain. 'Who are the scoundrels who've been scribbling in my book?'

'Well, that's torn it!' said Sam. 'Torn it from luff to leech!'

'We'll have to tell him now,' said Timothy.

'Tell me what?' cried the Captain.

'Everything,' said Hew.

'Then you were lying to me before, were you? Lying as well as mutineering?'

'Not exactly, sir,' said Sam. 'It was a difficult situation we were in, and it's going to be difficult to explain it. I think you ought to have your toddy before I start to tell you about it.'

The Captain was about to refuse indignantly, when he began to sneeze again. So he changed his mind, and told Sam to make it hot and strong and waste no time about it.

Sam hurried downstairs and the Captain, having thrown the frog-shoe and the seaweed out of his bed, climbed in and sat up against the pillows, and pulled the quilt over his knees.

'Give me my collar-box and the visitors' book,' he said, and sat there now looking at the jewels and now at the strange signatures in his book until Sam returned.

The jewels were real and that was very gratifying indeed, but the only possible explanation of the signatures—or so it seemed to the Captain—was that someone had written them for a joke. But who was that someone? Davy Jones's name was written in the narrow, pointed, ornamental way of the Elizabethans. Aaron Spens's signature was in the clear neat style of a much later date; and whoever had signed *Gunner Boles* had been able to copy the bold but laborious writing of a man who had taught himself to use a pen but had never had much time to practise it. It was quite clear that neither Timothy nor Hew nor Sam Sturgeon had written these mysterious names—and who else had been in Popinsay House while he was away? Restless and impatient because he was quite unable to answer his own questions, the Captain shifted from one part of the bed to another, tried this position and that to see which was the more comfortable, and suddenly exclaimed, 'Now what's this?'—Again he pulled down the bedclothes, and near the foot of the bed discovered a large pink shell.

'My bed's like the bottom of the sea!' he shouted. 'I'll find a foul anchor and a dead skate next. What's been going on here? Who brought that shell in? What sort of a game have you been playing while I was away?'

He was about to throw the Shell into the fire-place when Timothy cried, 'Don't do that! Oh, please take care of it! It's very valuable.'

'A common shell!' exclaimed the Captain. 'What value's in a shell?'

'Listen to it,' said Hew.

The Captain, sitting cross-legged with all the bed-clothes in disarray, the collar-box on one side and the visitors' book on the other, put the Shell to his ear, and the expression on his face slowly changed from anger and impatience to bewilderment and wonder. Sam came in with a glass of toddy on a little silver tray, and the Captain, because he had only one hand, said to Timothy, 'Come and sit beside me and hold the Shell.' Then he took the glass of toddy and slowly drank it, sip by sip, while Timothy held the Shell to his ear. Nobody spoke for quite a long time, and when his glass was empty the Captain took the Shell from Timothy and looked at it very curiously.

'I think,' he said, and now he spoke quietly and gently, 'you should tell me the whole story from the beginning.'

It took them a long time to tell him everything—there was so much to tell—but the Captain heard them very patiently, and because he had already listened to the Shell he understood without asking questions all those parts of the story which would otherwise have been hard to explain. They took it in turns to tell their tale, and when they had reached the end of it and Sam was describing the visit of Davy Jones and Aaron Spens, and how happy they had been in his bed, Mrs. Matches came in with the Captain's supper on a tray.

'Does she know?' he asked.

'I don't know anything that doesn't concern me,' she answered snappily, 'and what's more, I don't want to.'

'You're very wise,' said the Captain, and Sam put on his artificial hand for him so that he could eat his supper more conveniently.

'You can leave me now,' he said. 'You've given me a lot to think about and I want to think about it in peace. See that the boys go to bed in good time,' he told Sam, 'because to-morrow's Sunday and we're going to church.'

'Good night, Father,' they said.

'Good night,' he answered. He spoke in an absent-minded way, and when Timothy looked round the bedroom door, just before closing it, he saw that his father was not eating his supper, but listening to the Shell again.

Chapter Twenty-Six

A t half-past ten on Sunday morning a little procession came out from the front gates of Popinsay House and went down the road towards the parish church, which stood on a small hill nearly two miles away. Leading the procession were Captain Spens and Mrs. Spens, then came Sam Sturgeon and Mrs. Matches, and in the rear walked Timothy and Hew. Mrs. Spens, who was now quite well again, was wearing one of the new hats which she had made in South Africa, and Mrs. Matches was wearing another that Mrs. Spens had given her as a present. Captain Spens and Sam Sturgeon were very embarrassed at having to walk beside them, for the hats, they thought, were quite horrible to look at, and already a pair of terns, three lapwings, and a couple of black-headed gulls were flying above them, swooping and screaming and diving at what they evidently thought were strange and perilous foreign birds.

Before they reached the church there was a whole flock of lapwings and crows and terns and starlings and rooks and black-headed gulls crying angrily above them, darting at the dreadful hats, and now and then plucking a feather from them; but Mrs. Spens and Mrs. Matches paid no attention at all and walked proudly on, feeling very pleased with themselves. Sam Sturgeon, however, was by no means happy, for he felt like a scarecrow and thought the birds were attacking him. He had discovered, when he was about to dress himself, that someone had stolen his Sunday suit, and he was wearing clothes he had borrowed from the farmer who lived beside them. They belonged to the farmer's youngest son who was in the army, and the trousers were a good deal too short for Sam, and the sleeves of the coat did not come within six inches of his wrists. Timothy and Hew had told him that he looked exactly like a scarecrow, and they enjoyed their walk very much because they were hoping all the time that the birds would carry off either Mrs. Matches' hat or their mother's.

When they were half-way to church the bell began to ring, and the Captain looked at his watch and said they were in good time and there was no need to hurry. But the ringing of the bell had a very different effect on Dan Scumbril and Inky Poops, who were sleeping in the pulpit. It woke them up, and they looked at each other in the greatest consternation.

'What does that mean?' asked Scumbril.

'I'm afraid to tell you, Dan, I'm afraid to tell you,' said Inky with his hands over his ears.

'I thought,' said Scumbril, 'that they only rang the bell on Sunday morning.'

'That's right,' said Inky. 'They ring it to tell the people it's time to come to church.'

'But to-day's not Sunday,' said Scumbril. 'This is only Thursday—unless Pott was lying to us!'

'Perhaps he made a mistake,' said Inky. 'Oh dear, oh dear! Perhaps the newspaper he saw was quite an old one!'

'Why didn't you think of that to begin with?'

271

'I don't know, Dan, my dear, I don't know, I'm sure.'

The fact was that although Sam Sturgeon had been kind enough to give Pott and Kettle something to read while they were prisoners in Popinsay House, he had not thought that it mattered very much whether they read the day's newspaper or a paper that was a week or two old. Sometimes they had had one and sometimes the other, and the last one they saw had been three days old. This little accident had completely upset Inky's calculations, and now, instead of lying quiet and undisturbed in the pulpit, as they would have done had it been Thursday, they were to be surprised and surrounded by a congregation consisting of almost everybody who lived in the northern part of Popinsay. When they stood up in the pulpit, and looked through the diamond-shaped panes of the long church windows, they could see people coming towards them from all sides. Here was a man by himself, and there a family group; on the one side a cluster of girls, on the other a batch of children. Here were two ploughmen on their bicycles, there the minister and his wife, and there—in bowler hats and smart blue suits—Old Mattoo and James William Cordiall.

"Well, what are we going to do?' cried Scumbril. 'You brought us here! It was your fine idea that we could lie-up in a pulpit, and hide safely for a whole week, and what's the result? You've landed us in a trap!'

'It's not my fault, Dan; it's all the fault of the newspaper that gave us the wrong day of the week. You can't blame me for a mistake like that!'

'Blame or no blame, what are we going to do? We're in a trap, and how do we get out of it? You're the man with the brains, Inky, and if you don't use them—and use them quickly!—I'll beat them out upon the floor!'

'Give me time, Dan, give me time, and I'll think of something. I've never failed to think of something yet.'

'Time's short and getting shorter,' said Scumbril, and the bell cried, '*Ding-dong, ding-dong!*'

The two pirates crouched in the pulpit and now Scumbril, despite his bravery, was as frightened as Inky Poops. Inky's fingers were trembling and he was nervously licking his lips; but Dan Scumbril was beginning to hiccup. Then, quite suddenly, Inky looked a little happier and exclaimed, 'I've got it, Dan! I've thought of something. Oh, what a brain I've got! You can always depend on me, Dan, always!'

'Tell me,' said Scumbril. 'What is it you've thought of?'

'We're disguised, do you see? And they're good disguises, they couldn't be better! That's a fine suit of clothes you're wearing—if only you'd a pair of boots to complete it—and this dress of mine is just the sort of thing for a woman to put on when she's going to church on a Sunday morning!'

'And how does that help us?'

'Why, it helps us right out of our difficulty, Dan! Here we are, all dressed for church like respectable people, and here we are in church. There's only one mistake we've made, and that's to be in the pulpit where the minister ought to be. But if we go and sit in one of those pews, Dan, and if we choose that nice-looking one in the shadow there at the end of the church, and sit down like ordinary people, then nobody won't pay any attention to us! We'll just be two good, kind members of the congregation, Dan, and if we keep our feet tucked under the seat, there's nobody going to see that we haven't got any boots on. But you'll have to stop hiccuping, Dan, because that's not the way that people behave in church. You've got to sit nice and quiet until you start singing hymns and such-like, and then you've got to sing like thunder.'

Inky Poops had been living for a long time on the bottom of the sea, where he had seen no one but old sailors in their bathing-suits. He really believed that he and Dan Scumbril were well disguised and looked thoroughly respectable. But the truth of the matter was, of course, that in all Popinsay there was only one sight more horrible than Dan Scumbril in Sam Sturgeon's blue suit, and that was Inky Poops in Mrs. Matches' tartan skirt and her old black bonnet. There was no one to tell them this, however, and Inky felt very pleased with himself, and quite confident, as he led Dan Scumbril out of the pulpit and into a pew at the far end of the church. Scumbril, however, was still nervous and hiccuping occasionally.

The church was a small rectangular building, very plainly furnished. The pulpit stood in the middle of one of the long walls, and there were pews on either side of it, and across the aisle that divided the church in two there were more pews at right-angles to the others. The seats were all very narrow and uncomfortable, to prevent people from falling asleep during the sermon, and the wood was varnished. The pew that Inky Poops had chosen was at the end of the church farthest from the door.

For a minute or two they sat there all alone. On a fine day it was the people's custom in Popinsay to wait outside the church, talking and gossiping, until the bell had stopped ringing; and then everybody would go in together. On this particular Sunday no one was in a hurry to go inside, because everyone wanted to look at the curious hats that Mrs. Spens and Mrs. Matches were wearing; and when at last the bell stopped, and Captain Spens led the way in, only a few people noticed Inky Poops and Dan

Scumbril. The others could not take their eyes off Mrs. Spens's South African hats.

It was unfortunate for the pirates that an old man called Nicholas Bunn always sat in the pew which they had chosen; and Nicholas Bunn used to take his dog to church. It was a black-and-white collie, a very well-behaved dog, and usually it lay quietly at Nicholas's feet and disturbed no one. But when Nicholas sat down beside Dan Scumbril and Inky Poops, the dog began to growl immediately. The hair rose fiercely on its neck, it bared its teeth, and though Nicholas cuffed its ears and bade it be quiet, it continued to snarl and growl as though there were a couple of wolves in the pew. Dan Scumbril grew very nervous indeed, and hiccuped rather loudly.

The people in the pews in front stopped looking at Mrs. Spens's new hats, and turned round to see what was going on behind them. The people in the pews on the other side of the aisle leaned forward to get a view, and those on the far side of the pulpit stood up. No one had ever seen anything so strange and hideous as the two pirates—not even Mrs. Spens's hats—and within a minute or two everyone was staring at them in horror and bewilderment. Nicholas Bunn's dog was growling more loudly than ever, and Dan Scumbril was hiccuping like a cock crowing in the morning.

'Take me out of this!' he whispered wildly. 'The strain's too much for me. I can't stand it!'

Inky Poops, though by now he too was frightened, kept his head. 'Come along then, Dan my dear,' he answered, 'and I'll tell them you've taken ill and need fresh air. Keep calm, Dan, and we'll be safe enough.'

They stood up and pushed their way past Nicholas Bunn and into the aisle. Nicholas's dog began to bark, and would have followed them if Nicholas had not caught it by the tail.

'Excuse me,' said Inky to a woman in a pew across the aisle. 'My poor husband's taken ill with the hiccups, and needs fresh air.'

'*Hick! Hick-hick!*' cried Dan, crowing like a cock.

'It's the hiccups,' explained Inky to an elderly man who sat near the pulpit. 'My poor husband gets them terribly bad.'

He turned to repeat his apology on the other side of the aisle, and for a moment stood stock-still, unable to speak. For there, sitting with their parents, were Timothy and Hew, and beside them was Sam Sturgeon.

The boys, until now, had not seen the strangers who were causing so much disturbance, for while everyone else was leaning and craning forward to get a sight of them, and standing in their pews and jumping up and down, Captain Spens had said sternly, 'Sit still and behave yourselves!' He himself paid no attention to what was happening; Mrs. Spens and Mrs. Matches did not want to; and Timothy and Hew and Sam Sturgeon were not allowed to.—But now, right in front of them, stood the strangers who had so upset the quiet of a Sunday morning, and in spite of their curious disguise the boys recognised them at once.

'Inky Poops!' cried Timothy.

'Dan Scumbril!' shouted Hew.

They scrambled out of their pew, Sam Sturgeon with them, and at that moment Nicholas Bunn let go his dog, which rushed down the aisle, barking madly. But the two pirates had taken to their heels as soon as they were recognised, and though Old Mattoo and James William Cordiall, who sat near the door, had tried to stop them, they had both been knocked down and lay sprawling on the floor. The minister, a small fat man, had been about to enter the church as Scumbril and Inky Poops came

276

running out, and he too would have been knocked over if he had not very neatly ducked the punch that Scumbril swung at him. Now he stood at the door and saw his whole congregation hurrying towards him, as though the church was on fire. Leading the charge were Timothy and Hew, and on the aisle in front of him Old Mattoo and James William Cordiall were trying to defend themselves against Nicholas Bunn's black-and-white collie, which had decided to attack them instead of the two strangers.

'We're chasing two pirates,' said Timothy to the minister.

'Pirates!' exclaimed the minister. 'I have no pirates in my congregation!'

'Not now,' said Hew, 'but you had a few minutes ago.'

The minister wanted to argue, but the boys slipped past him, and Sam Sturgeon followed, and when he saw that everyone was of the same mind and determined to give chase to the two strangers who had tried to knock him down, the minister—who was a very reasonable man—turned round and went with them; and in two minutes the church was entirely empty.

But Dan Scumbril and Inky Poops had got a good start, and running to the north they were now three fields away.

Timothy and Hew and Sam Sturgeon were only a hundred yards behind them, but the dog, which should have been most useful, had become wildly excited and was too busy biting members of the congregation to remember the strangers who had first roused its anger. It was the minister who now organised the chase. He was a very reasonable man indeed, and seeing that his congregation were in no mood for a sermon he said to them, 'If those men are pirates they ought to be captured. So let's capture them as quickly as possible, and then come back to church.'

Taking off his black gown and his white collar—which was

too tight for comfort—he led the pursuit, and everyone followed except the very old, and a few who were very fat, and Captain Spens who could not run because he had an artificial leg, and Mrs. Spens and Mrs. Matches who did not want to lose their hats.

Some hurried across the fields, and some mounted their bicycles and raced along the road that led northward over the island, hoping to cut off the pirates' retreat. Inky Poops and Dan Scumbril were running strongly, and for some time they kept their distance ahead of Timothy and Hew and Sam Sturgeon. Scumbril had thrown off his stolen jacket, and Inky Poops had got rid of Mrs. Matches' tartan skirt and her old black bonnet. They had no plan except to keep away from their pursuers, and they ran till they were out of breath and could run no farther. This happened when they were passing the buildings of a farm called Hillocks, and Timothy and Hew and Sam Sturgeon lost sight of them completely. They were nearly out of breath themselves, and they had run a little way past the farm before they realised that the pirates had found a hiding-place.

'Perhaps they've gone into the house,' said Timothy, puffing and blowing.

'Or into the barn, or the stable,' said Hew.

'We've got them now,' said Sam, wiping his forehead. 'But we'd better wait till the others come up, and then we'll surround the whole place and make sure of them.'

All in their Sunday best, red of face and gasping for breath, the congregation came running across the fields, and when the minister arrived Sam told him that the pirates had taken refuge somewhere in the farmstead. The minister, who was always reasonable, agreed that the best plan was to surround the buildings, and the owner of the farm, whose name was Harcus, said there was no one at home and if they saw anyone stirring, or heard anyone making a noise, it must be one of the pirates.

'For we all came to church this morning,' said Mr. Harcus, 'everyone of us—except Benjie the bull.'

No sooner had he spoken than they heard a deep bellow of rage, a splintering crash, and through a broken door in the farm-yard Benjie himself came running out. He was a great rusty-coloured Shorthorn bull, and everyone immediately perceived that he was in an extremely bad temper. He stopped for a moment when he saw the congregation, all in their Sunday best, and pawed the earth with one of his little short, stiff fore-legs. Then he bellowed again, and putting his head down, charged. Scattering in all directions, the congregation fled, and Benjie chased them far and wide.

Inky Poops and Dan Scumbril had been lucky. They had gone into the byre to hide and rest themselves, and found it empty. After a few minutes, looking for another way out, they had opened a rough wooden door and found themselves in the bull-shed. They had been somewhat alarmed, but Benjie had been thoroughly frightened. Charging the outer door of the shed, he had broken through it, and then, by scattering their pursuers, he gave the pirates a new chance to escape.

Beyond Hillocks, to the north, there were two cottages not far away, and a deep ditch ran in their direction. Hurrying from the farm-yard, Inky Poops and Dan Scumbril got into the ditch, and crouching low, ran as fast as they could from the farm. None of the congregation saw them, for the congregation was intent only on escaping from Benjie. In one of the cottages, however, there lived a sharp-eyed elderly woman called Williamina MacAra who did not often go to church, but was always interested in what her neighbours were doing. She had been standing at her

279

kitchen window, watching the strange sight of a hundred people or more running across the fields in their best Sunday clothes; and when she saw two unknown men crouching in the ditch below her cottage she took the shot-gun that she always kept on her kitchen dresser, and loaded it, and went out to meet them.

Suddenly, not twenty yards away, Dan Scumbril rose behind a clump of yellow irises, and Williamina MacAra was so startled by his villainous appearance that, without stopping to ask who he was, she took aim and fired at him. Her aim was very bad, however, and instead of hitting Scumbril she killed a sheep that was tethered in the next field. The sheep belonged to Nicholas Bunn, who lived in the other cottage. Mrs. Bunn, who had stayed at home to cook Nicholas's dinner, was standing at the door. She had caught a glimpse of the pirates when they ran from the byre to the ditch, and when she heard a shot and saw the sheep drop dead, she thought it must be they who had killed it. So she hurried indoors to get her husband's gun, and running out again met Williamina MacAra.

'There they are!' said Williamina, pointing to the pirates who were now a couple of hundred-yards away.

'The murderers!' exclaimed Mrs. Bunn, and fired her gun in their direction. At such a distance she could do no damage, of course, but Scumbril and Inky Poops thought it best to run a little faster. Mrs. Bunn and Williamina MacAra followed as quickly as they could, but neither was young and both were fat, and the pirates were in no great danger of being caught by them. Far away to the west of Hillocks, however, Timothy and Hew and Sam Sturgeon had heard their shots, and looking in the direction from which they came, they saw Scumbril and Inky Poops running heavily across a pale-green field of young oats.

Benjie the bull had chased them till they were tired, and then

280

turned away to chase the minister. The minister, being one of the most reasonable men in Popinsay, had escaped by wading breast-high into a marshy pool, and Benjie had left him to chase Old Mattoo and James William Cordiall. The congregation were scattered over half a mile of country, but Timothy and Hew and Sam Sturgeon shouted loudly, and pointed to the pirates, and the pursuit went forward again in a long ragged line. Old Mattoo had not run away from Benjie, but stood to meet his charge, and hit him on his wet black muzzle with a heavy walking-stick. Benjie had pawed the ground, and bellowed once or twice; and then decided to chase a goat instead.

Dan Scumbril and Inky Poops turned eastward in their flight, for in front of them, beyond Popinsay House, the land rose over moor and rough pasture to the northern cliffs; and they had no liking for running uphill. But they had not gone very far to the east when they saw, coming towards them, Mr. Louttit the schoolmaster and a friend who was staying with him. Mr. Louttit and his friend, instead of going to church, had been walking round the loch to look for the nest of a pair of red-throated divers which had been seen there. They were both tall, sturdy young men, and Inky Poops and Dan Scumbril had no wish to meet them. So they turned to the north again, and now very wearily climbed the rising moor. Far behind came Williamina MacAra and Mrs. Bunn, who occasionally fired a shot after them; for each had filled her apron-pocket with cartridges before setting out.

Timothy and Hew and Sam Sturgeon led the chase, but they were still a quarter of a mile away when Scumbril and Inky Poops reached the cliffs and looked down at the green sea below them. Scumbril's face was as red as a sausage and gleaming with sweat, but Inky was as grey as an old waterproof and the sweat ran down his cheeks like rain off a roof. They looked back and saw Timothy and Hew and Sam Sturgeon running uphill, and behind them were Williamina MacAra and Mrs. Bunn, and to the east were Mr. Louttit the schoolmaster and his friend, and farther away, but coming steadily nearer, a long line of people, a hundred or more, all in their best Sunday clothes. There was no escape for them by land, and below them lay the deep green sea where Davy Jones's sailors might still be keeping watch.

'A plan, a plan!' cried Scumbril. 'A plan of escape, and quickly! Use your brains, Inky, and tell me what to do now. How do we escape from here?'

But Inky shook his head, and gasped for breath, and said, 'I've come to the end of my tether, Dan my dear. I don't know what to do, and that's the truth of it. Unless I make a speech, and tell them what a hard life we've had, and persuade them to give us another chance. I've got a silver tongue, Dan——'

'Boil my bones for mutton-broth if I'll listen to another word of it!' roared Scumbril. 'Your tongue's done me no good, and you no good either, and it's too late to hope for a change of luck now. No, no! It's the ocean again for us, the green sea again, and we must jump for it!'

'But Davy Jones may still be here! The sailors will be looking for us still, and keeping watch under the cliffs!'

'We'll take the risk,' cried Scumbril. 'The sea is broader than the land, we know it better than the land, and we've a wider chance there. So come, then—jump!'

He seized his shivering companion by the hand, and leaping from the cliff, dragged Inky with him. They met the water with a great splash, and disappeared. There was nothing to be seen but a whitish circle of melting foam when Timothy and Hew and Sam Sturgeon reached the edge of the land, and looked down at the sea.

'They've escaped!' said Timothy in bitter disappointment.

'Maybe,' said Sam, 'and maybe not.'

They stood, breathing heavily, and stared anxiously at the calm green water. A few puffins flew nervously to and fro, a fulmar sailed past and looked at them with a cold black eye; they saw nothing else. And then, fifty yards out, the head of an oldish bald man with red side-whiskers rose from the sea, and Gunner Boles lifted his hand in salute and shouted, 'Thank 'ee kindly, boys! Thank 'ee, Sam. We've got 'em safely now. Safe, and tied up all a-tauto!'

Then he disappeared again, just before Mr. Louttit and his friend reached the cliffs.

Four miles away, in the graveyard beside the parish church, Pott and Kettle lay in silent bewilderment and wondered what was going to happen to them. They had heard something of the uproar in church, and the beginning of their leaders' flight, but they had stayed quietly in the shed where the gravedigger kept his tools, and no one had thought of looking for pirates there.

Chapter Twenty-Seven

After breakfast on the following morning Sam Sturgeon and Timothy and Hew went over to the Hen with a basket of new-made scones and butter and raspberry jam for Cully. They found him lying comfortably in his pool with his arms securely anchored to eight large stones, and the yellow parasol propped up behind him, for the morning sun was shining hotly. William Button and Henry String sat opposite him at the edge of the pool, and with very glum looks were reciting the following verses:

'William the Conqueror, 1066,
Then William called Rufus—as red as old bricks—
And the First of the Henrys, but nobody reckoned
He'd ever be followed by Henry the Second;
For the Barons broke out, under Stephen and Maud,
To pillage and plunder, and rob and maraud!
There was fearful disorder till Henry could check it,
Who checked not the murder of Thomas à Becket.
Richard the First went to fight with Saladin,
But his brother King John was rather a cad, in

Whose reign the good Barons all signed Magna Carta
For fear they would suffer the fate of Prince Arthur ...'

'That's not a very good rhyme,' said William Button.
'It's good enough,' said Cully, 'Go on.'

'Henry the Third couldn't make the police
Arrest Simon de Montfort for breach of the peace;
Edward the First was polite to his wife,
But harried the Scots for the whole of his life;
Edward the Second, a very weak fella,
Was tipped off the throne by his queen, Isabella,
Who wanted a change.—It seems that she thought him a
Poor sort of fish, and much preferred Mortimer.—
Then Edward the Third very proudly appeared,
Who fought with the French in a very long beard;
The Black Death did a great deal of harm in his reign,
And his son, the Black Prince, fought some battles in
Spain.
But Richard the Second, he sat on the ground,
And asked his companions, "Why does it go round?
I'm not feeling well, I've a pain in my forehead,
Wat Tyler's a beast, and John of Gaunt's horrid,
There are Welsh in the west, and Scots in the north,
And I've got to make room for Henry the Fourth ..."'"

'Is that true?' asked William Button.
'Nobody, to my knowledge, has ever questioned the fact that
Henry the Fourth succeeded Richard the Second,' said Cully
coldly.
'What William really wants to know,' explained Henry String,

'is whether it's true that Richard asked silly questions and had a headache.'

'According to the poet Shakespeare,' said Cully, 'Richard was a brilliant young man. All brilliant young men suffer deeply and ask questions all the time, to which they never believe the answers. Go on. It's Henry the Fifth next.'

But now Timothy and Hew and Sam Sturgeon came forward, and Timothy, after apologising for their interruption, asked Cully what he was doing. Cully, still speaking very pompously, said he had discovered that the Powder Monkeys' education had been sadly neglected, and he was therefore teaching them a little English history, which every boy ought to know. But William Button and Henry String, who were by no means fond of lessons, said that now they must talk to their visitors, and Cully agreed with them when he saw the basket that Hew was carrying; for he much preferred eating scones and raspberry jam to teaching history. Hew sat down beside him to spread the scones, and William Button told Timothy and Sam that he had a most important message for them.

'It's from the Admiral,' he said. 'He's captured all the pirates now. He's got Scumbril and Inky Poops safe in his hands, and he's going back to his summer court to-night. He told me to tell you that the fleet will be passing west of the Calf of Popinsay about six o'clock, and if you like to come out in *Endeavour* you'll get a chance to see it, and the Admiral too, and you can wave good-bye to him. If you want to come, he said, you ought to take station about three cables west of the Calf, and not later than six.'

'We ought to go back at once,' said Sam, 'and tell the Old Man. He'll come for certain, and he'll want to see that everything's ship-shape and Bristol-fashion aboard *Endeavour* first. It's lucky we had her painted, but the Old Man won't be satisfied till she's as clean and smart as we can make her.'

'Are you and Henry going back with Davy Jones?' asked Timothy.

'No, we're staying to look after him,' said William, pointing to Cully in his pool. 'Gunner Boles is standing by the knot till someone comes to relieve him, and then, if Cully's able to travel, we'll all go south together, I expect.'

'I'm very glad we'll see you again,' said Timothy.

'So am I,' said William. 'You'll come out and have a talk with us now and then, won't you?'

Sam was impatient to return to Inner Bay and prepare for the great occasion of saying good-bye to Davy Jones, and to Cully's annoyance they stayed only a few minutes to talk to him, and then went home. Captain Spens, as Sam had foreseen, was very excited by Davy Jones's invitation, and told Sam to look out his full-dress uniform.

'And when you've done that,' he said, 'get hold of Old Mattoo and James William Cordiall and set them to work on *Endeavour*. They've got to scrub everything that can be scrubbed, and polish everything that'll take a polish. Tell them to wash and shave and put on their new jerseys. We'll need an ensign, because we'll have to dip it as the fleet goes past. There's a big White Ensign somewhere in the attics: we'll use that. But there aren't any flag-halliards are there? Well, you'll have to rig them, and to make sure they work you'd better do it yourself. And you ought to wear uniform, it'll look better. And the boys' hair needs cutting. You can cut hair, can't you? Well, cut their hair immediately after lunch. And now get busy, Sam, for we've no time to waste.'

Sam indeed had plenty to keep him occupied, but

everything was ready by tea-time, and shortly after five o'clock the *Endeavour* left the pier and headed westward. Her paint was gleaming, her brass-work shone in the sun, and Captain Spens, wearing a cocked hat, a frock-coat, his medals and a sword, looked very handsome indeed. Sam Sturgeon, his buttons brightly polished, was in his old blue tunic, now rather tight for him, and red-striped trousers; and Old Mattoo and James William Cordiall wore peaked caps and their new jerseys. Timothy and Hew, with their hair cut very short behind, wore their best grey flannel suits.

The *Endeavour* went out past the Calf and with her engine running very slowly kept a kind of sentry-beat, up and down, at about three cables' distance from the cliffs. They had arrived too early and had to wait a long time. Captain Spens was growing somewhat impatient when at last Sam pointed to the north and exclaimed, 'Here they come!'

A great finback-whale broke the smooth surface of the sea, and straight behind it, in the very centre of its wake, appeared another; and behind that another, and another, till the whole fleet was in sight and moving swiftly towards them. Old Mattoo swung the *Endeavour* broadside-on to the whales, her bow to the north. Sam Sturgeon stood by the flag-halliards, and Captain Spens, Old Mattoo, James William Cordiall, Timothy, and Hew arranged themselves in line on the port side, and faced the west. As the leading whale approached, the Ensign was dipped and Captain Spens stiffly saluted.

In the howdah of the leading whale were Davy Jones, a couple of his Councillors, and a dozen sailors, now also standing at attention. Davy Jones raised his great arm in salute and shouted, 'Well done, *Endeavour!* We shall remember you!'

All his sailors cheered. Whale after whale came surging past, the sea breaking white under their great blunt heads, and the sailors stood tall and sturdy in their howdahs, and cheered the *Endeavour*. Timothy and Hew waved their hands and cried 'Hurrah!' till they were hoarse, and Old Mattoo and James William Cordiall, looking very pleased with themselves, made deep noises in their throats like the bears at the Zoo when visitors throw buns to them. Sam Sturgeon cheered, and Captain Spens, quite forgetting his dignity, took off his cocked hat, waved it wildly in the air, and shouted 'Hurrah!' more loudly than anyone else.

In the middle of the fleet, standing closely together on the basking-sharks of the supply column, were the captured pirates. They were roped one to another, and looked monstrously grim and ill-tempered, but none so fierce and surly as Dan Scumbril and Inky Poops, who were tied back to back on a shark that carried only them and their guards. There was silence while they passed, and then from the rear of the fleet came a great noise of singing. The sailors were singing their marching song, and on the last whale of all stood Aaron Spens, shouting his greetings and love to the boys, and kissing his hands to them, while his sailors chanted in stentorian voices of Nelson and Drake and prize-money and rum.

And then, as soon as he had passed the *Endeavour*, and Sam Sturgeon had hoisted the Ensign again, Aaron Spens sent his whale down in a long steep dive, and looking to the south the boys and their father saw that all the fleet had disappeared, and the whole sea lay empty and shining under the sun.

'Never in my life,' said Captain Spens, 'have I seen a finer sight! Never!' he repeated, and with a great gesture threw his cocked hat into the sea.

'Nor have I,' said Timothy, and snatching Sam Sturgeon's blue cap, threw that into the sea.

289

'Nor have you!' cried Hew to Old Mattoo and James William Cordiall; and whipped off their peaked caps and tossed them overboard.

Then they all shook hands with each other, and Old Mattoo headed the boat for home. But when their excitement had dwindled they began to feel a little sad and dispirited, because Davy Jones and his sailors had gone, and Popinsay, when they landed at Inner Bay, seemed quiet and empty.

'I wish they had stayed here,' said Timothy.

'So do I,' said Hew. And every day, for a fortnight at least, they said the same thing.

But they had plenty to occupy their minds besides thinking of Davy Jones. The weather was fine, and they often went fishing for cod and haddock in the *Endeavour*. More often they fished for trout in the loch, and every morning they swam in Inner Bay. They discovered, to their great disappointment, that they could no longer swim under water for any length of time, because the oil that was made of sixty-nine different ingredients had long since dried on their skins, and was no more use to them. But in the ordinary way of swimming they were twice as strong as they had been, and in the Atlantic swell that broke under the cliffs they could dive like seals. Nearly every day they talked with Cully and the Powder Monkeys, and the days went by with surprising speed.

In the evening Sam Sturgeon used to go and talk to Gunner Boles on the Hen, and one night he came into the boys' room, and woke them up, and said, 'They're leaving to-morrow. Gunner Boles's relief has come, and arrangements have been made for taking Cully down south. I don't quite know what time they're setting out, but you'll have to say good-bye to them in the morning.'

Very unhappily they set out after breakfast, Timothy and Hew and Sam Sturgeon, with a large cake for Cully that Mrs. Matches had baked for the Captain's birthday—which happened to be that very day—and two Zulu assegais, that also belonged to Captain Spens, as presents for William Button and Henry String. They would, thought Timothy and Hew, be very useful for pricking basking-sharks.

They crossed to the Hen, and as they approached the pool where Cully usually lay, they heard him singing; and heard another voice which they could not identify. They stopped to listen, and then, going down on their hands and knees, crawled to a ledge of rock, overgrown with seaweed, from which they could see the pool and Cully's companion, and hear the words of their song. Great was their surprise when they recognised his visitors, who were nine in number.

Opposite him, between William Button and Henry String, sat Miss Dildery, and on the seaward side of the pool were her eight nephews and nieces. They sat in a row, behaving very well, but they did not seem to be enjoying themselves. They looked like octopuses who had been compelled to dress-up for a party when they wanted to go paddling.

Miss Dildery was very busy, in a homely but elegant fashion, for with four of her arms she was embroidering two table-mats in gay colours, and with the other four she was winding two balls of bright silk from skeins that William Button and Henry String held for her, one on either side. And at the same time she was singing a duet with Cully, to which the eight little octopuses, with shrill voices and rather grim expressions, added a chorus. It went as follows:

CULLY

You say that you love me—I'm sure that you do!

291

I myself feel exceedingly tender to you!
In your beautiful eyes I would drown when I look,
If I could be sure that you knew how to cook,
And I want to remind you, before we are wed,
That you always must bring me my breakfast in bed.

CHORUS

Breakfast in bed! That is what he desires!
A capable wife is the sort he admires,
And love doesn't last if it isn't well fed,
So remember to bring him his breakfast in bed!

DILDERY

You adore me, dear Cully—I know that you do!
And I am most deeply attracted to you!
To serve and attend you will be my delight
If you'll always admit my opinions are right!
Be sure to agree with whatever I've said,
And of course I shall bring you your breakfast in bed.

CHORUS

Admit she is right! That is what she desires!
A unanimous husband's the sort she requires,
So never look black, though she makes you see red,
Or she won't often bring you your breakfast in bed.

CULLY

A bargain, dear Dilly! I promise, I do,
If you wait upon me, I shall listen to you!
If you do as I wish, you can say what you please—
Believe, if you like, that the moon's made of cheese—

You can think that black's white, you can stand on your head,
If only you'll bring me my breakfast in bed!

CHORUS

Stand on your head! He won't care at all!
Love cannot live but in Liberty Hall!
And with Freedom of Speech you can Butter your Bread,
If you faithfully bring him his breakfast in bed!

DILDERY

A bargain, my cabbage—*mon cher petit chou!*
If you listen to me, I shall wait upon you!
I'll cook and I'll darn, and I'll nurse when you're ill,
If in all other matters I get my own will!
I shall not be driven, I must not be led,
If you want to make sure of your breakfast in bed.

CHORUS

She will not be driven! She'll have her own way!
If it's comfort you value, you'll just have to pay!
Good fortune's a jewel, but it hangs by a thread—
Oh, I wonder how long you'll get breakfast in bed!

There was a little pause when they had finished, and then Cully said, 'The children sing very nicely, my dear, but a good voice isn't everything. Children ought to show respect for their elders—great respect, unfailing respect, loving respect!'

'And they do!' Miss Dildery declared. 'They've been very well brought up, and already they respect you deeply.—You do respect your Uncle Cully, don't you, children?'

293

'Yes, Aunt Dildery,' they answered, and stared coldly at their elders.

'Well, they don't look as if they did,' said Cully—and then Timothy and Hew and Sam Sturgeon stood up behind the ledge of rock, a few yards away, and Timothy and Hew shouted, 'Good morning, Miss Dildery! How do you do?'

Miss Dildery dropped her table-mats and the two balls of coloured silk, and held out all her arms towards them. 'My dear, dear friends!' she exclaimed. 'Oh, what a pleasure to see you! Little did I think, when I had the joy of entertaining you at Coral Villa, that we should meet again on your own beautiful island! Life is so full of surprises, isn't it?'

Timothy introduced Sam Sturgeon, and Hew asked her, 'Are you going to look after Cully now?'

Miss Dildery blushed all over—coral pink and rose pink in some places, pillar-box red in others—and, looking shyly at Cully, murmured, 'You tell them, dear.'

'She thinks it would be a good thing if we got married,' said Cully in an off-handed way. 'What's in your basket, Timothy?'

'A cake,' said Timothy.

Miss Dildery was displeased, as well she might be, by Cully's manner. She said shrilly, 'He's been pleading with me to marry him for years and years, and when I heard how brave he'd been, and how terribly injured he was, I hadn't the heart to refuse him any longer. So I took the earliest chance to come and tell him so. We travelled by basking-shark—so comfortably! The children did enjoy it—didn't you, children?'

'We were sick,' said one of the little octopuses.

'Not all the time,' said Miss Dildery. 'And in any case it was well worth a little discomfort to make your poor uncle so happy.'

'Are you going to live at Coral Villa?' asked Timothy.

'Coral Villa is going to be the happiest house in all the sea,' said Miss Dildery.

'How is Dingy?' asked Hew.

'*Horace,*' said Miss Dildery firmly. 'You mean Horace. Horace is splendid, quite splendid, and very, very happy. The children adore him—don't you, my dears?'

'Except when he ties us into knots,' said one of the little octopuses.

'He plays with them,' explained Miss Dildery, 'and sometimes they don't quite understand the rules of the game.'

Cully had been looking fixedly at the basket on Timothy's arm, and now he asked, 'What sort of a cake is it?'

They had wrapped it up carefully in a napkin and brown paper, and when Timothy undid it and Cully saw that it was a birthday cake, magnificent in white sugar icing, his spirits revived and he suddenly became as cheerful as he had been when the boys first met him.

'What a lovely cake!' he exclaimed. 'Oh, I do like birthday cake! There's nothing better, is there? But it won't keep, I'm afraid, it looks far too rich, so we'd better cut it now, in case it goes bad. You've got a knife, Mr. Sturgeon, haven't you?—Oh, Dilly, my dear, take the children down to the water and play with them for a little while, will you? I shall be busy for half an hour or so. We've a great deal to talk about.'

'But you must give the children some cake!' said Miss Dildery. 'They adore birthday cake, and so do I.'

'It's very bad for children,' declared Cully, 'and you shouldn't eat sweet things at all. They make you fat.'

'Nonsense' said Miss Dildery. 'Cut *nine* slices, Mr. Sturgeon please, and then the children and I will go and have a little picnic, and leave you to talk.'

'Thin ones,' whispered Cully anxiously. 'Thinner than that—much thinner!'

It was a large cake, fortunately, and after good slices had been cut for Miss Dildery and the eight little octopuses, and for William Button and Henry String, there was still half of it left for Cully. He enjoyed himself immensely, and talked as vigorously as he ate.

'She's a fine octopus, isn't she?' he said. 'I'm very fond of her, we've been friends for years, but I'd never marry her so long as I could swim. Oh no! No, no, no, no! I was always glad to see her when we met, and I enjoyed thinking about her when we were two or three thousand miles apart. But I didn't want to live with her all the time, not when I could swim for myself. Why should I?—But it's different now, of course. Quite, quite different! It was devotion to duty that undid me. I became a hero, and now, in consequence of that, I've got to get married. Oh dear! Dear, dear, dear me!—Do be careful, boys, if ever you're tempted to behave like a hero. You may lose a leg or an arm, all the ladies for miles around will fall in love with you, and if you've lost a leg you won't be able to run away. One thing leads to another, and a crippled hero is bound to be married whether he likes it or not.—Don't say that's the last slice, Mr. Sturgeon? Well, well! It was a beautiful cake, and there'd have been almost enough if it hadn't been for all those children.—You'll come and see us in Coral Villa, won't you, if ever you travel under the sea again? I shall be a quiet, respectable, married octopus, but we'll talk about old times, and I dare say we'll enjoy ourselves in one way or another. I *think*—I'm not quite sure—but I *think* she's a very good cook.'

The flow of words was stopped by Gunner Boles, who suddenly appeared out of the sea and came stumbling up the weedy rocks, shaking water-drops from his red whiskers.

'It's time to go, Cully,' he said. 'Timothy and Hew, my dears, we've got to say good-bye.—I've seen my orders, Sam, and it's an easy job for me this time. I'm going to have a spell of duty at the Admiral's court, and these two worthless, good-for-nothing, young Powder Monkeys are coming with me. Though why Davy Jones should want them about his house, I can't think.'

'You've handed over the knot, have you?' asked Sam.

'To a good man,' said Gunner Boles. 'My relief's a good sailor and a good man, and he'll look after the knot well enough. But I don't suppose you'll ever see him, Sam.'

'No, it isn't likely,' said Sam, 'unless you've trouble again at the bottom of the sea.'

'I don't want any more trouble,' said Gunner Boles. 'I want a quiet life, and peace to smoke my pipe and contemplate the wonders of the deep. That's all I ask for.—Now then, Cully, heave yourself out of that pool. Show a leg, my lad.'

'Don't be ridiculous,' said Cully. 'You know perfectly well that I'm quite incapable of doing a hand's turn for myself, and I don't ever intend to try. I've earned my rest!'

'I shall look after him,' said Miss Dildery. 'It is my duty and my privilege!'

She made her nephews and nieces take hold of his arms, one on each, and haul together. They were strong little creatures, and pulled Cully out of the pool without much trouble. Then he said good-bye to Timothy and Hew and Sam Sturgeon, shaking hands with all of them at the same time, and Miss Dildery thanked them very prettily for having been the means of bringing her and Cully together again.

'We owe our happiness entirely to you,' she said, and blushed like a fine sunset.

The little octopuses pulled Cully down to the sea, and swam with him to the basking-shark that was waiting a couple of hundred yards away. Miss Dildery swam beside them, and turned round at least a dozen times to wave to Timothy and Hew.

William Button and Henry String were very pleased with their Zulu assegais, and Sam had brought a new pipe for Gunner Boles. The Gunner had told him, a few days before, that they could keep the Shell, which he had left in Captain Spens's bedroom on the night of their party, on condition that no one ever listened to it but themselves. And now he made them promise again to remember that.

'For it's a great secret that it tells,' he said, 'and it wouldn't do at all if everybody got to know about it. So take care of the Shell, boys, and don't forget the sailors under the sea!'

'We'll never forget,' they answered, and very sadly indeed they watched him, and William Button and Henry String, wade out into the calm green water, and then, as neatly as seals, dive down into the depths. When they were a hundred yards away Gunner Boles came up to the surface, his bald head shining in the sun and his red whiskers gleaming like fire, and waved to them, once, twice, and again. And that was the last they saw of him.

Chapter Twenty-Eight

'**A**nd now,' said Timothy as they walked up the short drive that led to Popinsay House, 'life is going to be very dull.'

'Your mother doesn't think so,' said Sam, and pointed to three men who were working on the roof of the house, renewing slates and repairing the chimneys. There were other men painting the windows, and inside were paper-hangers and carpenters, as busy as they could be. All over the island, indeed, people were painting their doors and papering their walls and planting fine flowers in their gardens, for Captain Spens had discovered that everyone in Popinsay was a descendant of some sort, or married to a descendant, of one or other of the men who had sailed with Aaron Spens, and therefore entitled to a share of the treasure according to Aaron's old agreement with his crew. Many people did not get very much, but what they got they quickly spent with great enjoyment.

'No,' said Sam, 'your mother isn't going to find life dull for the next few months—and your new gardeners won't have much time for idling, not if I know her.'

There had been no gardener at Popinsay House for many a year, but now there were two. They were hard at work, and

Timothy and Hew and Sam Sturgeon stood for a couple of minutes to watch them. They were two of the ugliest men that anyone in Popinsay had ever seen, but they were hard workers and very grateful to Captain Spens for employing them. He had found them in the cellar one day. They were afraid, they said, to stay any longer in the shed where the grave-digger kept his tools, and they could think of no other hiding-place. So they had returned to the cellar where once they had been prisoners, because they had been given plenty to eat there, and usually a newspaper to read. The new gardeners were Pott and Kettle.

The house was in great confusion and there was hardly anywhere to sit down except the study; for Captain Spens refused to let it be painted, papered, decorated, or renovated in any way. The weather was fine and warm, however, and when the postman came Mrs. Spens took her letters into the garden to read them. Every day she received a great many letters and parcels, for she was always buying new things for the house and sending away for catalogues of furniture and china and curtains and garden tools, and so forth. When she had looked through the four catalogues which had just arrived, to see if there was anything new to be got, she read her private letters, and presently calling Timothy and Hew, said to them, 'I've some very interesting news for you. News that will give you great pleasure, I hope.'

'What is it?' asked Timothy doubtfully.

'Have you bought a pony?' asked Hew.

'No, it's something far more important than that. I've made arrangements for you both to go away to school in September.'

'But we go to school here!' said Timothy.

'Why do you want us to go to another school?' asked Hew.

'We learn a great deal from Sam Sturgeon,' said Timothy.

'Which we couldn't learn anywhere else,' added Hew.

300

'You can't always stay in Popinsay, can you?' asked Mrs. Spens, speaking very calmly and reasonably. 'Popinsay is only a small island——'

'It's a very nice island,' said Timothy. 'I don't see why we shouldn't stay.'

'It's a very interesting island,' said Hew. 'All sorts of things happen here.'

'But many more things happen in the great world,' said Mrs. Spens, 'and when you grow up you'll want to see the world. You'll want to travel, and meet all sorts of people, and see foreign cities, and understand what's going on there. And to prepare you, if only a little, for the world, I think you should go to a larger school than we have here. You can't learn much about the world by what goes on in Popinsay....'

Timothy and Hew, she perceived, were not listening very closely, and Mrs. Spens felt that her own attention was wandering. There was a noise in the house: a noise that grew louder and louder. It came from the study.

'Your father sounds annoyed,' said Mrs. Spens. 'Something must have upset him. Did he get any letters to-day?'

'No,' said Timothy, 'only a newspaper.'

'That's quite enough, of course.'

They heard a crash, as though a large piece of furniture had been knocked over, and Mrs. Spens said, 'I think you should go and see what's the matter—and tell him I've got a headache coming on.'

Timothy and Hew found Sam already in the study, and Mrs. Matches listening outside the door. Captain Spens had overturned his writing-table, and was walking up and down waving a newspaper in the air. 'Scoundrels and nincompoops!' he shouted. 'They're the cause of all the trouble, and the world's full of them.

Full of barefaced scoundrels and whimpering nincompoops!'

'Mother says we've got to go out into the world,' said Timothy.

'Then choose your company, and choose it carefully,' said the Captain; and crumpling his newspaper into an untidy ball, threw it into a corner of the room.

Gunner Boles's Shell lay on the chimney-piece, and picking it up, Timothy held it to his ear and listened. 'We got into all sorts of company under the sea,' he said.

'And enjoyed it,' said Hew.

'Perhaps we'll enjoy going to school,' said Timothy.

'I expect we shall,' said Hew, 'though it's a nuisance having to leave Popinsay.'

'Who said you were going to school?' asked Sam Sturgeon.

'Mother.'

'I meant to tell you,' said Captain Spens to Sam. 'I didn't expect her to make the arrangements so quickly. But she's quite right—we've been talking it over since she came home—and she's quite right! They ought to go.'

'It's to prepare us for going out into the great world,' said Timothy, 'which is full of scoundrels and nincompoops, so Father says.'

'I don't say there aren't good men as well,' declared the Captain, 'but they usually seem to be outnumbered.'

'Scumbril and Inky Poops thought Davy Jones was going to be outnumbered,' said Timothy.

'Because they didn't know about the sailors—and us!' said Hew.

Surprised at their arguing with him, Captain Spens stared at them, and frowned, and considered what they had said. Then, a little grudgingly, he admitted, 'Yes, that's true enough in a way. It's quite true, I suppose.—The boys are right, Sam!'

'Yes, sir,' said Sam, 'I've done my best for them. I've tried to bring them up on sensible lines, and I only hope that going to school doesn't unlearn what they've been taught by me and Gunner Boles.'

Captain Spens began to pace up and down again. He had not quite recovered his temper, and when he perceived that someone had knocked over his writing-table, and thrown a bundle of untidy newspaper into a corner of the room, he grew angrier than ever and shouted at Sam: 'Have you nothing better to do than to stand here, gossiping and idling your time away? Pick up my table, and try to make the place look tidy. I hate an untidy room!—And you, boys, what are you going to do this afternoon? Everybody else about the house is working, and working hard. Can't you find something useful to do?'

'I and the boys,' said Sam, in a very determined voice, 'are going fishing.'

THE END

A NOTE ON THE AUTHOR

Eric Linklater was born in 1899 in Penarth, Wales. He was educated in Aberdeen, and was initially interested in studying medicine; he later switched his focus to journalism, and became a full-time writer in the 1930's. During his career, Linklater served as a journalist in India, a commander of a wartime fortress in the Orkney Islands, and rector of Aberdeen University. He authored more than twenty novels for adults and children, in addition to writing short stories, travel pieces, and military histories, among other works.

Made in the USA
San Bernardino, CA
06 September 2016